HEMINGWAY LIES AND THE SEARCH FOR SAM

William H Strickland

This is a work of fiction. Names, characters, businesses, places, events, and incidents are either the products of the author's imagination or used in a fictitious manner. Any resemblance to actual persons, living or dead, or actual events is purely coincidental.

ISBN: 1499244916
ISBN 13: 9781499244915

For my good friend, the recently departed James Robert MacArthur, better known as "Jimmy Bob"—a drinker, a thinker, and a lover of books.

Contents

CHAPTER ONE

Wrecked

Hawken Turner wanted the simple things in life. He wanted to be a good father and a role model to his three sons. He wanted to give his love to a woman and share his life with her. He wanted respect from his community and business associates. But that was not the way his life had evolved. There was whiskey on his breath and bitterness in his heart. Home was a battered passport filled with stamps from places he could not remember. He was estranged from his boys, broken from failed relationships, and losing control of his business. His once-handsome face was unshaven and his eyes were red.

Hawken Turner was a dead man. There was only one question left. *Was he going to heaven, or was he going to hell?*

***

The screeching tires left pavement, gathering speed as they slid across dirt and gravel, failing to find a grip. At the last second, he was confronted by a massive oak tree racing toward him as the headlights drew it from the shadows. The speeding Porsche slammed to a stop with an explosion of flying plastic and crumpled steel. The winding engine gasped for air, choked, then began hissing eerily with steamy disgust. The road was pitch black once more. There were no streetlights or houses on the narrow and twisting country road. Hawken took inventory of the damage to his body. His left wrist was bent backward, and there was a gruesome angle to his forearm. His right foot was twisted at the ankle and unable to respond to his plea for movement. He was unable to move his right arm; the shoulder had dislodged from its socket. Burning pain inside his torso indicated that something inside was broken, but he could not pinpoint the source.

The cabin filled with toxic fumes, like gunpowder mixed with gasoline. Blood filled his mouth and seeped onto his lower lip, as it joined more blood flowing from his shattered nose. The reality of the collision took hold as Hawken sat transfixed by the textured weave of the deflated bag that had delivered the blow to his face. The bag was in his lap, lying limp after exploding into the last-second shield that was meant to save his life.

As Hawken regained his senses, a flicker of flame appeared on the backside of the broken dashboard pressing against his chest. The flame flickered in unison with the dripping sounds of melting plastic and grew steadily with each flaming drop. Regrets seeped into his mind, along with the awareness that fire would soon connect with fuel, a combustible combination destined to explode and leave him trapped inside a coffin of fire.

Hawken stared at his cell phone lying on the passenger floorboard, just inches away but impossible to reach. Never in his life had he wanted anything more than to reach the phone and call his sons to tell them that he loved them. He winced at the thought of his boys growing up with no explanations of things that needed explaining. There had been too many women, too much liquor, and not enough time spent fishing together. It was too late to be the father he had wanted to be, but if he could just reach the phone, if he could tell them the truth, maybe they would not make the mistakes that he had made. *If only*... Hawken Turner blocked the pain from his broken body and searched his soul for the story he needed to tell.

CHAPTER TWO

Sam

The story that Hawken Turner longed to tell his boys was not entirely about Sam, but it did begin with Sam. The moment Samantha Patterson walked onto the campus of the privileged River Oaks Academy prep school in January 1968, Hawken Turner fell in love with her. She was bending over, picking up a pencil from the sidewalk during the changing of classes. When she straightened up and shook her long chestnut hair into place, Hawken Turner stopped dead in his tracks. It did not matter that she was two years older than he was, or that the look she gave him was only a look of curiosity because he was staring at her. All that mattered was that she triggered the flame deep in his soul that warms the loins of men, and Hawken Turner felt it for the first time in his young life. It was inexplicable, undeniable, and unfaltering. It was Adam seeing Eve for the first time. Sam was the prettiest girl Hawken had ever seen, and the prettiest he would ever see. She was the one, and from that day on, she always would be.

Sam entered the school midterm as a transfer student and a new addition to the slightly snobbish student body who had all grown up together and attended the prestigious school from the beginning. She might not have had the classical features of a prom queen, but she carried an intoxicating look of innocence, with her flowing hair parted down the middle, and a touch of hippie flower child in her appearance. She wore flared blue jeans that hung low on her hips and challenged the dress code in a school filled with doctors' kids and academic overachievers.

Everything about Sam was sweet. She moved through the crowded halls between classes like a girl strolling the aisles of a fall carnival. She always appeared amused as she held her books pressed to her chest with both hands, glancing from side to side as she spoke to friends passing by. She often looked over her shoulder, speaking to one of the girls following behind her like an entourage. She was the new girl in school, a little different, and she had become instantly popular. Sam did not walk; she glided…nonchalantly, like an angel with subtle curves and a seductive smile.

Hawken Turner was smitten.

A few days after Sam had arrived, the gods smiled on Hawken. He was seated in the cafeteria at lunchtime when a brown paper bag plopped on the table and Samantha Patterson sat in the empty seat beside him. He nearly choked on his sandwich. It was fate. That seat was usually taken by one of his football buddies or hunting pals, but there it was, empty; and there she was, the new angel at school, sitting beside him.

She opened her lunch bag and took out a sandwich while Hawken wiped the crumbs from his face. He looked at Sam from the corner of his eyes as he began searching his spinning head for something clever to say.

"Hey, can I have a bite of that sandwich?" he asked, his voice sounding two octaves higher than normal. "It looks better than mine."

"Is that the way you greet all the new students at this school?" she asked.

"No, but it looks good. Can I have a bite or not?"

"Sure. Do you like ham?" she asked as she offered the sandwich to him.

Hawken opened wide and inserted the sandwich as far as he could into his mouth. He took a bite that nearly consumed half the sandwich and nodded his head approvingly, waiting on her reaction. When Sam said nothing, Hawken sheepishly offered his pimento cheese to her.

She took a bite. "Hey, that's good," she said, handing it back to him.

Sam looked into his eyes as if she was trying to decide if he was crazy or just playing with her. Hawken held his breath while he awaited her decision.

"Did you make it?" she asked.

"My mom made it. I'll tell her you like it, but I don't know your name."

"My name's Sam."

"Well, welcome to River Oaks, Sam. I'm Hawken Turner. Did your mom make that?"

"No, I made it myself," Sam said.

"It could use a little more mustard." Hawken smiled an innocent smile.

"Okay, more mustard next time," she said. "Just for you, Hawken Turner."

Sam must have figured that Hawken was only playing with her that first day at lunch, because, from that day forward, she sat with him in the cafeteria every day for the entire remainder of the school year. Whoever arrived first saved the other a seat. Hawken abandoned his jock friends and hunting buddies for his new lunch partner, and Sam declined invitations from cheerleaders and gossipers to sit with Hawken. The ritual began each day when they opened lunch bags and compared meals. They became food critics and started an unstated competition to see who had the tastiest or most exotic meal for the day. Sam brought quiches, yogurt, and smelly cheese from Europe. Hawken brought venison, smoked mullet, and oyster stew. By the end of the school year, the competition had escalated to the point where Hawken brought his charcoal grill to cook hamburgers, venison tenderloins, and steaks on the lawn near the football field.

As the school year wore on, Hawken and Sam drifted toward an undefined relationship in which they became more than friends but less than lovers. They never passed in the hall without a smile or some flirtatious exchange of affection, yet in spite of their mutual affection, their age difference was always a buffer—but a good buffer that allowed them the freedom to act flirtatiously and share thoughts openly without complications. Sam must have seen the adoration in Hawken's eyes, and she must have known that he had a crush on her. She treated him with care, yet welcomed the attention he gave to her. She became his mentor, with her age advantage and big-city experience from her previous life in Pittsburgh. She was like the big sister who shared her carefree perspective on life and taught him about girls. It was no secret when Sam went out with other boys, and that always gave him a sinking feeling in his gut, but sharing Sam was better than not having her at all, and Hawken Turner had big dreams for the future.

Maybe it happened because Sam was new in town, or maybe she just understood him better than anyone else did. For whatever reason, Sam asked Hawken questions that others in Lewisville only talked about behind his back in the beauty parlors and church parking lots. One Monday afternoon in the school cafeteria, Sam joined him at their usual table. She reached into her book bag and brought out a book.

"We got a new book to read in English class today," she said. Sam slid the book across the table.

The paperback book had the author's name in bold print, overshadowing the title. Ernest Hemingway, *A Farewell To Arms*. Hawken studied the book and hesitated before speaking.

"Never read it," he said.

"Why's your face turning red?" Sam asked.

"It's not turning red. I've never read the book."

"I heard that your family knew Hemingway," she said. "Everybody says he came to Lewisville and stayed at your grandfather's house a few years back."

"Who told you that?"

"Mrs. Cooper told us in English class."

"Is that the only time you've heard it?"

"I think I heard it mentioned once or twice before… somewhere."

"They met him on safari in Africa—a long time ago. That's all."

"That's amazing. Hey, maybe I can talk with your mom when we have to do a report on this book. Would you mind if I did that?" Sam asked.

"No. I'm sure she'd love it. She loves to talk about Hemingway. All the time. Ernest did this. Ernest did that. But only the good parts about him. What else did you hear?"

"Nothing important," Sam said.

"That's good because there's more stuff to the story."

"What kind of stuff?"

"A big fight kinda stuff. It's sorta embarrassing. Can we talk about it later?"

"Sure we can."

Hawken was often puzzled but ultimately pleased by Sam's collection of revolving suitors. She seemed to have a talent for finding boys who would treat her badly. There were not many secrets in their small school. During one typical winter day at lunch, Hawken sat next to Sam, his mind on her latest boyfriend from one of the neighboring towns.

"Let me slay that dragon for you," he said.

"What dragon?" Sam asked.

"That conceited asshole you're going out with on Saturday. Keith Plummer."

"He's a nice guy."

"He's a pig."

"No, he's not. He smells good," she said.

"For two dollars at the dime store I can smell just like him. And I'm a lot nicer," Hawken said.

Sam sat silently for a few seconds as she contemplated a response.

"You know…I wish you were older," she said. There was no smile, nor playfulness in her eyes.

"I'm getting older every day," Hawken replied.

"Yes, but so am I." The smile returned to Sam's face. "I have an idea. You can be number two. Just like your football number. And your baseball number. My number two. I can have a number one and a number two."

"Number two is the same as *loser.*"

"No, it's not."

"Yes, it is. But if it doesn't work out with number one, then I'll be number one?" Hawken asked.

"Yes, of course," Sam said.

Hawken pondered her offer. "What are the benefits that come with being number two?" he asked.

"Well...what do you want?"

"Kissing?" Hawken said.

"Later."

"On the lips?" he asked.

"Okay."

"With feeling?"

"Of course."

"Okay. Number two is all right—for now."

It was not exactly the position that Hawken was dreaming of, but it amused them both, and the kissing part was a promise that Hawken would not let her forget.

Hawken and Sam saw each other nearly every day throughout the summer. Hawken was still number two, but he had not fallen by the wayside as all the number ones before him had done.

When Sam began her final year of high school, nothing changed. They flowed seamlessly from the lazy days of summer into the busy fall. They chatted between classes and met in the cafeteria every day where all the students knew the seats that were theirs. It was during one of their cafeteria rendezvous that Hawken had the idea to introduce her to hunting.

"I'm going deer hunting on Saturday," he said. "Why don't you go with me?"

"You and your deer hunting. Is that all you think about?" Sam asked.

"That—and you, of course. Come on, you might like it."

"I don't have anything to wear," Sam said.

"I have everything you need."

"I'm not getting up early," she said. "You know I like to sleep in on Saturdays."

"I know, but we *have* to get up early. We need to be in the stand before first light. It won't kill you."

"You want me to carry a gun?" she asked. "Are you serious?"

"No, I'm not giving you a gun. And I'll do all the shooting… if there's any shooting to be done."

Sam stopped eating and rolled her eyes. "I've never been hunting in my life. How can you shoot anything as beautiful as a deer?"

"Hey, the family's got to eat," Hawken replied.

"Well, now, I wouldn't want your family to starve. I've been to your house and seen all the starving children. It's a wonder how you all survive."

"Saturday morning then. Come over to my house at five, and we'll drive my Jeep to the farm."

"I guess, but I'm not too sure about this," Sam said. "Why do you want *me* to go?"

"I want to impress you with my hunting skills so you'll see me as good husband material. And—I'm inviting you so that you can keep me warm in the tree stand."

"Oh, Jesus. Yes, of course! I have to see my future husband shooting animals. That's *so* important to me. You better call and wake me up."

On Saturday morning, two hours before sunrise, Sam knocked at Hawken's door just as she had promised. He came to the door with an armful of outdoor hunting gear for her to try on and handed her a long-sleeved insulated T-shirt that he had outgrown two years before.

"Here, this will keep you warm," he said.

She removed her red down jacket and pulled the thermal top over her sweater. Hawken held open a heavy camouflage hunting jacket, two sizes too large, while Sam inserted first one arm and then the other. Hawken snugged the jacket closed around her chest and zipped it from her waist to her chin. He placed a camouflaged hat on her head, complete with insulated flaps that he pulled down to cover her ears.

"Perfect. That ought to do it. Now you look like a hunter."

"I'm going to freeze," Sam said.

"You'll warm up. Come on and let's go. It's going to be light soon."

A crusty white frost covered the field. Hawken drove the Jeep around the edge, stopping on the far side where a narrow path led into the woods. He carefully slid the rifle from its oiled leather case, then quietly closed the door. They started down the narrow path to the tree stand with Hawken leading the way and Sam following close behind. The sky was still dark but the stars yielded just enough light to follow the worn trail cut between head-high pines on one side and towering hardwoods on the other.

Hawken glanced at the pines and measured their height with his eyes. He had planted the seedlings along with his grandfather, Colonel Cade, when he was only twelve years old. He felt pride knowing that someday the land would provide for the family when they sold the timber. The pines had grown to eight feet tall, making thick cover for the deer.

The hardwoods provided acorns and green browse for deer on the low branches. A shallow creek twisted its way through the hardwoods, and provided a source of water. The thick pines on one side and the creek on the other formed a natural trail between the bedding area and a cornfield. At the convergence of the pines and the hardwoods and the small creek was a tree stand.

Hawken stopped to hold a branch out of Sam's way. She had the hat pulled down tight over her ears, and she walked with both hands shoved deep into her pockets.

"Why don't you use the flashlight?" Sam asked.

"I'm letting my eyes get adjusted to the light," Hawken whispered. "We might see something going in." He turned his head to the side as he listened to the sounds of the woods.

When they reached the stand, they quietly climbed the wooden ladder and sat on the cold bench. It was narrow, barely wide enough for two. Hawken propped the rifle in the corner, and Sam tucked her hands between her legs to brace against the cold.

Dawn began to break as the soft pastel light of blue and pink replaced the black sky, and the woods began to reveal creatures cautiously emerging from their beds. First, the jays flew down from their roosts and searched the leaves and soil for seeds, nuts, and small insects. The squirrels came next. They scampered down tree trunks, scratching at the bark and chattering when they encountered sights or sounds that alarmed them. Then the squirrels settled on the ground and rustled the leaves. Hawken studied each new sound to identify its source.

The two hunters propped their feet on a rest and waited as the minutes stretched into an hour or more. Though Hawken remained sharp and alert, Sam slept soundly, her head resting on his shoulder.

In the distance, a flicker of white caught Hawken's attention. He turned in that direction and waited for it to move again.

"There," Hawken whispered.

Sam opened her eyes for the first time since she had settled in the stand. "Where?"

"Out front. Coming down that hill. See it? It's a doe. She's behind that tree right now."

"I don't see anything."

"Shhhhhhh. You're talking too loud. There—she's right behind that tree, coming this way."

"Oh, I see it," Sam whispered.

The doe was cautiously making her way closer to the stand. She was nuzzling the ground for acorns, stopping often to raise her head, twisting her ears to catch a sound, and working her nostrils to smell the air for danger.

"You're not going to shoot her, are you?" Sam asked.

"No, but look at the way she keeps looking behind her. That means that there's a good chance that a buck is following her."

The deer continued stop-and-step movements toward the stand. Sam was fully awake and excited now that she knew that Hawken was not going to kill the doe. She sat quietly on the edge of the bench seat and watched the graceful movements the deer.

"And there he is," Hawken said. He looked straight ahead, carefully hiding his movements, as he reached for the rifle.

Just as Hawken had hoped, a buck had eased stealthily into the open food plot following the doe. Hawken could see the thick neck and muscular bulk of the body. The antlers stood outside his ears, a sign of mature age, and the mass of the antlers was heavy at the base of the skull. The buck was a shooter.

"Be very still," Hawken whispered. "He'll come right to us."

Hawken brought the gun closer, pushed the barrel toward the buck, and rested it on the railing of the stand while he waited for the deer to move closer. He moved the gun slowly and deliberately when the deer's head was down so the sharp eyes of the buck would not catch the movement. The doe wandered off, but the buck was moving closer toward the stand, one step at a time. The minutes went by like hours while Hawken waited for the ideal opportunity to take the shot. His thumb sat ready on the safety, his finger on the trigger.

"Hey!" Sam yelled out without warning. With the lightning flash of white tail and three crashes of exploding brush, the deer was gone. Hawken leaned back, stunned.

Sam turned to him with puppy dog eyes.

"Sorry," she said.

Hawken stared blankly at the spot where the buck had stood in his sights just seconds before. He looked into the thick woods to see if the buck had stopped, but the deer was gone. Hawken had little to say. The hunt was over. Even if there was a chance to see another buck, there was no chance to take the shot—not with Sam along. He stood in the stand, stretched his back, and unloaded the rifle. He would have been angry with anyone else who cost him a shot at a trophy deer, but this was Sam, and the anger never came. Disappointment, but not anger.

"I should've known better. That was the best buck I've seen in years," Hawken said. "You don't get many opportunities like that."

"I'm sorry," Sam said again.

Hawken climbed down from the stand, the helped Sam down the ladder. He shouldered the gun and they started down the path back to the Jeep without speaking a word. He kept his eyes on the ground and looked for deer sign on the trail while Sam walked far ahead, as if anxious to get back to the warmth of the Jeep and away from the hunting for good. Before reaching the Jeep, she stopped and looked back at him.

"You're mad, aren't you?" she asked.

"I'll get over it."

"You know, I told you that I've never been hunting before. What did you expect?"

She walked back down the trail toward him until she stood so close that her chest was touching his. She looked up at Hawken with her sweet face and disarming smile.

"That was a trophy buck," Hawken said.

"Why don't we go to see the animals in the zoo?" she asked. "I love the zoo. We won't have to shoot anything there."

"I don't go to zoos," Hawken said.

"And why not?"

"I don't like to see animals suffer," he said.

Sam rose to her tiptoes so that her nose was nearly touching his. "Oh…you don't like to see animals suffer? You were just about to shoot one dead ten minutes ago, and now you're an animal lover?"

"That's right. I'd rather see them fighting for survival, like real animals, out here in the wild, than see one caged up for kindergartners to gawk at. Did you see that buck this morning? Did he look sad? Animals in the zoo look sad to me. I can't take it."

"Well, that buck would've been sad if you shot him," Sam said.

"No, he wouldn't. He would have been dead."

"You're crazy," she said. She put her arm inside his and they started back on the trail.

"No, I'm not," said Hawken. "But I believe that killing them and eating them is better than putting them in a zoo."

Sam squeezed Hawken's arm and rubbed her cold nose on his shoulder. The tension dissipated and they walked to the Jeep as if nothing had happened. There was no hunting trophy for Hawken, but the fresh, cold air of the outdoors felt good on his face. The smell of the woods and the encounter with nature was the thing. Not the killing. Sam was no hunter, but she did not complain. She would probably never go again, but she had tried it. And Hawken was happy to see that she kept the clothes.

Obviously, hunting together was not a good idea if he was looking for something special to share with Sam, so Hawken decided to try a softer, more sensitive approach. He knew that Sam loved poetry. She quoted poetry, wrote poetry on the covers of her notebooks, and always seemed to have a book of poetry lying in the seat of her car. Even though he struggled with romantic words, Hawken Turner had no problem making words rhyme, and when he blended the words just right, the poetry was pretty damn good.

One frantic Monday morning at River Oaks, Hawken stood in the gymnasium, bellied up to the bleachers while he sweated over homework due for his next class. He had five minutes to get it done. He flipped the pages of his history book, writing answers to the questions as fast as he could. Just then, two soft breasts pressed gently into his shoulder blades, arriving simultaneously with the familiar scent of his favorite perfume. Sam's hair brushed the back of his neck as her lips reached his ear and she whispered, "I love that poem you wrote me."

"That's good," Hawken said. "I should have been doing my homework instead of thinking poetic thoughts, but I guess that some things are just more important than school."

"You're lucky that nobody saw it fall out of my book, or maybe I would've been asked to read it to the whole class," Sam said. "When did you put it there?"

"When we were standing by the lockers before school this morning. I stuck it in your book while you were flirting with Baxter."

"Sneaky. Finish your homework, and I'll see you at lunch," she said as she laid a folded note on the bleachers next to his book. Hawken closed his history book and opened the note. A handwritten poem read:

Surprise, surprise—you are very sweet
I found your poem around my feet
I know number two is not much fun
But write more poems, and you'll be number one

Love ya, Sam

Hawken liked writing poetry. He loved hunting, but he liked writing poetry. From that day on, when Hawken climbed the ladder and settled in his deer stand, he propped his rifle in the corner and took pencil and paper from his pocket. He killed deer and he wrote poetry—but only for Sam.

When hunting season ended, it was time for spring sports. Sam played second base for the softball team, and Hawken played third for the baseball team. Both teams had practice after school, and that led to a convenient ride-sharing arrangement after practice.

With the brown winter fading and the bright colors of spring creeping into the landscape, Hawken found himself wishing that the days could last forever. He loved playing his baseball, and when baseball was done for the day, he loved the ride home even more. As every spring day grew longer, the thirty-minute ride home grew longer as well.

Hawken drove a late-model Jeep, black with a tan convertible top. When the weather was warm, the top was down. Sam drove a yellow 1972 Corolla with a broken radio antenna and black faux leather interior. The Corolla was worn and ugly, but for Hawken, sitting next to Sam in any car was a luxury ride.

They never went directly home. They took the long way home. The long way that went by the river where they stopped and threw rocks into the water. Sometimes they drove the dirt roads, or found some other distraction that milked every second of daylight from the sun. They talked about everything and everybody, deep dark subjects and meaningless banter, white lies and hard truth, dreams of the future and disappointments in the past. And while they joked and drove around and shared their deepest secrets, the little thin line between friendship and love began to dissolve.

After practice, one late April afternoon, Hawken emerged from the locker room and saw Sam arguing with Charles Baxter in the parking lot. She was leaning into his car, and the two were snipping back and forth. After the tense conversation, Sam walked away and Charles screeched the tires of his Camaro and sped down the road.

"What was that all about?" Hawken asked.

"Don't ask."

"Okay, I won't ask. But Baxter doesn't look too happy."

"Do you have a date to prom yet?" Sam asked.

"Not yet."

"Good. You're going with me," she said.

"I thought you were going with Baxter?"

"He's a jerk," she said.

"What if I don't want to go with you?" Hawken asked.

"You're going with me. Now come on and let's go."

On the way home, Sam stopped by the river and drove down the dirt road beside the bridge to the clearing where they liked to park and talk. Hawken walked to the back of the Corolla and pulled two beers from a cooler they kept in the trunk. He handed a beer to Sam, and then picked up a rock and skipped it across the water. He sat next to Sam on the hood of the car while they watched the river flow.

"So, tell me about the fight," Hawken said.

"He's so immature," Sam said.

"It took you this long to figure that out?"

"I guess," she answered. "You know, he's jealous of you. He says that we spend way too much time together."

"I'm sorry about that," Hawken said. "Well…not really sorry."

"I don't care so much about him being jealous, but he said ugly things about your family. That's just immature."

"What kind of ugly things?" Hawken asked.

"I don't like to repeat it."

"Tell me."

"I think you know."

"Then tell me."

"He said that everybody in Lewisville thinks that your mom had an affair with Ernest Hemingway. But he said it in a very ugly way."

"Ahhh…the Hemingway lies."

Hawken took a long gulp from his beer and sat silently staring into the river.

"Doesn't it bother you that people say those things?" Sam asked.

"Not at all."

"Yes, it does," said Sam. "I see it in your face anytime somebody mentions Hemingway. These gossipy people make me so mad. I swear, sometimes I hate this two-faced town."

"Okay, yeah…it's embarrassing. But this is a good town with good people. You'll love it after you've been here for a while. It's just that…well, there's not much to talk about. When Hemingway dropped in for a visit, he caused all kinds of chaos, and that gave people something to talk about, that's all. People gossip."

"I know it's just a rumor," she said. "I'm just sorry that you have to live with it all."

"The only thing that bothers me is that people think that it bothers me. I've heard the whispers behind my back. I don't care if they say it out loud, but I hate the whispers."

"Then what about the fight you had with Dillingham last year on the football field?" Sam asked. "I heard that was about the gossip."

"I couldn't let somebody on the football team say stuff about my mom. So the fight part was true. Can't even say that I won. Son of a bitch gave me a black eye, but I don't think he'll say it again. Anyway, he's an asshole. The whole team thought it was great—a freshman punching a senior."

"I'm sorry for your mom, too. Those are her friends that say that stuff—not really her friends, people pretending to be her friend."

"Don't worry about her. Maggie Turner can take care of herself."

"But doesn't it bother you that your friends say these things?" Sam asked.

"I don't want to talk about it," Hawken said. "The whole thing is embarrassing. Have you heard the country club story?"

"Just bits and pieces."

"Well…Hemingway stopped by on his way out west from the Keys to see the Colonel and Uncle Roy. They all went out to the country club for dinner—Maggie and my dad were there too. Anyway, something happened at the country club and a huge fight broke out. There was lots of drinking and stuff going on. The police showed up, and it got to be a big mess—so they say. It was a big story around town but I was just a baby then. My dad died soon after that and the story died too. But every now and then, I catch somebody cutting their conversation short, or closing the door to keep me from hearing them talk. I'm sure it's about all that stuff."

"I'm sorry. And I'm sorry about your dad, too. He must have been young. Do you remember him?"

"Not really. I was only three when he died. Have you ever seen a picture of him?" Hawken reached into his wallet and pulled out a crumpled photograph. "That's us together at church just before he died. Do you know the courthouse building downtown?"

"Sure."

"My dad designed that."

"So that's why you have a drawing of the courthouse hanging in your room."

"Yep."

"What about Maggie now?" Sam asked.

"What about her?"

"She's so young and pretty. Do you think she will ever get married again?"

"She'll never marry again. She lives in the past with her old photographs and love letters…she lives in a dream world."

"Does she ever date?"

"Hey—now you're getting personal and you're embarrassing me. Why don't you drink your beer?"

"Because I have to know everything."

"Why?"

Sam leaned over and rubbed her nose against his. "Because I want to know."

With the exception of his father, Arthur Turner, everyone in Hawken's family loved to hunt and fish. Conversely, nobody in Sam's family hunted, or fished, but she was willing to give it a try. After their one day of hunting together turned into a disaster, Hawken was thrilled when he discovered that Sam loved fishing.

She started fishing with Hawken in the lake by his house. With her appetite wetted, she soon joined him on weekend trips, fishing the rivers and tidal creeks down on the coast. Once Sam mastered coastal fishing, they ventured out into the Gulf of Mexico, where the water was bigger, the fish were stronger, and the tackle was heavier. That was Sam's favorite kind of fishing. Fishing and beach combined into one.

When the first day of summer came, the mackerel were running and the weather forecast called for a hot day with light wind and calm seas. Hawken drove into Sam's driveway with Uncle Roy's twenty-five-foot Mako hooked behind the Jeep. Sam was in the kitchen packing a lunch for them to eat on the boat. The morning air was fresh with a cocktail of blended smells rising from coconut sunscreen, fresh coffee, and toasted bread.

"You want one or two?" Sam asked.

"I'll take two," he answered.

"You want your bread toasted?"

"Sure."

"Grapes, apples, or both?"

"I don't care," he said.

"Okay. You get both."

Hawken propped himself against the kitchen counter with a mug of coffee, chatting with Sam's mother while Sam moved about the kitchen packing the boat provisions. Nothing could go wrong on a day like that. It was too perfect. Just the two of them boating the blue water of the Gulf, basking in the warm sun with the smell of salt air in their noses. One of the best days of Hawken Turner's life.

Sam was quite accomplished at boating and fishing. When they arrived at the marina, she began launch preparations without hesitation. The Mako slid off the trailer and into the water, and Sam took up the mooring lines and secured the boat to the dock while Hawken parked the Jeep. Hawken climbed aboard, cranked the engine, and studied the gauges. Sam arranged the fishing rods into the designated rod-holders and began stowing the food, towels, and tackle box beneath the deck. When she secured the gear, Hawken engaged the throttle and Sam joined him at the helm.

They stood side by side as Hawken eased the boat through the glassy calm of the harbor, into the rippled water of the bay, and finally into the gentle swells of the Gulf of Mexico.

As soon as Hawken steered the Mako past the jetties and into the Gulf, he spotted a tight group of boats on the horizon circling a patch of churning water. An acre of feeding mackerel drew his attention. Seagulls were diving and picking bits of baitfish left behind as frenzied fish tore them to pieces. Excitement building, Hawken slowed the boat and began rigging lines for trolling. Sam removed her swimsuit cover-up and began applying a coconut-scented sunscreen. Hawken glanced up from his rigging and scanned her tanned figure, barely covered by the string bikini. He looked away quickly as he rarely thought of Sam as a sexual object, but certain parts of his body thought otherwise. When she finished caressing the lotion into her skin, she turned to Hawken and began to rub sunscreen onto his back with slow, circulating palms. Hawken nearly forgot about the school of fish and the circle of competing boats. The touch of her hands on his back as she smiled at him while wearing next to nothing was far better than the fishing would ever be.

Hawken steered the Mako hard to port and maneuvered her into an opening among the circle of boats. They set out three lines to the rear, and it did not take long for a mackerel to strike the bait. Hawken slowed the boat to a stop as Sam took the rod, bent her knees, and braced herself for a fight. The hooked fish stripped yards and yards of monofilament line from the screeching reel as the rod bowed and jerked toward the water. Hawken snatched up the other two lines, preventing them from becoming tangled as the fish made another run and began streaking from side to side. It was a full ten minutes later when Sam finally cranked the twenty-pound mackerel to the boat. Hawken leaned over the gunwale, sank the gaff into the mackerel's silver belly, and swung the fish into the boat. Sam smiled with a look of satisfaction.

"That's one for me," she said.

"That's one for *us*." Hawken corrected her, even though he was much happier that she had been the one to catch it.

With the lines baited and reset, Hawken found another opening among the congested mass of trolling boats. He maneuvered the Mako between them and directly through the center of the feeding fish. Two of the rods bent toward the water and began jerking violently. Hawken raced to the stern and began retrieving the line from the idle rod, and Sam took control of the nearest rod as line stripped from the reel. Hawken stowed the empty rod and grabbed the third rod, which was also singing out as the line was quickly disappearing from the reel. Two fishermen and two fighting fish.

"Hawken!" Sam yelled.

"Reel!"

"Hawken!"

"Just reel him! I've got this one."

"I can't!" A tone of desperation resounded in her cries.

Hawken looked over and dropped his jaw when he saw Sam's predicament. Half of her long chestnut hair was tangled in the reel. In the excitement and confusion, Sam had continued cranking the handle and wound her head all the way down to the point where her ear was touching the reel. She could reel no more, nor could she free her hair.

Caught in the chaos, and without thinking out the situation, Hawken put his rod in the holder, raced over to Sam, took his fillet knife from his belt and sliced her hair from the reel. Sam's head snapped free, and she slowly rose up from the reel with a look of astonishment. She reached to her head and pulled at the stubble as if she were trying to make it long again. She gasped for air and sank down into the cushioned deck chair without saying a word.

Hawken had no words to console her. Without looking in her direction, he cut the line and freed the fish from the reel loaded with twisted hair. Quickly, he reeled the other mackerel to the side and swung it into the boat. *One for me*, he thought of saying, before better judgment prevailed.

The damage was done. There was one thing Hawken knew about Sam—she was obsessive about her hair. Now, half that hair was wound around a fishing reel perched in a rod holder several feet from her head. He saw anger in her eyes. It was a look he had never seen before, and he knew her anger was directed toward him. It was killing him inside, but there was nothing he could do.

It was not yet noon, but the fishing was done for the day. The boat ride to the dock was silent, and neither Sam nor Hawken looked toward the other. Sam spoke not a word when they docked the Mako and loaded the gear into Hawken's Jeep. He was careful to shield the reel from Sam's eyes as it still contained the matted strands of hair that once belonged on her head.

Sam rode silently in the Jeep, wrapped in a windbreaker, her arms crossed over her chest. She leaned her half-haired head against the passenger door and slept—or pretended to sleep—the entire two-hour drive back to Lewisville.

When they arrived at her home, Sam gathered her bags, stepped out of the Jeep, and closed the door without a word. Hawken sheepishly followed her to the front door. As she opened the door and stepped inside, she turned and spoke for the first time since the incident.

"You take care, now," Sam said.

"Sorry about the hair," Hawken said. He barely spoke the words when the door closed behind her.

For the next three days, every time Hawken passed by the telephone at home, he stared at the black box as he fought the urge to pick it up and call Sam. He thought it was best to give her some time. Surely, three days would be enough time for her to forgive him. After three days, he had to call her. Sam's mother answered the phone.

"Is Sam there?" Hawken asked.

"No, Hawken, she's gone shopping with Jennifer for some school clothes."

Hawken almost asked about her hair, but decided it was best to avoid that subject.

"Can you ask her to call me, please?"

"I'm not sure when she's coming home, but I'll let her know that you called."

Hawken studied every word Sam's mother said, trying to interpret the exact meaning. *Was Sam avoiding him? Was she never going to speak to him again?* Sam's mother had been polite as always, but she was vague with her answers.

Three more days passed, and Sam did not return his call. Hawken kept calling and left two additional messages, but she failed to respond to any of them. He knew that she would be leaving for college soon, and a feeling of desperation came over him as he thought of the emptiness of life without her. At the least, he had to say good-bye.

A week after the fishing trip, the phone rang.

"Hawken! Sam is on the phone." Maggie held the phone out as Hawken jumped from his seat and took the heavy black receiver from her hand.

"Hello," Hawken said.

"Hey. What are you doing?" Sam asked.

"Nothing. Just got back from the weight room at school. Where have you been?"

"Getting ready for school—shopping for new clothes, packing up. You know…getting ready. Do you want to go get something to eat?" Sam asked.

"I thought you were mad at me."

"Do you want to get something to eat, or not?"

"Sure," he said. "When?"

"How about I come by in about thirty minutes?"

"All right. Thirty minutes."

Hawken never asked where they were going to eat, because they had a routine and it was always the same. The Tastee-Freez on Main Street was one of those classic diner-type establishments that had endured over the years, serving burgers and ice cream from classic recipes handed down through the generations. They sat at their usual booth near the back where they had a hint of privacy in the busy diner. The booth had red vinyl seats with tall backs and a large window with a view of the drive-through. It was Sam's choice. She liked to wave at friends and make idle comments about the occupants of cars as they picked up their orders.

Sam blushed with embarrassment as they sat down. She bobbed her hair in her hands to show Hawken her cropped hairstyle with both sides finally balanced. She smiled as if she liked the new style, but changed the subject quickly as if she was afraid she had acted badly on the boat.

Sam picked at her food and was less talkative than usual. Hawken put ketchup on her fries and ate them himself while he waited for her to protest. She never did.

After a long stretch of silence, Hawken finally spoke. "I know it's not the hair. What's wrong with you tonight?"

"I'm leaving tomorrow," she said.

"I thought you weren't going until next month?" Hawken asked.

"My sister's roommate moved out and the apartment is ready. Dad's going that way for business and wants to follow me up there to help me move in."

Hawken stared at his milkshake and said nothing. He tried to think of some way to stop her—some way to delay her, but her words had a tone of certitude. So…it was good-bye.

They walked outside and Sam pulled him by the arm and turned him to face her. The summer night was heavy and sticky hot without a hint of a breeze. Hawken leaned against his car and Sam kept holding his hand. There was a long silence as though neither knew what to say next.

"Let's go swimming," Sam said.

The Turner family swimming pool was their favorite oasis when summer nights were thick with sweltering heat. The pool sat in the center of the twenty-acre property—far from the houses, close to the edge of the lake, and shadowed by the tall Georgia pines. At night, they could see the scattered lights of neighborhood houses in the distance and they could watch the occasional cars pass along the distant road. It always seemed that the pool was theirs and theirs alone.

They met at the pool and changed into bathing suits in the pool-house bathrooms and Hawken turned out all the lights except the one in the pool that glowed like an emerald eye tucked into the shadows. The moon hung over the lake, and slivers of light shimmered across the water. They eased themselves into the pool and glided toward the deep end until the water reached the tops of their shoulders.

Hawken dipped his head backward to wet his hair. When he opened his eyes, he saw Sam looking at him with a look he had never seen before. Her lips parted as if she was searching for something to say but lacked the nerve to say it. Then she turned and glided into the deep water, swam to the far end, and returned to face him. There was steam rising from the water, and the moonlight created slow dancing lines as the waves gathered the light and bounced it around the pool. There was no splashing or playfulness that night. Hawken was caught in her stare but she did not speak. She nodded her head backward, calling him to her and she reached out her arms and drew him closer. He pressed his body against hers and she tilted her head to the side. His lips met hers and they joined together tighter and tighter. They had kissed often, and had touched each other as lovers before, but that night it was more. Hawken felt love in the kiss and his chest was pounding. He felt as if they were alone in the world and free to go where they had never been before.

The long, slow and deep kisses lasted for minutes. Like never before, Sam tasted like a woman. She moved like a woman. He felt her nails pressing into his back. She was no longer the care-free schoolgirl he knew, but a seductive and impassioned woman and she reached her hand to the back of his neck and kissed him with purpose. Then she suddenly stopped kissing him and backed away. She reached behind and unlocked the clasp of her bikini top. Hawken watched as her top slowly, very slowly, slid from her breasts and floated from her body and then slowly settled to the bottom of the pool. She reached out to him and drew him close again.

Hawken lowered is head and closed his eyes and when he opened them, he saw the bottom of her suit suspended near the bottom of the pool. There was nothing left to hide. He let nature take hold, and two souls reached out to each other as they bound themselves together by a moment and a secret destined to last forever.

CHAPTER THREE
The Storm

Sam left early the following day for Southeast Missouri State without saying good-bye. Maybe saying good-bye was too sad for Sam. She had finally grown fond of the small South Georgia town, her circle of friends, and, of course, Hawken. Maybe she felt that their last night together was something that should be put away to mature and define itself with time. Or maybe, like Hawken, she felt it was just too perfect to spoil with words.

Whatever the reason, Sam just left. She was starting a new chapter in her life, and perhaps the excitement of moving out on her own and starting college eased her sadness of leaving. Hawken knew he would miss her but he felt strong enough to let her go without words. She would be back, one way or another, and he knew fate would play that card.

The next year and a half was a test for Hawken Turner. He had to know if he could make something of himself when his heart was aching, and he had to know he could make the leap from boy to man.

He plowed through his senior year at River Oaks without Sam. He was often sullen with her gone, but despite the loneliness, it was a good year for him. He easily made his grades and earned All-Region awards for both football and baseball. He walked the halls of school with the same easygoing gait that had served him well his entire life. There were no love notes in his locker, no food tastings in the cafeteria, and no long lazy drives on the way home. Hawken kept her in his thoughts always and they occasionally spoke on the phone, but she was seven hundred miles away, and it might as well have been seven thousand.

When high school was over, Hawken decided to study architecture at the University of Georgia in Athens. It was only a little closer to Sam, but UGA was a state school, he had friends there, and it was the best choice for Hawken. It was the unwritten plan for the upper-middle class in Lewisville—graduate from high school, go to college, get a degree, start a family, and work until retirement. A boring plan in Hawken's mind...unless the plan included Sam.

When he arrived at UGA, he found university life was much the same as his last year in high school, only with bigger classes, more students, and better football. He made new friends, joined a fraternity, and spent enough time studying to make passing grades. He dated a few sorority girls out of a sense of obligation, but he had no intention of looking for Sam's replacement. He lived the life that was before him at the moment, confident that time would bring him full circle to the place he was destined to be...hand in hand with Sam.

Southeast Missouri State was fertile ground for Sam's subtle charms and easy style. She was popular there, and having an older sister at SMS helped her to make friends—particularly among male students who wanted to date her. She was open and honest about her dating when she and Hawken spoke on the phone or she sent the occasional letter. At times Hawken sensed their relationship drifting apart, but when they met in Lewisville for a holiday or some special occasion, the magic always came back.

After Sam's father retired, and moved to Missouri, she didn't travel home to Lewisville very often. Neither did Hawken. However, they did make plans to meet in Lewisville for Christmas break during Hawken's sophomore year at UGA. When she called to make the plan, her voice seemed to carry a heightened note of anticipation.

With the smoldering fire stoked once again, Hawken filled his car with gas, packed his dirty clothes, and left for home two minutes after his last exam. He was cooking a hamburger on the kitchen stove when there was a knock at the door, followed by the familiar voice.

"Hey, is Hawken home?"

"He's in the kitchen cooking. Come on in, Sam. It's so good to see you," Maggie said.

"Cooking? I've got to see this," Sam replied.

The sound of her voice put a lump in Hawken's throat. Without looking up from his cooking, he felt her presence when she entered the kitchen and announced her arrival with the familiar placement of breasts snuggled into his back.

"You're doing it all wrong," she said. "You have to mash all the grease out." She took the spatula from him and pressed the hamburger into the pan, producing a sizzling of grease when the juices poured from the meat.

"Hey, I like the juice," he said. He turned to face her and noticed that her smile was even more alluring than he remembered. It was the big, friendly Sam smile, not the serious sexual smile from their last night together.

"I don't want you to get fat," Sam said.

"Okay. I'll start my diet tomorrow."

Hawken scooped the hamburger from the pan and placed it onto the bun. The meat was undercooked and raw inside, but that didn't stop him. He squirted ketchup on one side, mustard on the other, and placed three pickles in the center.

"Let's go outside and eat this," Hawken said. "It's sunny today, and I need a little fresh air."

They walked outside and sat on the hood of Sam's car. The yellow Corolla was parked in the driveway, like so many times before.

"Damn, it's good to see you," he said. "Have you missed me?"

"I always miss you, but I'm not so sure that you're missing me. You must have a girlfriend at school now, or maybe the telephones don't work there in Athens. I think you've been having lots of fun without me," Sam said.

"No, I'm still waiting for you," he replied. "No fun at all."

"Yeah, right."

Their conversation drifted back and forth with news of family, school, and updates from friends. Hawken could see by Sam's smile that she was happy, but there was a hint in her eyes that she had something more serious to say. There were nervous moments of silence while they sat on the car and Hawken ate at his burger.

"What?" he asked, finally.

"What?"

"You have something to say that you're not saying."

"Well…I do have some news," she said.

"What news?"

"I have a boyfriend at school now."

Hawken took a bite of his burger to hide the disappointment on his face. The awkward announcement gave him a sinking feeling, and he tried to finish his hamburger, but it seemed like sawdust in his throat. He kept chewing, determined not to show his true feelings. "Serious boyfriend?"

"Yes, a serious boyfriend."

Sam slid close to him and leaned her head on his shoulder. She seemed relieved to have confessed her news, and Hawken could see that she was trying to hide her excitement, but it was obvious that she was in love.

"Well…am I still number two?" he asked.

"Of course," she said. "If you still want to be."

"I guess so," Hawken said. "But I'm moving you down to number two on my list."

"Number two? Who's taking my place?"

"I haven't found her yet…but I will."

"No, you won't," Sam said.

"I know."

"But you can…if you want to."

They sat on the car and exchanged meaningless conversation for quite some time before Sam got up to leave.

"I have to go now," she said. "Jennifer is home and we have some catching up to do. Maybe we can see each other again before I go."

Hawken said nothing.

"Okay?" Sam asked.

"Yeah. Sure," he replied.

Two days later, Hawken met Sam at the Tastee-Freez. She was wearing a diamond necklace. Hawken figured he had to ask. "Did he—your boyfriend—give you that for Christmas?"

"Yes, do you like it?"

"Lovely," Hawken said. "So...is this one a jerk?"

"A jerk?" she asked.

"You know that you're a jerk magnet. So what's wrong with this one? Child molester? Womanizer? There's got to be something."

Sam was wearing a smile as bright as Hawken had ever seen on her face. The look helped to ease the churning in his gut.

"Maybe all those old guys were jerks, but I really like this one. He's perfect. I think you'll like him too. He plays tennis."

"Oh, shit. A tennis player. Great."

Sam fondled her necklace as they continued the conversation in the greasy, fry-scented red-vinyl Tastee-Freez as they had so many times before. They shared a hot fudge sundae, and waved at friends driving by, but there was no romantic touching of the hands. There was no sharing the spoon, and no locked legs beneath the table. They were back to old friends, and that was it. The reunion that Hawken had hoped for melted faster than the sundae. Nevertheless, Hawken was never going to give up, and the news of the new boyfriend did not deter him. A temporary change had occurred—that was all.

Hawken endured the long separation from Sam after the holidays and did not hear from her for several months. He dealt with the separation the best way that he knew how—he drank and partied like a drunken sailor. Whenever he had the urge to call, which was often, he found one of his Kappa Sig fraternity buddies for a night on the town. Hawken knew that he would see Sam again, and he knew that she would choose the time. Three months later, Sam finally called him—but she did not sound happy.

"Hi, Hawken. How're you doing?" she asked.

"Well, look who's finally calling. I thought you'd forgotten about me."

"You know that will never be true, my sweet boy. I've been busy with studying and all that school stuff," she said.

"And how about the tennis pro—Mr. Prince Charming?" he asked.

"We broke up."

The statement was abrupt and spoken with a crack in her voice, causing Hawken to refrain from showing any joy from the news.

"I'm almost sorry to hear that. Whose idea was that?"

"It was his. It's hard to say why, but we weren't seeing eye-to-eye about the future, you know? We said we'd see other people while we worked things out, but it only took him two weeks to find a new girlfriend. You know we were living together, don't you?"

"I suspected that."

"Well, he wants me to move out. I think he wants this new girl to move in with him. He hates to live alone. He needs somebody to mother him." She was sobbing into the phone.

"I'm going to move back home, Hawken. Maybe go to school there. I have no place to live up here, and I don't want to stay here anyway. I need to get out of here. He was so perfect, Hawken. I was really in love with him. Why don't you come here to visit me first? I want to see you. You always make me smile, you know."

"When?" Hawken asked.

"Come now—tonight if you can. Please? We'll do something crazy."

Hawken fought back the urge to leave at that very moment, knowing that he would see her soon enough. "I don't think I can right now, I'm getting ready for exams. When are you moving back home?"

"Next week. On Friday."

"I can meet you at home for the weekend. I'll just bring my books," he said. "Then I'll go to Missouri and kill that asshole for you."

Sam managed a broken laugh. "Yes, please."

"Good, but you have to visit me when I go to prison."

"Thanks, Hawken. You know, you've always made me happy."

"Listen—you'll get over this. I promise. I'll see you soon, okay?"

"Okay. Next week."

"Okay. I'll be there."

Ken Tucker was the kind of guy that every boy should have as a pal, and he had been Hawken's best friend since grade school. They had done it everything together as young boys—played baseball, swam in the creeks, hunted, fished, and spent long summer days canoeing and camping as Boy Scouts. Tucker was also attending the University of Georgia, and Hawken could always count on seeing his buddy with a beer in his hand and a joke to be told.

When Ken knocked on Hawken's door at two in the morning, there was no beer and no joke. He stood in the doorway, standing like a soldier, as he delivered the news. His voice shook and he looked straight ahead with glazed-over eyes.

"Sam's dead. She hanged herself at school."

The rest of the conversation merely consisted of words escaping Ken's lips and evaporating into air. When he was done,

Ken left, and Hawken closed the door. He could never again think of his friend without remembering that look on his face and those first words that he spoke. Their friendship would never be the same. Ken Tucker was part of the memory that Hawken could never accept.

That was the night that the storm clouds first appeared. The night that the moorings ever-so-slowly surrendered their knots and the drift began. Like a boat with a broken rudder, he lost control, and yet did not know it at the time. He was unable to resist the current that slowly gathered his shattered soul and drew him along the river into the unknown. He was lost, alone, and completely unaware of his own existence.

CHAPTER FOUR
Chat

There was no architect to guide him. Hawken returned to Athens after the funeral. He put one foot in front of the other to walk to class. He read each page of his textbooks, sometimes as many as four times before he could move to the next page. He took notes without knowing what he had written. He called an old girlfriend who had once been able to divert his thoughts away from Sam, but when they went to dinner, he kept looking over her shoulder, as if expecting to see someone he knew. The pain was in the shadows, floating, hiding, and sometimes rising to the surface when he least expected it. He could not sleep at night. He wanted to be alone—alone in some place where he could face the pain and fight the demons.

Springtime passed. Then summer. Still Hawken remained in Athens. When fall came around, a weather front moved into Athens, and the clouds hung low and gray. Hawken began to wonder if he would ever see the sun again, or if he cared. One December day, he climbed into his truck, started the engine, and let the truck find its way back home.

When he arrived in Lewisville, Hawken drove to his house but he didn't stop. He saw Maggie's car in the drive and imagined the sympathetic words she would say to him. He drove to the Tastee-Freez, but when he spotted Jennifer's car in the parking lot, he didn't stop there either. He had to keep moving. If he kept moving, the heartache would not catch him, and if the heartache never caught him, he would live as if nothing had ever happened.

Hawken drove out to the family farm and the woods that had provided so many warm memories from his childhood. He was safe there in the woods. His survival instincts came alive in the woods, and he could breathe without thinking. He had his rifle lying across the backseat of the truck, but he was not hunting. If he killed a deer, he would need to process the meat, and processing meat meant seeing people he knew. Lewisville was a small town, and people knew what had happened. They would say kind words to him and touch his shoulder with compassion, but Hawken didn't want that. He wanted to be alone. The woods were good for that.

There was no one in sight when Hawken pulled his truck inside the gate and started toward the rear of the property. The farm was nearly a thousand acres, and Hawken knew every creek and valley. He had forged his relationship with the Colonel on that piece of land. They hunted and fished there and planted trees for future harvest. And it was there in the woods where the Colonel had introduced him to Chat.

Chat was a wiry old black man who had come to work with the Colonel after years of service as a dog handler for Lovett Plantation. Nobody knew exactly how old Chat was, not even Chat. He had a slight build, a salt-and-pepper mustache, and he always seemed to be smoking a cigarette, or in the process of rolling a cigarette. Most days he wore a faded camouflage jacket, handed down from "Mista Colonel," except on Sunday when he wore the finest suit ever seen at his country church—another handed-down gift from the Colonel—that was at least one size too large. A Stetson fedora, which he wore tilted from right to left, complemented the suit.

Chat knew about everything there was to know about handling dogs for a quail hunting plantation, but what Chat really liked was hunting deer. The wealthy plantation owners were northerners who came down South during the winter months to hunt bobwhite quail. They hunted from horse-drawn wagons while matched pairs of English pointers bounded across open pine forest in search of hidden coveys of quail. Deer often raided the food plots planted for quail, so the plantation owners encouraged Chat to hunt deer when the hunts ended and the dogs were put away.

Chat claimed that he learned about hunting from an Indian, raised in the swamps around Tallahassee, who helped look after the horses on the plantation. Chat swore the man was an Indian even though he was "just as black as me," as Chat used to say. Hawken wasn't sure about the Indian heritage, but the stories were interesting, and Chat did know a lot about the woods and hunting deer. Actually, Chat knew a lot about everything. His simple mind and his dark eyes had piercing insight into life's most complex mysteries. The Colonel had taught Hawken to shoot, but Chat taught him to hunt.

Hawken could recall the day when he was eleven years old and Chat told him about smelling deer. "I'm gonna teach you to smell them deer, jes' like that Injun taught me," Chat said. He reached down into a deer scrape and scooped up a handful of dirt soaked with deer urine and rubbed it onto Hawken's cheeks.

"Jes' keep dat on your face," Chat said. "It'll make you smell like a deer, an' you'll get use ta knowin' what them deers smell like, too. Yo' granddaddy, Mista Colonel, don't believes I can smell them deers, but you watch what I tell you."

Chat was right; you could smell deer. Hawken learned that skill by the end of the first season that he and Chat hunted together. He loved it. From then on, he walked silently in the woods, sifting the wind for scent and following his nose just like the deer. It was his game of survival.

Chat also taught him to listen for the jays and the squirrels. "They gonna tell ya where them deers are. They goes to chatterin' jes' so when they's a deer aroun'," Chat said. "The only way you gonna get a deer while you walkin' here on the ground is to see 'em 'fore they see you. Less you catch 'em when they huntin' a girl-frien'. You can kill you a big buck easy then. Jes' like a man—they jes' lose all sense when they in love like dat."

Hawken drove to the edge of the woods and found himself wishing that Chat were still around. He could tell Chat everything, and Chat would have the simple answers to the burden that was weighing heavy on his soul. He stopped the truck at the exact spot where he had stopped with Sam the first and only time they went hunting together. He eased his rifle from the leather case and gently closed the truck door so it did not make a sound.

Hawken did not need a rifle, but it felt good in his hands. He loved the old style Winchester .30-30 that had once belonged to his grandfather. The Colonel gave the gun to Chat, and then later the gun became Hawken's when Chat had died. It was a straight shooter with lever-action and iron sights. It was an old gun with modest value on the open market, but it was a treasure to Hawken. Its walnut stock was worn, darkened, and dented, but he kept the rifle clean and well lubricated so that it worked with smooth precision. The weight was well balanced and the stock fit his shoulder perfectly.

Hawken walked the same path to the deer stand that he and Sam had walked two years before. One step at a time. His body moved by instinct, and his mind refused to think. He walked around the tree stand and probed the ground for signs of deer as he had done so many times before. A feeling of emptiness took hold, and he thought of Chat's graveled voice when he shared his simple thoughts full of truth and unseen wisdom. But Chat was gone. And Sam was gone, too. The woods had become only woods. His hell was not the fiery underground depicted in books and stories, but the hollow heaven on earth, and a crushing feeling of worthlessness.

When darkness approached, Hawken stepped out of the woods. He put away his gun and climbed into the Ford. He opened the glove compartment and brought out the driving whiskey. Again, he thought of Chat.

Chat had introduced him to driving whiskey at an early age, and Hawken never forgot the first day Chat passed him the bottle. "I keeps this drivin' whiskey here for three things," he said. "For dis' toothache, for cold wind, and for drivin'. You wanna try some? You old 'nough now."

Chat passed the bottle. Hawken held it and hesitated.

"Don't you worry none," Chat said. "I ain't got nothin' 'gainst drinkin' after white folks."

Hawken put the bottle to his lips. He choked when the fire ran down his throat.

"You ain't s'pose to swaller it like dat," Chat said. "You pours a little in yo' mouth, and lets it crawl down to yo' belly. Warms ya all da way down dat way."

There would never be another Chat. And there would never be another Sam. When Hawken finished the whiskey, he crossed his arms, closed his eyes, and tried to imagine her face. The face never came. Darkness came instead, and a night with no stars. Then the hazy light of morning came, and Hawken awoke with a stiff neck and cramped legs. The field was white with frost, and the windshield was covered with ice. Hawken stretched his legs, cranked the Ford, and drove slowly and silently back to the college. He stopped along the way to replenish his supply of driving whiskey. *I keeps this drivin whiskey for three things: to forget about yesterday, to make it through today, and to prepare for tomorrow.*

When Hawken Turner arrived in Athens, there was a crumpled yellow envelope waiting in his mailbox. It must have been lost in the mail and sitting in limbo until someone had found it. Hawken's hands began to tremble when he recognized Sam's writing. He checked the postmark—*she sent it on the day that she died.*

CHAPTER FIVE

Opportunities

Opportunities can come along when they are least expected, and Hawken's opportunity came in the fall of his fourth year at college. Since Sam's death, he had drifted aimlessly in school, putting her memory far back into the recesses of his mind so that he never felt the pain. He spent most of his time at his Kappa Sig fraternity house drinking beer, playing sports, and joking around. No one ever suspected he carried a heavy burden.

Hawken rarely went home to Lewisville, preferring to stay in Athens as much as possible. Even the summer semesters he spent at school, going through the motions and waiting for a new version of his life without Sam. He never answered his phone when he suspected that it might be family or some friend calling from home, and he rarely returned messages. It was only by chance that his mother reached him early one morning before class to tell him more bad news.

"Where the *hell* have you been?" Maggie asked. "I've got some bad news to tell you."

Hawken braced himself as he searched his mind for what might come next.

"Your Uncle Roy's had a heart attack. He's going to be okay, but they had to do four bypasses."

Hawken was fond of his Uncle Roy, who had been a Spitfire pilot during World War II and gone on to become a major in the air force. Roy had lived all over the world and had fascinating stories to tell. When he retired from the air force, he had taken advantage of his worldly experiences and opened a travel agency, Lewisville Travel, along with his wife, Louise. Aunt Louise handled the typical vacations—cruises, Hawaii, Italy, and such. Uncle Roy developed an outdoor adventure division, Lewisville Safaris, offering hunting and fishing trips all over the world. He was admired throughout the sporting community and soon became well known as *the* authority for safari travel—a dream job in Hawken's eyes.

Maggie talked on about the surgery and Uncle Roy's doctors until she finally got to the point. "Louise wants to know if you would be interested in helping them out until Roy can get back to work."

"I don't think so," Hawken said.

"Hawken, it would be good for you to come home for a week or two," she said. "You haven't been here in a long time, and everybody wants to see you. I'm worried about you. You never answer your phone."

"I know, but I'm close to finishing now, and I want to stay here until I graduate," he said.

The conversation ended without Maggie convincing Hawken to return home, but she planted a seed into his conscience. When he was growing up, Hawken had traveled with Uncle Roy on a few outdoor trips, and now he thought back on those dove and duck hunting days in Mexico—the grueling journey with its border crossings, police shakedowns, cold Mexican beer, dusty roads, and the best wing shooting Hawken had ever experienced. He remembered the salmon fishing in Alaska at a remote lodge on the Kenai River where they flew a yellow floatplane at treetop level in dense clouds for two bumpy hours until they reached camp, a hundred miles past the last dirt road. They fished gin-clear lakes and rivers loaded with salmon and trout. He thought of the redfish trip to the Louisiana bayou and tarpon fishing in the Keys. The memories of those experiences with Uncle Roy began to work their way into Hawken's mind. He had less than a year before graduation, and his sanctuary at college was not going to last forever. He needed something intriguing to occupy his mind. Maybe that job was the answer.

Perhaps the most appealing aspect of Uncle Roy's business was not Mexico, Alaska, or the Keys, but the probability that he would work with Brenn Von Snierden, owner of Zimato Safaris. In his early sixties, Von Snierden was a professional hunter and a good friend of the family. Tall, with a slim but muscular build, Von Snierden was of European descent. He had lived in Africa for most of his life. The man looked as though he had been born in sweat-stained khaki, and wore it wherever he went. His clothes were faded but he owned them like scarred fur on a battle-weary lion. He had dozens of tales about elephant hunting and man-eating lions, though he never spoke from a braggart's point of view. He was one of the first big-game operators in Africa, and...he earned a reputation when he became Ernest Hemingway's safari guide.

On occasion, Von Snierden came to Georgia to visit with Uncle Roy, as they had a war connection through some kind of secret alliance that neither spoke about. Hawken had met Von Snierden more than once and was fascinated with his stories.

There was a family history with Von Snierden as well. Mysterious history. Von Snierden guided the safari for Hawken's family two decades before. The safari that started all the rumors. The safari with Hemingway.

The thought of hunting in Africa with Von Snierden was an enticement that Hawken could hardly refuse. The thought of finding answers to buried questions from the past was unavoidable. Answers that would take time. Answers that Hawken was sure he would eventually find.

He stayed awake thinking of his pending graduation from college and the possibilities of moving forward with his life. The promise of unlimited travel and exploring new cultures seemed like a world where he might live without care. The following day, Hawken picked up the phone and called Maggie.

"I've been thinking," Hawken said. "That job with Uncle Roy sounds pretty good. Ask them when I can start."

CHAPTER SIX
First Trip to Africa

awken never regretted his decision to return home to work at Lewisville Travel. Well-funded clients were plentiful, and exploring untamed destinations for an occupation kept him on the road and happy. He kept close to home at first, then slowly expanded his range. He drew on his passion for hunting and fishing to sell clients on distant adventures to hidden destinations. Mexico, Alaska, Costa Rica, Argentina, and, of course, Africa held the best opportunities.

Uncle Roy never returned to work after his heart attack, and two years later, Aunt Louise followed him into retirement, leaving control of Lewisville Travel in Hawken's hands. After they reached a buyout agreement, at twenty-three years old, Hawken was not only in control of the business, he owned it.

Hawken inherited an experienced staff that included a hardworking office manager, June, who took care of the corporate travel and most of the bookkeeping chores, the mundane tasks Hawken despised. June was the backbone of the business, and Hawken was the visionary. The safari travel was Hawken's responsibility, and the core income from managing corporate travel was under June's control. The arrangement worked harmoniously, and they soon became friends as well as coworkers. June not only managed the office but also looked after Hawken. She arranged his visas, booked his flights, checked his inoculations, and even took care of his home and domestic responsibilities when he was traveling.

Hawken was talented at assessing his clients' needs, judging the right destinations, and choosing compatible outfitters. He inspected all of his offerings before selling them to clients so that he always had firsthand knowledge of the operations. Whenever possible, he traveled with his clients to ensure that he delivered a trip that met, or exceeded, their expectations. He routinely went on scouting trips to find new destinations rarely seen or experienced by American adventurers. An undiscovered safari was the prize, and provided Hawken Turner the one thing that always appeased him—a deep sense of solitude.

During long flights between the continents, in his search for the perfect trip, Hawken often thought of Hemingway. He tried to imagine what he could have done if he had been born before Hemingway. He could have been the one to pioneer offshore fishing for great blue marlin, or the first to catch bluefin tuna in the Bahamas. He could have been one of the first to shoot a rhino in Africa. But Hemingway got there first, and he wrote about it so notably that no other man could claim it.

Still, maybe one day Hawken Turner would find the undiscovered trophy. Maybe he would find a smoky river gently flowing beneath a jungle canopy, loaded with finned predators. A place where no white man had ever fished. He liked to dream about casting a plug into such waters…the hiding monsters, the nervous anticipation, rippled water, then the sudden explosion when the beast attacked. Maybe someday…but at that moment in time, he had Africa, and he had a good client he would take there—Wilson Green.

Green was an elderly gentleman, nearly eighty years old, with an intense appreciation of hunting. He had a gleam in his eye whenever he spoke of Africa. Not a boasting gleam, but the same gleam as a grandfather speaking of his beloved grandchildren. Green had taken all of the big five—elephant, lion, rhino, leopard, and Cape buffalo. He had taken those trophies many years before, when Africa had first captured his soul. He no longer sought the trophies as before, but he loved the wildness of the country and the abundance and variety of game there. Green was not a rich man. He had lost his wife to illness five years earlier, and some might have thought he had little left to live for. But Green lived for Africa, and sacrificed every penny of his retirement savings to hunt there. He was the kind of man both Hawken and Von Snierden treasured as a hunting companion.

When Hawken and Wilson Green arrived in Johannesburg, Von Snierden met them at the airport. From there, they boarded a Piper Cub and made a two-hour flight to the landing strip beside Brenn's safari lodge. The main lodge, in the center of the camp, held a dining hall and kitchen. A round building made of whitewashed mud and straw, with a thatched roof that fit like a Mexican sombrero, the main lodge was crafted from native timbers—sturdy, but aged by years of seasonal rains followed by relentless drought. Crooked places in the walls and doorways followed the natural shape of the wood. With its weathered shades of tan, brown, and gray, the lodge blended perfectly with the surrounding landscape.

There was a fire pit outside of the main lodge made from sandstone rocks arranged into a six-foot circle surrounded by canvas chairs and a stack of twisted limbs for firewood. Facing the lodge were four canvas tents pitched over wooden platforms covered with woven rugs. Each tent contained two beds with creaseless woolen blankets to provide warmth on the cool African nights and mosquito netting hung over each one.

It had been a long trip for Hawken and his elderly client—nearly twenty-four hours—and after a relaxing dinner of superbly prepared game meat and vegetables, Wilson Green excused himself and retired to his tent to read his Bible before sleep. Brenn poured a pair of scotches and led the way outside to sit by the fire and discuss the schedule for hunting.

"How's your Uncle Roy doing?" Brenn asked. "I call him from time to time, but it appears that he's enjoying his retirement. He and Louise are rarely at home."

"Yes, that's true. He's doing fine, but I think he's done with the business now. He spends most of his time fishing and playing golf."

"How are Maggie and the Colonel? It's been quite a while since I last saw them, but we speak on the phone a bit. They're quite the pairing, those two."

"Doing well. They don't shoot much anymore, but they still talk about the safari."

There was a bit of silence as Brenn took a drink from his scotch and poked at the fire.

"I actually spoke with Maggie not long ago, and she seems to be a bit concerned about you taking over this business and staying airborne so much. She thinks you've taken on quite the project, but Roy tells me that you're handling the business well."

"She's a worrier," said Hawken. "I fly all over the world and she wants to know where I am at any given moment." Hawken laughed. "It would make her crazy if she knew some of the places I've been."

"What about the girl? Maggie says you experienced quite a loss sometime back, and she feels that you haven't been the same since then. Everything's okay with you?"

Hawken took a drink from his scotch. "I'm surprised she shared that with you. But yes, of course. Everything's fine. Life goes on, you know."

"Well then, life will go on, and we'll have a bloody good hunt. There are scads of kudu and sable just outside the camp at this time, and the weather's been superb," Brenn said. "We should have no problems with the tracking. Have you ever hunted Africa before?"

"No. I've sent a few experienced clients, but this is my first."

"You're going to love it here. And Green is a good man to hunt with," Brenn said. "Let me go and freshen that drink for you."

Brenn gathered up Hawken's glass and returned from the lodge with fresh glasses, a bucket of ice, and a full bottle of MacLachlan scotch. The two men spent the next hour discussing rifles, provisions for the Range Rover, and the stalking tactics they would use to hunt the plains game with Green. It was nearly midnight, and both men were loosened with alcohol, when the conversation turned back to a personal nature.

"Was she beautiful?" Brenn asked.

"Was who beautiful?"

"The girl you lost."

Hawken took a long drink from his glass before answering. "You know...sometimes I can't remember her face. Like now. I can't tell you what she looked like."

"I know." Brenn poured more scotch into his glass. "It's inexplicable how the heart tries to force you to let go. It's good to forget, but I think there's a process that needs to take place before you can bury that sort of thing forever, or it will simmer just below the surface and eat away at you. You have to pay a price for love."

"I can't remember her face, but I distinctly remember her smell—not the way she smelled with perfume and shampoo, but the way she smelled when she buried her head in my chest like she used to do. And the way she would come up behind me, rest her chin on my shoulder, and whisper something in my ear...the Sam smell."

Hawken took a long drink from his glass and swirled the ice around while he stared into the fire. "Strange how I've lived all these years, and done so many things that I shouldn't have done, and the one thing I should have done...and I didn't." Hawken took another drink. "I knew something was wrong the day that she died. The hair was standing up on the back of my neck, a feeling like I'd never known. Came from nowhere. I should've gone to her that day."

"You can't blame yourself for something like that."

"I don't blame myself. I just wish...I'd done something."

"Bloody shame. I wish that I could tell you that there are more fish in the sea, as they say, but I've found that to be untrue. My Bessie was my one and only. I can never imagine that there is another just like her. I'll never understand what it is that she saw in me, but I can't fathom life with another. Life can be cruel, and this life leaves scars, Hawken."

Brenn took a log from the woodpile and tossed it into the coals, creating a crackling sound and a shower of sparks that rose high into the black sky. "Look at the lions. They're magnificent and proud, but when you see them up close, all the brave ones are covered with scars. That's what love does to them."

"I'm not sure I want to see one that close, Brenn. Not a live one anyway."

The two men continued to drink beside the fire until Hawken finally asked a question that had been on his mind since his arrival.

"Tell me something, Brenn. What was he really like?" Hawken asked.

Brenn looked at him with a furrowed brow.

"Hemingway," Hawken added. "What was Hemingway really like? And how was it he was here when the Colonel, Uncle Roy, and my mom came?"

"It was an accident that they were here at the same time. I only planned for Roy, your grandfather, and your mom. Then the day after they arrived, in pops Ernest Hemingway in all his glory."

"It's a shame that my father couldn't make the trip," Hawken said. "But he wouldn't fly. Never. And he didn't hunt either."

Brenn took a drink. "Ernest loved the pageantry of a good safari. I think it was the life-and-death struggle that captivated him. He was always at the center of the action. No...he *was* the action. And a gentleman. Many people don't appreciate the gentlemanly side of him. He loved to entertain people, and he had great stories, as you might imagine."

"I know. That's what my mom says."

"I remember the night when Ernest first met her. She had just returned to her tent after washing up and found a bush snake in her tent. She was calling for Motumba to bring her a gun and cursing like a sailor."

"I'm sure she was. We Turners don't like snakes. And we do sometimes talk like sailors."

"Anyway, Maggie was cursing up a storm and calling for artillery when Ernest walks into her tent, grabs the snake behind the head, and frees it into the bush. Like he was gathering an acorn from the ground. That was their introduction."

"I am surprised Hemingway didn't shoot the snake...from what I've heard."

"He had that reputation as a brutal man, but in truth, he was an animal lover. And he was very generous. You've seen my rifle? He gave me that rifle as a gift. The Holland and Holland double. He loved that gun and saw that I admired it as well. He made a superb shot on a buffalo one day—two hundred meters and he put it right between the eyes. Ernest turned to me and said, 'You should have a rifle like this.' And he handed it to me."

Brenn studied Hawken's face, kicked a twig into the fire, and continued. "He could become quite cantankerous when he drank, but he drank very little here in Africa. Ernest was a dreamer. He sat around the fire in that very spot where you're sitting now, and stared into the distance, leaving me to wonder what he was thinking."

"My mom talks about Hemingway like he was a god. I think she's memorized every word from his books. We have shelves at home that are filled with them. All Hemingway. Nothing else. I've seen her reading a letter. More than once. And she's secretive about it. I think Hemingway wrote it to her, but I've never asked." Hawken took a drink of scotch. "Do you believe that certain family traits are inherited and passed through the generations?"

"Like what?"

"Like the Colonel being a tough old son of a bitch just like his father. And like the Hemingways. The curse. You know…the mental stuff, the suicides. And the drinking."

"I think Ernest was cursed by life experiences. He was scarred by the suffering that he witnessed and his inability to forget the things that he knew." Brenn's eyes grew misty. "I only wish he had died sooner."

"How can that be?" asked Hawken.

"He wasn't the same man toward the end, and he knew it. Bloody tragic, it was. He lived hard, and the body can't withstand so much hard living. It's sad to think of him that way when you can remember his greatness. You can't beat yourself up and expect to die a pleasant death. I felt pity for him in the end."

Brenn tossed the remains from his glass into the fire and looked at the empty bottle of whiskey. "We'd better retire to the tents now if we're going to be on point for Mr. Green tomorrow. He's a good man, and we don't want to disappoint him. I'll see you in the morning."

"Okay, Brenn."

The following day, an hour before dawn, the safari camp came to life. Dry grass and twigs grew into crackling flames when placed upon the smoldering coals from the previous evening's campfire. The smell of biscuits, fried eggs, and cured meats seeped from the open door of the lodge as the men gathered ceramic mugs of aromatic coffee and stood around the fire. After breakfast, the men climbed into the heavily provisioned Range Rover and drove off into the brisk African morning.

"We're going to see if we can put a stalk on some gemsbok today," Brenn announced after driving for nearly an hour along the rutted dirt road toward the plains.

The hunting proved challenging, but the day was magnificent. The grasslands held zebra, giraffes, and herds of impala. The air was pure and clean, and the men hunted mostly in silence, as the landscape produced its own conversation.

The lead tracker, Motumba, was a Maasai who had worked with Von Snierden for more than thirty years. Motumba never smiled. He studied the tracks and broken branches along the game trails as if his life depended on it. Hawken and the others followed behind him in the Rover.

"What about Motumba?" Hawken asked Brenn. "He never says a word."

"Motumba has been here since he was a boy. There's no better tracker in Africa. Or…perhaps I should say that there's no tracker I'd rather have on safari than Motumba," Brenn said. "He was Hemingway's favorite, too."

"He certainly looks capable. I'm sure Hemingway had his pick."

"He did. I used to joke that they were brothers. He saved Ernest once, and those two hunted together from that day on."

"He saved him?" Hawken asked.

"Yes. He saved his life. The fool Hemingway was standing firm as a raging bull elephant was about to smash him to bits. Ernest just stood there with an empty rifle, aiming at the beast like the gun was still loaded." Brenn took a drink from his canteen. "Motumba—he was about your age then—came crashing through the brush and stayed tight by his side, firing into the elephant until he fell dead at Hemingway's feet. The two were inseparable after that."

"Damn," Hawken said. "How long has he been with you?"

Brenn passed the canteen to Hawken. "He's been here since the winter of 1938. Found him wandering alone in the bush when he was only eight. His entire family died in the border wars. Motumba was hiding in the bush while he watched them butchered with machetes. Terrible story it was. He's been with me ever since. He's a good man, but I don't think he'll ever forgive himself for living while his family died as they did."

With each passing hour, the sun baked the plains and a cloudless sky provided little relief. Crisp khaki shirts bore wet stains spreading from their armpits as the hunting party walked for miles in the heat and oppressive humidity. It was late in the afternoon when Green finally got his gemsbok—a mature male with a thick neck and tall horns. The camp staff arrived, butchered the buck, and returned to the lodge to prepare dinner.

"I don't know about you fellows, but I could use a sundowner," Brenn said.

Green removed his sweat-stained hat and wiped his brow with a red bandana. "That's exactly what I was hoping to hear you say."

Thirty minutes into the drive back to the lodge, Brenn slowed the Rover and pointed toward shadows ahead. A hippo staggered along the middle of the dusty road, a baby by her side. The mother hippo was wounded. Dried blood streaked down her leg from a gash on her hip.

The injured hippo was something of concern, but Brenn was watching something else. "Look at the lions following them," he said. "There are four, five, six of them. I don't know why they are stalking. The hippo isn't going anywhere with that wounded leg. I'm afraid this won't be a good outcome for the hippos."

The men sat and watched as the lions closed the distance. The lions walked slowly and looked from side to side as if bored with the pitiful hippos, until finally, one of the lions with a thick brown mane rose up on his haunches and sank his claws into the mother's back. The other lions tensed and moved closer, surrounding the hippos. Green wiped the lens of his binoculars and Hawken gulped as the attack began.

"Look. The baby is just standing there, at his mother's side. Why are the lions ignoring the little one?" Green asked.

Another lion sprang on the back of the mother, using all of his weight to topple the struggling hippo. The hippo buckled under the weight but did not fall. The lions began to bite into the wound, and a fresh stream of crimson ran down the hippo's leg. Still the baby stood close by his mother.

Three of the lions finally brought down the mother hippo and began tearing at her flesh. The other three turned to the baby. One of the lions pawed at the baby's back, as another bit into his face in an attempt to bring it down. As the claws and teeth did their damage, the baby began a bleating cry for mercy. Hawken had seen cruel acts in nature, but he had never seen anything this horrific. He looked over at the Holland and Holland double rifle, loaded and racked between him and Brenn. Hawken reached for the rifle, but as his hand closed on the gun, a steel-clawed grip grabbed his wrist and stopped him.

"No," Brenn said. "There are too many lions."

Green and Brenn raised their binoculars while Hawken stared at the rifle. He snatched the rifle from the rack; stock went to shoulder, cheek went to stock. Hawken notched the sight and squeezed the trigger. The bullet struck precisely one inch below the baby hippo's ear with a loud *thwack* and a puff of blood. The .375-caliber projectile tore through the brain cavity, collapsed the legs, and dropped the baby hippo as if it were broken in half.

The lions scattered into the bush. They stood off, dazed, but did not go far. They would be back to finish their kill. Without saying a word, Hawken racked the rifle, Brenn started the Rover, and the men continued to the lodge. It was late in the afternoon, and the dusty African sky turned to pink, then orange, and finally a magnificent shade of blood red. That day, with the lions and the killing and the sunset, was Africa at its purest.

Later that evening Brenn, Green, and Hawken finished dinner and took their drinks outside to sit beside the fire. "That was a hell of a shot you made on that hippo today," Brenn said. "You have a steady eye, and you handle a weapon well. But you need to learn the ways of Africa."

"I can't believe you were going to stand by and watch the hippo suffer, Brenn."

"That's the art form of survival here, Hawken. If you cannot accept that, it's a sign of weakness. And weakness will get you killed in Africa. At least you knew the proper one to kill. We can't have you shooting at our lions if you shoot that well," Brenn said. "It was the same with Hemingway. He would've killed all the lions if I had allowed him."

"Tell me," Hawken said. "Was he a good shot?"

"He was a superb shot," said Brenn. "And he hid his weakness much better than you do. And I remember the way he would growl every time he shot a lion."

"Well, I'm sorry if I couldn't just sit there and watch that animal suffer."

"I have told everyone that there should be no mention of the incident. This pompous government here has adopted some useless laws preventing the killing of their animals now. It's not like the old days. We have animal rights groups now who want to control the hunting from afar," said Brenn. "I'll wager that they don't advertise scenes like we saw today to their benefactors who are crying about saving the lions. Today the lions eat the hippo. Tomorrow maybe the hippo kills the lion. The next day it will be the buffalo's turn to kill. Africa can be brutal at times, but I hope that you fellows don't lose sleep thinking about it."

"I'll sleep just fine," Hawken said. "Where's Motumba? We should have him over here for a drink."

"Motumba doesn't drink."

"Good for him. What's he doing now?"

"He's walking the perimeter. He listens to the bush and tracks the animals by sound. Sleeps outside...with his eyes open, I think."

It was true, Hawken Turner slept just fine in Africa. And he dreamed. In his dream, he heard drumbeats drawing him toward the river. When he reached the river, the drumbeats stopped, as if he had reached the place he was supposed to be. Brenn Von Snierden, Motumba, and Wilson Green were there waiting for him in a place where the flowing water turned from a lazy wide river with yawning hippos at the edge, and crocs sunning on the banks, to a narrow, dark, fast-moving river with dense canopy growing overhead.

Beside the river was a small boat with a wooden paddle. When he stepped into the boat and shoved off into the swift current, he became aware of the blackness ahead. His instincts told him that he had to survive the stretch of darkness before he reached the ocean. As he drifted deeper into the darkness under the jungle canopy, monkeys chattered and lions roared. Just when he felt that the ocean was around the next bend, he awoke to the smell of coffee and the crackling sounds of the campfire.

CHAPTER SEVEN
The Good Life

H awken Turner had nearly forgotten any thoughts of finding love again, but then love walked right in his front door. It had been nearly four years since Sam's death, and Hawken was bartending at the Turner family Christmas party in Lewisville. Robin Campbell was the first of her family to enter the house. The statuesque beauty was visiting Lewisville for the holiday. Taller than average, with an athletic body, an aristocratic nose, blue eyes, and flowing blond hair, she was a head-turner. It didn't take long for Hawken Turner to engage her in conversation and he soon discovered a charming personality to match her good looks.

"Can I get you a drink?" Hawken asked.

"Sure. I'll have bourbon with a splash of water."

Hawken hesitated for a moment as they looked at each other with the unspoken acknowledgement that it was a man's drink. *I like that*, Hawken thought as he stepped behind the bar. Hawken admired the form-fitting red sweater hugging the shapely breasts in a tasteful but provocative manner. She sat on a tall stool at the bar and crossed her shapely legs.

"How long are you here for?" Hawken asked. He handed her the drink and sat on the stool beside her.

"Through the holidays, and then I'm going back to Nashville. So...a few days, I guess."

"Well...has Lewisville changed since the last time you were here?"

"We moved when I was five, so I really don't remember much. But my parents love it here and it seems nice enough. A little quiet maybe."

"Nashville, huh? I heard it's a fun city. What do you do up there?" Hawken asked.

"Don't laugh—I'm a librarian. I know it sounds boring, but as soon as I get my real estate license, I'll have more time for my second job—a part-time fitness instructor. Which I love."

The combination was intriguing. "Nice. A bourbon-drinking, rope-skipping librarian."

They both laughed.

"That's right. I love books and bourbon." She flashed a warm smile.

"Do you wear glasses at work?" Hawken asked. He had a hint of mischief in his eyes.

"No." She spoke with a low voice as she leaned to his ear. "Not all librarians wear glasses."

"Your favorite author?" Hawken asked.

"I'm reading a new author right now that I like a lot. Her name's Danielle Steel. It's not exactly great literature, but she keeps me turning the pages."

"Thank God," Hawken said.

"Thank God for what?" she asked.

"Thank God you didn't start talking about classic literature. Sooner or later my mom would find out, and you'd be in for a long, long conversation on Hemingway."

"Oh, really? She's a big fan?"

"Yes, but it's a long story. Just do me a favor and don't ask her."

"No problem."

A few more party guests arrived and Robin's mother drug her away to meet their new friends in Lewisville. Robin seemed somewhat bored and occasionally looked over to Hawken as if saying, "Come save me, please." Hawken was more than happy to do just that.

"Hey look, there are some parties planned for the next couple of weeks. You should come with me to a couple," Hawken said.

"I'm not sure what the family has going on, but I'd love to get out a little. Call me."

"Sure."

And that was how it went from casual conversation to courtship, like a grass fire in high wind. Hawken invited Robin to a Christmas party the following night. Then another. And then another. They complemented each other during the parties. They bantered back and forth with sarcastic conversation, and soon physical attraction coupled with mutual interests brought romantic feelings and transformed the two strangers into a couple. They were among the first to arrive and the last to leave. They always found the mistletoe, and with each ensuing rendezvous beneath the leaves and berries, their kisses grew longer and deeper until they reached a point where other party guests turned to stare with wide eyes and slack jaws. Ritual kisses led to sensual kisses, sensual

kisses led to passionate kisses, and passionate kisses led to a freef-
all into mindless bliss.

The festivities of the holidays mixed with alcohol and hormones took them to a place that they could not deny. At the end
of the holidays, Robin was pregnant.

It was supposed to be the happiest day of his life when Hawken
married Robin. And for the most part, it was. She would never
replace Sam, but obligation erased that need, and any thoughts of
delaying the marriage were drowned out by alcohol-fueled party
toasts and festive prewedding parties.

The country club scene could not have been better scripted
as the two families filled their respective sides of white wooden
chairs arranged in perfect rows on the lawn beside the eighteenth
green. They had eight bridesmaids and eight groomsmen chosen
from childhood friends and college roommates. Everyone at the
high-noon wedding wore a smile on their face—everyone except
the girl standing in the distance, the invisible girl, the one seen only
by Hawken. The girl that he truly loved.

When the "I dos" were spoken, nieces and nephews,
grandmothers and grandfathers, cousins and friends all drank
and danced merrily to the ten-piece orchestra. By all measures,
they were the perfect couple—good looking, college educated,
respected families and common goals for a future together. There
was, however, one curious moment, which seemed insignificant at
the time, but hinted at consequences for the future. Hawken and
Robin were standing side by side, chatting with friends and family.
For a brief moment, the couple turned to each other. Their eyes
met, smiles faded, and the look of mutual doubt was undeniable.
Then Hawken looked down to the midsection of the white silk

dress and the bump in her belly that was holding them together. The smile returned, doubt faded, and the married couple returned to handshakes and kisses from drunken friends and relatives.

When Hawken and Robin settled into married life, the future looked promising. The marriage was good. The life was good. Hawken hired two assistants to help with his safari business, and Robin took a position as assistant librarian at the Lewisville library. She worked part-time at the library, leaving time for tennis with friends and shopping trips to Tallahassee. With additional staff at the office, Hawken spent more of his time hunting and fishing with his buddies. Neither complained about the time spent apart.

They lived in a modest three-bedroom ranch located on the west side of town, but a year after the marriage, Uncle Roy and Louise moved to Florida, leaving their house on the family estate available for purchase. Hawken jumped at the opportunity to buy a place of their own, especially one filled with his childhood memories.

The years slipped by quickly and happily, and after ten years of marriage, Hawken and Robin had three healthy sons to fill the house. They had never discussed the idea of having children, but they never took precautions to prevent it, and consequently, Garrett, Thomas, and Hayden were born. Hawken found that he loved the role of father and with each passing day, he became the father that he wished he had known. He traveled less and stayed at home more, doing the things that boys do—fishing, baseball, building forts, and playing in the dirt.

There was no single moment when he and Robin began to drift apart, but there was one evening when Hawken became aware that it had already happened. As bedtime for the boys arrived, he carried each of them to their room for the nighttime ritual. He told them a bedtime story about a bear that stole his salmon in Alaska. They were tucked beneath the covers, hanging onto every word, their eyes wide open as Hawken spun the tale. When he ended the story, he pulled the covers under their chins and rubbed each of their heads with his hand as he wished them sweet dreams.

Hawken didn't join Robin after he turned out the lights. Instead, he walked quietly into the kitchen and took a tall glass from the cabinet. He opened the liquor cabinet and took out the half-empty bottle of MacLachlan. He dropped a chunk of ice into the glass and was about to pour a stiff drink when Robin called to him from the bedroom.

"When are you coming to bed?" Robin asked.

"I'm going to relax for a minute. I'll be there soon."

Hawken took the glass and bottle of scotch and settled into a large cushioned chair on the back porch overlooking the lake. In the glow of the moonlight, he could see the shadows of the tall pines and the gently shimmering ripples dancing across the lake. He tried to clear his mind of thought as he drank his whiskey. He looked at nothing, but his eyes faced across the lake at the distant swimming pool. A black hole surrounded by a concrete deck. The sounds of frogs and crickets permeated the screened porch. He refused the memory, but the memory was there. He swirled the ice in his glass and took another drink. Then another. And another.

Hawken was no longer married to Robin, he was married to the porch and the drink that he drank there. Robin never said anything about Hawken's drinking, but it was too late to stop him anyway. Night after night, after Hawken put the boys to bed, he took the bottle from the cabinet and walked out onto the porch.

He held the bottle like a warrior holds a shield. He drank his whiskey, looked at the pool, and dared the memories to haunt him. When the weather was cold, and sometimes when it was not cold, he put on his letterman jacket from high school—the one with the number "2" on it, the one that Sam liked to wear. The one that still smelled of Sam.

At the office, Hawken began to confide in June when his marriage began to slip from love to friendship, and, eventually, to something less than that. June was only a friend, but the friendship became intertwined with business, and they spent many hours together at the office, and on the telephone. So much time that Robin began to take notice.

"Is that June again?" Robin asked.

Hawken hung up the phone after a lengthy conversation. "Yes, it was June. We've got a large group going to Argentina tomorrow, and the weather isn't looking good for the flights."

"That's not something that you could talk about at work?" Robin asked.

"We did talk about it at work, but the clients are calling her, and the weather is getting worse. Do you have a problem with that?" Hawken asked.

"No, I don't have a problem, but you seem to spend a lot more time with June than you spend with me."

"It's work."

"I know it's work, but she doesn't have to call the house."

"You do the same thing, Robin."

"What do you mean?"

"Well, for example, you spend a lot of time with your tennis friends. I came home the other day and you were sitting in the driveway with Paul. That's the same thing."

"He gave me a ride home from the courts because Lisa finished her match and left early. Do you have a problem with that?"

"No, but if I do something like that, it seems to turn into a big problem."

"Tennis gives me a chance to do a little something for myself. And I like to stay in shape. Paul is just part of the group. What are you insinuating?"

Hawken took a beer from the refrigerator and sat at the dining room table. "I'm not insinuating anything. I'm saying that you spend a lot of time playing tennis. It doesn't matter with whom."

"And you spend a lot more time than that working with June," Robin said. "Then you're constantly on the phone with her."

"Because I have to."

"You can talk all day at the office. But when you're home, you spend a lot more time on the phone with June than you do talking with me. So whose fault is that?" she asked.

"Oh, it's my fault," Hawken said. "But it's *our* problem."

"I'm glad you finally acknowledge that there's a problem. Do you remember the last time we had sex?" she asked.

"I'm not sure. When was Hayden born?"

"It's not funny, Hawken. You're good with the boys, but you ignore me all the time. I'm so tired of the way I'm treated around here. You spend all of our time with a drink in your hand."

"Well, it's difficult to deny that while I'm holding this beer."

"And you never go to church with me. You're always fishing, hunting, or playing golf. Why can't you go to church with me more often than just the holidays?"

"Sunday's the best day for me and the boys to spend time together."

"Exactly. You should spend it with them in church."

They sat silently for some time before Robin spoke. "We should go to marriage counseling."

"We don't need some high-priced counselor to tell us what's wrong with our marriage."

"What do *you* think is wrong with our marriage, Hawken?"

"Okay, Robin. I don't know, but if you think it will help, I'll go to the counseling. But I think we should just give it some time."

Robin made the appointment with Dr. Arnold Goodman, a man she had met in her circle of tennis friends. When they met at Dr. Goodman's office, it was obvious to Hawken that Robin had already laid out the therapy plan. Dr. Goodman gushed at the sight of her, and barely acknowledged Hawken's presence. He asked Robin into his office alone, and forty minutes later, she walked out with a smile, and left. When Hawken entered the office, he felt like he was walking into a trap.

"Mr. Turner, your wife has taken most of the time for this first session, so it's possible that…"

"Look Dr. Goodman, why don't you just tell me what she says I'm doing wrong and I'll work on it. No need to beat around the bush."

Dr. Goodman looked up from his notes and crossed his arms. "All right. Your wife says that her friends are constantly questioning the amount of time that you spend hunting, fishing, and playing golf rather than spending time with her."

"Okay." *I do those things with my boys,* Hawken thought to himself.

"She mentioned a time when you went to an FSU baseball game instead of a dinner party. You were the only husband that didn't attend."

"Okay." *I promised the boys I'd take them before I knew about that party.*

"And you refused to dress in costume for the costume party with her tennis friends?"

"True." *I don't like her pretentious tennis friends.*

"She said that you never hold her hand, or show any sign of affection when you're in public. Wives need their husbands to show their love in the company of others."

Oh yes, the fakery.

"And she is very concerned about your drinking."

Got me there, Doc.

"Do you think you can work on those things?" Dr. Goodman asked.

"Sure," Hawken said. *Like a trained seal.*

When he left, Hawken went straight to a nearby bar. He could imagine Robin at home, confident that a professional counselor had pointed out all Hawken's flaws while holding her blameless. He tried to find something he could hold against her, some way to shift the blame, but several drinks later—he gave up.

Robin was not happy when Hawken came home drunk.

Soon after the session with Dr. Goodman, while Hawken and Robin were still trying to save their marriage, the Colonel was hospitalized with a brain tumor. The man had never been sick a day in his life, and then he was told that he only had weeks to live. It was painful to watch, and Hawken suffered greatly as he witnessed the once-robust presence dwindle into a frail skeleton. Hawken drove slowly and took the long route to the hospital. When he entered the room, he cringed at the jungle of medical tubing and monitors, unable to face the dying man. He hid his face to hold back his tears, though he longed to put his head on the bed and weep. The colonel was a tough man, and Hawken would not allow himself to cry in his presence. There was no chance of recovery, and Hawken found himself wishing for the end.

The cloudy day of the Colonel's funeral was a fog of respectful friends in dark suits, weeping women, and stone-faced preachers reading from the Bible. Bright flags, flowers, and a shiny casket decorated the gravesite. Too colorful for a man who loved the purity of nature. Robin held out her hand to comfort Hawken, but the grip was limp and the touch was cold. They spoke sadly with friends and relatives before leaving the graveside, but they never once looked at each other.

The day after they tossed the Colonel in the dirt, Hawken Turner went fishing—but he never came back. A different man came back.

CHAPTER EIGHT
The Lake

Hawken was sure that his three sons saw nothing out of the ordinary when he announced that he had planned a "guys only" vacation. Just dad and the boys—Garrett, thirteen, Thomas, eleven, and Hayden, eight.

"Where're we going, Dad?" Hayden asked as he jumped into Hawken's outstretched arms in anticipation of some unknown adventure.

"It's a secret," he said. "Did you bring your bathing suits?"

"Yes, sir."

"Well, that's all you need. I've got everything else. I checked the oil and battery in the Jet Ski. I've packed the cards and poker chips. We've got Monopoly and the sleeping bags. The grill is loaded on the truck. I've relined the fishing poles, organized the tackle box, and…I want to leave in about an hour, so get your stuff together."

"Come on, Dad. Where are we going?" Thomas asked.

"Still a secret. Thomas, you and Hayden pack those drinks from the refrigerator into that red cooler and then put the ice from the freezer on top. Garrett, come help me hook the Jet Ski to the truck."

The boys followed his orders with enthusiasm. They would have cooperated under any situation, but the excitement of an undisclosed destination added incentive.

"How long is the drive?" Thomas asked.

"About seven hours, and I don't want you little bastards doing any cussing on the way up there."

"Hell, no," Thomas said.

"I won't say a damn cuss word," Hayden said.

"Shit, no," said Garrett.

It was late afternoon when the truck, loaded with gear and towing the Jet Ski, pulled onto the steep, wooded drive leading to the lake house. The house was set high on a sloped bank overlooking the lake. Trees and thick foliage nearly blocked the lake from view, but the crisp blue water was visible through an opening in the trees, leaving just enough view to take in the dock and swimming platform that was theirs for two weeks.

"Tomorrow, Garrett and I will go around the bend there and pick up the pontoon boat I rented. Then we can explore the lake and look for some good fishing spots," Hawken said.

"Can we go swimming now?" Hayden asked.

"Sure. Just as soon as we unload the truck."

Hawken was proud of his boys. He liked to think that he had taught them proper manners and right from wrong at a young age, although they most likely received their obedience and kindness from their mother. It was not difficult for him to find time for them. He loved them dearly, and always had. It was only a bonus for him that they shared his love of the outdoors and adventure.

While Hawken arranged the gear in the lake house, the boys made their way down the sloped bank to the dock.

"Dad! Dad! Bring the poles! There's a huge fish under the dock!" Thomas was obsessed with fishing. "What kind of fish is it?"

Hawken peered beneath the dock and spotted a large fish lurking in the shadows. "I think it's a carp. You can't catch one of those with a hook and line."

"Why not?"

"I'm not really sure. That's just what I've always heard. But go ahead and try if you want to."

"Yes, I do, he's huge!"

The carp had no value as a desirable table fish, but fish were fish to Thomas, and the bigger the better. Thomas had fishing skills and was innovative in his approach. If he tried a lure that didn't work, he kept trying until he found one that did. If no lures worked, then Thomas found live bait—worms, crickets, grasshoppers, or anything else that he could imagine a fish might like to eat.

After an hour of fishing for the carp under the dock, Thomas gave up. Hawken cooked four racks of pork ribs on the grill while he watched his boys from the deck. The boys swam and fished until the sun dipped below the horizon on the far side of the lake and the sky turned dark. The charcoal fire sent savory tentacles of thin blue smoke down to the hungry boys. They bounded up the wooden steps leading to the house, barefoot and exhausted.

"We'll eat on the screened porch since you're still wet," Hawken said.

The burning coals had cooked the meat to tender deliciousness. The steady consumption of cold beer enhanced Hawken's feeling of happiness as the alcohol eased into his bloodstream. It was a good day for Hawken Turner, but the beer and tranquility of the lake could only postpone the heartbreak of the impending news that he had to tell his children.

The boys settled around the wooden picnic table and devoured the ribs until their faces looked like clowns with red barbecue sauce spread on their cheeks. Thomas laid out his strategy for catching the carp, and when he was convinced that he had a plan that would succeed, the conversation turned from fishing to hunting.

"Dad, are we going hunting this fall?" Garrett asked.

"I think I can put something together. What kind of hunting would you like to do?"

"I want to go deer hunting," Hayden said. He was not yet old enough to hunt, and he surprised Hawken with his request.

"Hayden, you've never fired a rifle before. Do you think you are ready for deer hunting?" Hawken asked.

"Hell, yeah."

"Hayden, I'm telling Mom about your cussing," Thomas said.

"Go right ahead. You've been cussing too."

Hawken thought it best that he should caution the boys about their cussing. "Hey, I don't think cussing makes anybody a bad person, so I don't care what words you say around me. But you had better watch your language around adults. And especially around ladies you don't know. Or any ladies for that matter. Understand?"

"Yes, sir."

Hawken returned to the subject of hunting. "Well, there's a lot of preparation that you need to do before you're ready to hunt deer."

"I've shot the twenty-two before," Hayden said.

"Well, that's not the same as a deer rifle," Hawken said. "And besides, I don't want you to make the same mistake that I once made when I was just a little older than you."

"What did you do?" Thomas asked.

"Well, I was hunting deer with Granddaddy once down at the farm. It was me, him, and Chat. It was early in the season, and I hadn't been out shooting at all before the season started."

"How old were you?" Thomas asked.

"Oh, thirteen or fourteen, I think. Anyway, I had taken the .243 with a Leupold scope. I should've done some target shooting before the season to check the scope and look at some patterns, but I didn't." Hawken took another beer from the cooler, twisted the cap, and took a long drink. "So I'm sitting in one of my favorite tree stands in the morning, and I don't see anything for two or three hours."

"Were you by yourself?" Hayden asked.

"Yes. Granddaddy wasn't too far away on another stand. So, just about the time he's ready to come get me, I start seeing deer. The does came in first, which is usually the way it happens. I notice that they're looking behind them, which is a good indication that a buck is following them. Then I see him…a nice young buck coming into the food plot. It's the rut and he's nearly running, 'cause he's chasing those does. The bucks are always a lot more careful than the does—except during the rut. If you want to kill a nice buck, you need to hunt him during the rut. Chat taught me that. That's when the bucks lose all sense of caution and all they think about is mating with the does. All day long, they chase the does around. They forget about eating, their necks swell up, and they make all their mistakes during the rut. Just like a man—but you'll learn about that for yourselves one day."

Thomas put his hands around Garrett's neck as if checking for swelling. The boys all laughed.

"So I'm trying to put the scope on the buck, but he's running around and won't stop long enough for a good shot. I have a touch of 'buck fever,' and I'm shaking, trying hard to keep him in the scope."

"What's 'buck fever,' Dad?" Garrett asked.

"That's when your instincts kick in. Your adrenaline gets so strong that you start to shake and you can barely speak. It's like a bird dog on point. When they get close to birds and start pointing, bird dogs get all twitchy. Primal instinct takes over the body."

The boys slid in closer to their dad as the story continued.

"Anyway, the buck hesitates for a second, and I have a narrow shot right between two trees."

"How many points does the deer have?" Thomas asked.

"Six points…a nice rack, but he's young. Too young to shoot. You should always try and shoot a buck that's past his prime. That's what keeps the herd healthy." Hawken took another drink of beer.

"But I take the shot. And it's not a clean shot. I know I hit him, but he runs off. Big, big mistake, and I'm feeling like shit about it. I wait for about fifteen or twenty minutes, hoping he'll bed down and bleed out without me spooking him. When I get down from the stand and go to the place where he had been standing, I find a few drops of blood and start following the blood trail. I want to find him in a hurry because I don't want Granddaddy to know that I took that shot and wounded a deer."

"Did he find out?" Garrett asked.

"Yes, he did. And he was mad as hell. Granddaddy was like a drill sergeant and he never accepted poor discipline. You see, Granddaddy grew up during the Great Depression. When he was young, he saw people struggling to keep food on the table. They hunted for food. To Granddaddy, that's the reason for hunting—food, and you didn't take a chance on losing food. He taught me the right way to hunt, and I knew he would get over it eventually, but I felt bad that I had disappointed him."

"Did you find the deer?" Thomas asked.

"Yes, I did. I had to trail him for what must have been a half a mile or so. He was lying in a creek. His body had given out and he couldn't go any farther, but he was still alive. He was on his side in a shallow creek with blood flowing downstream, and he was holding his head up out of the water and looking at me. Looking me right square in the eyes."

"What did you do?" Hayden asked.

"Well, I put the crosshairs right on his neck and shot him again. But I felt terrible. I swore right then that if I ever shot another deer it would be right through the heart, and if I couldn't do that every time I was going to quit hunting."

"Have you ever missed once since then?" Garrett asked.

"I didn't shoot too many after that. But when I did, it was always a clean shot. I don't want you boys to make that same mistake. That's why we're going to practice, and I'm not letting you hunt until you're ready."

Hawken looked at his sons' sad faces and flashed them a smile. "Maybe we should stick to the fishing. You can always throw them back after you catch them."

The two weeks at the lake house went by in a blur of lazy days spent swimming, fishing, skiing, and exploring the lake. Hawken taught Garrett and Thomas to operate the boat and Jet Ski without his help. They were fast learners and heeded every warning that Hawken issued with a maturity not seen in many boys of their ages. They were at home on the lake and rarely left the water except to eat, or at nighttime when they would play cards and fall asleep on sleeping bags spread together on the living room floor.

Hawken was proud of his sons. They were turning out to be fine boys. Garrett was thoughtful and considerate of his younger brothers. He was predictable, and Hawken knew every move that he would make before he made it. He had a good heart and a willingness to pitch in. Even without asking, he was quick to help Hawken load vehicles, rig fishing poles, or cook on the grill. He was good with his hands and never shied away from work. Thomas, a typical middle child, was intelligent and a survivor. When he saw something that he wanted, he didn't quit until he got it, and then he basked in the satisfaction of achieving his goal. Hayden was the mystery son. An old soul at a tender age, he had a stoic demeanor and sometimes seemed consumed in deep thought. He had no problems joining in with his older brothers, and he fit in nicely, but there was sometimes sadness in his eyes. Hawken had crushing news to share with his sons, and he was deeply worried about Hayden's reaction.

Hawken awoke on the last morning of vacation with a slight hangover and the sound of Thomas yelling from the dock.

"I've got him! I've got him!" Thomas had gone for one last chance to catch the carp that had been taunting him for two weeks. The carp had finally succumbed to a piece of bread wrapped around a hook and tipped with a tiny piece of bacon. Thomas had schemed until he found the perfect combination of light line, barbed hook, and smelly bait. It was a fitting end to the vacation, but Hawken's pride was tempered by the thought that their time together was soon to end.

"Okay. You boys get your bags packed. We've got a long way to travel, and I don't want to get home late at night," Hawken said.

"Can we go skiing one more time before we leave?" Thomas asked.

"Nope. We need to get on the road. Thomas, you and Hayden roll up the sleeping bags. Garrett, come help me pull the Jet Ski out."

The boys slept in the truck for most of the ride back home. The truck was quiet enough for Hawken to think about the wonderful vacation they had taken, but he could not think. His mind was blank as the truck covered mile after mile of bare highway and invisible scenery. The comfort that he embraced in the company of his children had vanished, and a feeling of emptiness took its place. The last few hours of the trip to his soon-to-be empty home were nearly unbearable.

"Hey, boys. I need to talk with you about something," Hawken said as the boys began to awake.

"What did we do?" Thomas asked.

"You haven't done anything. It's what I've done."

"What did you do?" Thomas asked.

"Well, it's actually about something that's going to happen," Hawken said. "Your mother and I are getting divorced."

His sons sat in silence.

"Who are we going to live with?" Hayden asked.

"You're going to live with both us," Hawken replied. "Just not in the same house."

CHAPTER NINE
The Bend

When Robin realized that the marriage was over, she rightfully laid the blame on Hawken, and whether or not she intended it, she punished him. He had lied to her when he told her he would stop drinking, and the efforts she took to stop him were useless. Hawken knew that she was better off without him, but he never expected what she did next. She gave the dog to the neighbors, packed up the boys, and moved to Nashville. Hawken adored his boys, and they loved him as well, but she was a strong woman. He begged and pleaded with her not to go, to take them so far from him, but she took them anyway. Maybe, he thought, she was trying to jolt some sense into him. Maybe she was still in love with him. Whatever the reason, Hawken got what he deserved.

Hawken found Lewisville, Georgia, to be a lonely place for a man with no friends, and after his divorce, he had no friends. Everyone in Lewisville was married, soon to be married, or divorcing so they could marry someone new. When the leading women of Lewisville took Robin's side after the divorce, they made sure their husbands did the same.

In contrast to the decline in local social activity, Lewisville Safaris was expanding, and Hawken was traveling all over the world meeting interesting people with intriguing stories. His clients became his friends, and he enjoyed the camaraderie when traveling with them—most of them.

One of his best clients, Charles Murphy, relied on his administrative assistant to plan his travel and work out the details for his frequent trips. Melissa was an intelligent and highly educated assistant who was obviously overqualified for her position and subtly complained about booking hunting trip instead of doing her real job, but she had a cheerful disposition and Hawken enjoyed working with her to fulfill Murphy's outdoor excursions.

"Hello," Hawken said when he answered his office phone.

"Hi, Hawken, it's Melissa. Murphy needs to plan another trip to shoot some animals. Can you help me out?"

"Of course I can. What are we going after this time, fur, feathers, or fish?"

"Feathers, I think. What is it you slaughter down there in Argentina?"

"You make it sound so heartless," Hawken said. "You need to leave that office and go with us some day so you can get a true appreciation of hunting."

"The only things that I'm hunting on my vacation are Italian shoes, and the only thing I'm killing is my American Express card. I don't know why you don't just go to the grocery store, buy some frozen chickens, throw them up in the air, and shoot them. That would be much easier."

"I can plan that trip if you want. The Grocery Chicken Safari. Run it by Murphy and see what he says. Of course, we'll have to build a camp so we can stand around drinking and poking at the fire while we tell big lies about our hunting and fishing conquests. And I'm not sure how good that grocery chicken mount will look on his wall."

"Men."

"What about men?" he asked.

"Just send me the Argentina information, and I'll run it by Murphy."

"How about I just give it to you at dinner?" Hawken asked. The question seemed to slip out of his mouth before he thought about it. He had always been attracted to the sound of Melissa's voice, which blended perfectly with her sarcastic personality.

There was a moment of hesitation before she asked, "Are you asking me out on a date?"

"No. I just want to go over the itinerary in detail and show you pictures of dead animals and proud men holding their guns and smiling. Of course, I'm thinking we'll need some wine and soft music in the background to set the proper mood."

"That sounds a little more interesting," she said. "What night did you have in mind?"

"How about Friday night?"

"I'm doing dinner with the girls on Friday."

"How about Saturday? Are you washing your hair?"

"No, I'm not washing my hair. I mean—I will wash my hair. Oh, you know what I mean. If you're serious, Saturday night sounds fine. I'll bring Murphy's calendar."

"Great, and bring his checkbook, too," said Hawken. "After all these years of talking on the phone, we can finally meet face to face. Give me an address, and I'll pick you up at seven."

"Don't forget the pictures," she said before hanging up the phone.

Hawken had once seen a photograph of Melissa on her company's brochure. She was an attractive woman with stylish dark hair and blue eyes. Previous conversations had led to the discovery that she was a divorced mother of two, spending more time with her job and children than seeking a relationship with a man. Despite that fact, Hawken was still interested.

The quaint Italian restaurant that Hawken chose for dinner was small and dark with red-checkered tablecloths and flickering candlelight. Hawken sat across the table from Melissa and the restaurant was crowded so they leaned in close as they spoke in near whispers. The dinner lasted long into the night and would have lasted longer had they not been asked to leave by the anxious waiter waiting to sweep the floors and go home.

The first dinner led to a second dinner, and the second led to a third. Soon, Hawken and Melissa were seeing each other every weekend for dinner, drinks, or coffee.

After a month of going out, the friendly relationship took a turn toward romance. The evening began at their favorite Italian restaurant where they sat at "their" cozy table by the window. When dinner was over, Hawken invited her to his home to build a fire by the lake and contemplate the mysteries of the world with a flask, a cooler of beer, or a bottle of wine, if the mood was more romantic. That night was clearly a wine night.

When they got to his house, Hawken gathered a bottle of Cabernet from the wine rack, and they rode double on his ATV to the shed. There, Hawken stacked a mound of firewood over a layer of kindling and started a fire while Melissa opened the wine. They clinked their glasses together and stood shoulder to shoulder looking into the burning flames. There was no denying nature with the scene as it was set—man and woman on the banks of the lake, moonlight seeping through the cracks of the live oak trees, and the lapping glow of the fire as it lit the faces of two people awakening to the tide of carnal instincts.

They hardly spoke a word after they finished the wine. There was no need. The weather was turning cool and Hawken took his jacket off and put it around Melissa's shoulders. There was no need to speak when they returned to the house and Hawken took her hand and led her to the bedroom. He felt he was falling in love with Melissa. Maybe not the Sam kind of love, but the kind of love that takes place in candle-lit restaurants and ends up in bed. The moment they entered the room, he encircled her slender body in his arms and the couple came together, serenaded by the rhythmic singing from rain frogs outside the open window.

As the relationship continued to grow, Hawken and Melissa began to change some habits. Hawken had always spent his personal time doing what he loved to do—fishing, hunting, and boating. Melissa was intellectual, sophisticated, and very cultured. She spent her time visiting museums, reading, cooking, and lunching with her friends. Fortunately, they were both open to new experiences. Melissa was soon driving the ATV around the lake, building campfires, and walking barefoot in the woods. Hawken spent time relaxing at Melissa's house, reading her books, discussing politics, and trying recipes from gourmet cookbooks. He adored her intellect and sharp wit. Her modest home was cozy and getting cozier every day. Each time Hawken walked through her front door, he was greeted with a warm kiss, delicious smells spilling from the tiny kitchen, and an open bottle of wine sitting on the counter. Conversation was easy and pleasant. They talked about sports, food, wine, politics, and travel. And there was always the anticipation of ending the evening together in bed.

Although Melissa was a welcome addition to his life, Hawken was still determined to be a nurturing father, and the limited time he was spending with his boys was his first priority. He spent hours each day thinking of weekend excursions and family activities that would make their time together seem like the life he wanted for them. Hawken was not a man who communicated well by telephone. Try as he might, he could not convey his true feelings when speaking to a distant voice connected with copper wiring. He needed physical interaction with his sons. Cards and letters were better, but they only enforced the feeling of separation, and often left him more sad than happy. It was vacation time that brought out the best in Hawken. Those were his opportunities to teach his sons the lessons that Maggie and the Colonel taught him. The same kind of growing up lessons that he wished he had learned from his father.

One crisp October day, Hawken picked up his boys in Nashville for a long weekend, the highlight of which would be a trip to see FSU play football against the University of Miami in nearby Tallahassee. The truck echoed with laughter and disparaging comments about the Miami Hurricanes and predictions of their humiliating beating by the boys' beloved Seminoles. College football in the Deep South didn't get any better than that. Hawken had five tickets to the game—his ticket, three tickets for the boys, and a ticket for Melissa. It would be the first time that the boys would see him with a woman other than their mother and Hawken was nervous.

"Hey, boys, did I tell you that we're going to have some company at the game on Saturday?" he asked.

"Who?" Thomas asked.

"I have a date. Miss Melissa is going with us. You don't know her, but she's a nice woman. You guys will like her." Hawken knew this to be true because his boys liked everyone.

"Is she your girlfriend?" Hayden asked.

"We've been going out quite a bit. You know I get a little lonely living at home by myself. I don't know if I would call her my girlfriend. Not yet. But I want you boys to be nice to her. Okay?"

"Does she like football?" Garrett asked.

"She's not a Miami fan, is she?" asked Thomas.

"Yes, she likes football. And she's a big FSU fan," Hawken added. "I've been thinking of a plan to make sure you all remember to be on your best behavior, so tell you what: I'll give each of you twenty dollars to spend at the game if you're nice to her. Special nice."

"Oh, yeah, I can do that," Thomas said. "Souvenir time!"

"FSU hat," Garrett said.

"And…whoever is the *nicest* to her gets an extra twenty."

"That's as good as mine," Thomas said.

"I don't think so," said Hayden.

"And no cussing," Hawken added.

"Hell, no," Garrett said.

"Shit, no," said Hayden.

The fall air was crisp, the sky was blue, and thousands of fans streamed into the stadium waving pom-poms and wearing FSU's garnet and gold. Seventy thousand fans filled every seat in the stadium, and the crowd was electrified. FSU won the closely con- tested game, much to the delight of the Turner boys and Melissa. Despite the excitement of a close game, the boys' manners were impeccable as they worked hard to impress Melissa.

"Miss Melissa, can I bring you something?" Thomas asked as he stood to go for a Coca-Cola.

"No, thank you, Thomas," Melissa said.

After Thomas left, Melissa leaned into Hawken and whispered, "Your boys are so polite."

When the other two boys overheard the whispering, they figured they had better start acting or Thomas would win the contest.

"Dad, can I sit next to Miss Melissa?" Hayden asked.

"Sure you can," Melissa answered before Hawken could speak.

"Do you like the game, Miss Melissa?" Hayden slid over into the seat left unoccupied when Thomas left.

"Yes, I do. And it's so much fun being here with you guys.'

"You can wear my hat if the sun is in your eyes," Garrett said. He offered his hat from two seats away.

"That's okay, Garrett. I'm doing just fine." Melissa looked over at Hawken and beamed.

The boys continued their charade throughout the game, and when it was over, there was no way Hawken could choose one as the winner. He split the extra twenty between the three, which he paid out when Melissa left for the bathroom. Hawken was afraid that the boys nearly overplayed their politeness, but Melissa seemed happily entertained by the three angels.

"Hawken, your boys are so polite. It's really incredible," Melissa said. "I think they like me better than you do."

With money in hand, Garrett, Thomas, and Hayden ran straight to the souvenir stand beneath the stadium and began choosing their prizes like starved wolves on a deer carcass.

"Look at them now," Hawken said.

"They're such good boys," Melissa said.

"Well, Melissa, it's like ole Chat used to say, 'You got to treat dem childrens like you treat a bird dog. You can't train 'em up too much. You got to leave a little of da wild in 'em. Dey hunt better dat way.'"

"Is that the creed you live by, Hawken?" Melissa asked. "You hunt better with a little of da wild in you?"

"Well, it seems to be working pretty well at the moment," Hawken replied.

One evening at Melissa's, after a home-cooked meal of spaghetti, Hawken and Melissa settled into the sofa with a bottle of Cabernet. Melissa had a question that had been on her mind since she had met Hawken's boys and seen the affection that the boys showed toward each other and toward their father.

"What did you do to make her hate you?" Melissa asked.

"Who?"

"Your ex-wife."

"How do you know she hates me?"

"It's obvious how much you care about your boys. You must have done something that made her want to hurt you so badly that she'd move away to Nashville."

Hawken set his glass of wine on the coffee table, crossed his arms, and turned to Melissa.

"Well...I probably deserved what I got. She's a good woman and I'm not sure that was exactly her plan. We had started drifting apart and I thought maybe we needed a separation—just give it some time. When she first moved, I thought there was a possibility of us getting back together. I thought maybe she was trying to force reconciliation, but I wasn't sure. We got into a big fight over custody and that made her angrier and more hateful. The next thing I know, she's got a new fiancé. Nine months later, she's married to Stan. I've got to admit—he's a handsome guy—looks like a model."

"That's too bad. For your boys, I mean. It has to be tough on them."

"It's been tough on all of us. Now the time is slipping away. They're growing up so fast, and I'm stuck trying to catch a little time here and there. I'm going to try for a change of custody again when they are a little older. Probably useless, but I think boys need to be close to their father. Good or bad, I think they need to know their true father and know where they came from. Don't you agree?"

"Yes, I do."

"I need to get the business in shape so that I have more time for them. All this traveling isn't good for parenting. And it would be tough for the court to consider any changes as long as I'm single."

"So you want to get married again?" Melissa asked.

"Does that scare you?"

Melissa's face turned red.

Hawken reached for his glass on the table and took a sip of wine. "So, how about you?" he asked. "You've never mentioned your ex."

"My ex-husband ran off with a stripper. Two kids in high school and he runs off with a twenty-three-year-old pole dancer."

"Damn. I guess that's about all you can say about that."

That was enough talk about the past for both of them. Hawken took another drink of wine and set the glass down on the coffee table. He slid close to Melissa, placed his hand on the back of her neck, and joined lips with the woman who was winning his heart.

If Melissa was going to be Hawken Turner's girlfriend, she was going to have to learn to fish. Hawken barely had time to run his business, be a father to his boys in Nashville, date Melissa, and fish, too, so he had to combine whatever he could. He bought Melissa a fishing license.

"Wow. I can't wait to tell all my friends that I have a fishing license!" She tried to sound sarcastic, but Hawken was sure that she would proudly inform her sophisticated friends that she was a licensed fisherperson the next time they got together for lunch at some fashionable restaurant.

"It's only the first of many," he said. "Laugh now, but I think you're a fisherperson at heart. Just wait and see."

Hawken often fished from a Carolina Skiff that he kept on a trailer so that he could explore the tidal wetlands and inshore fishing along Florida's "forgotten coast". The shallow-water fishing was a couple hours south of Lewisville, but well worth the drive for Hawken. He loved to quietly drift the flats and creeks, casting plastic lures or live shrimp to redfish and trout as they held close to the thick grasses lining the channels.

Just as Hawken predicted, Melissa loved to fish. They spent Saturday afternoons on the boat with wind in their faces, sun on their skin, and the smell of salt in the air. The scenery along the creeks and rivers was spectacular. They waited anxiously when they rounded each bend and saw alligators, egrets, osprey, and even bald eagles. The shallow water was clear and clean, and they saw shells, crabs, and minnows on the sandy bottom.

When they stopped to fish, Hawken baited the hooks, tied lines, and told fishing tales with a cold beer in hand while they waited for the bite. He taught Melissa how to let fish take line, then lean back against the rod and to set the hook at the precise time. He taught her to reel the line steady to prevent backlash and to bring the fish to the net without lifting it from the water. Melissa learned quickly, and Hawken was gratified as he watched her fishing skills improve with every outing.

On one Saturday afternoon in the early fall, when the sky was gray and the temperature was cool enough for jackets, Hawken and Melissa set off for a casual day of fishing. They had spent two hours baiting hooks and catching trout when Hawken noticed a nervous ripple disturbing calm water near the tall grasses off the stern of the boat.

"Look at that. A school of redfish. *Big* redfish," he said.

"Where? I don't see anything."

"Over there near the bank. Tailing. You can just see the tip of a tail sticking out of the water."

"Oh! I see them."

"I'm going to throw a spoon in there and see if we can get one to take it."

Hawken put his rod down stealthily to prevent banging the bottom of the boat and reached for the tackle box. Without taking his eyes off the fish, he unlatched the lid and reached deep into the bottom, hoping to find a gold spoon. As he shuffled the clutter aside, he found a plastic Ziploc bag. He lifted the bag from the tackle box and held it to the light. Carefully coiled chestnut brown hair—Sam's hair. He stopped breathing. His heart pounded.

"What is it?" Melissa asked.

He was too stunned to speak. He nervously returned the bag to the deepest darkest corner of the tackle box and closed the lid tightly.

"What was that?" she asked again.

Hawken never answered her. He had long forgotten the tangled locks of hair, cut from Sam's head and stored in the tackle box so many years ago. He recalled how he had coiled the hair when she was not looking and placed it in the bag, hoping that someday it would be just a humorous story, something they would laugh about many years later—or at least after her hair grew back. Hawken felt weak in the knees. Melissa said something about the weather, but he wasn't listening.

"I'll just cast what's on here," Hawken said. He carefully moved the tackle box under the console as far away from him as he could manage.

"They're gone," Melissa said.

"Lucky fish," Hawken said. He slid the tackle box to the bow of the boat with his foot. "Let's go home."

Hawken continued to see Melissa. Their relationship was easygoing and comfortable. They found sanctuary in each other's company, with compelling conversation and mutual affection—but things began to change, ever so subtly. He became restless and searching. The drumbeats returned to Hawken's head, calling him to the river. *I need some time to myself,* his voice began to say. *I need to tell Melissa.*

He spent all night trying to choose the words to tell Melissa about Sam without hurting their relationship. At the end of the week, he no longer wanted to tell, but he had to tell her some reason why he had ignored her for a full week. The next day was Monday, he would call her on Monday.

Monday came and he started toward the phone, yet he did not call. Tuesday came, and Hawken was busy with work and returned home late in the night, too late to call. Wednesday came, and

Hawken called his boys that night, spending the evening catching up on the news from each of them. Afterward, he started to call Melissa. But that never happened. Melissa called him on Thursday, and left a message. Hawken never returned the call. Each day that passed swept Hawken Turner further away from Melissa. He stared at the phone at night but never moved. He ignored her to the point where he felt ashamed to call. Maybe he would lie and say he was sick. Maybe he would tell her the whole truth and see what happened.

Five days of ignoring Melissa turned into a week. Then a week turned into two weeks. After two weeks, the phone was out of reach, and Hawken Turner reached for the bottle instead. He never called Melissa again.

CHAPTER TEN

The Dentist

Looking in from the outside, Hawken Turner had no reason to complain. At thirty-seven, he had more clients booking safari trips than he could handle. He would leave with one group for a week or more, return, visit his boys, take care of office work, and then he was off again with another group. The calendar hanging on the wall at his office was filled the names of each country—Mexico, Costa Rica, New Zealand, Spain, Brazil, and, of course, *always* Africa.

Maybe it was having a teenage son, and two more near that age. Maybe it was the fact that he was approaching forty. For whatever reason, Hawken began to change. He stopped hunting the trophies, and he no longer photographed his kills. He continued to hunt, but only for food and the memories and the feeling of a bond primal ancestors who had long since vanished from earth. Hunting was his reminder that life was fragile and only death was certain. He loved the animals...but he continued to kill them just the same.

Hawken could not deny Africa. Plains game, antlered trophies, dangerous buffalo, hippos, and the big cats—they were all there.

The continent nurtured an environment that fed the souls of hunting purists like Hawken and Brenn Von Snierden. Brenn was still there, and he had answers to questions that haunted Hawken Turner.

Africa was Hawken's prized destination, his great love, but he very nearly ended his ties to the Dark Continent due to a dentist. One of Hawken's good clients had referred the man, so Hawken accepted the booking on his behalf. Big money kept the poachers at bay, and the dentist paid big money. He paid twenty thousand dollars to shoot a lion in one of Von Snierden's concessions where hunting lions was still allowed.

Hawken was reluctant about the hunt from the start. Perhaps he was becoming more cynical with age. Five minutes after meeting Dr. Trammel in the airport, Hawken knew that he despised him. Trammel was loud and anxious. He was dressed in fancy safari clothes from a trendy catalog, exposing him as an imposter in the hunting world. Hawken noticed the sales tag still attached to the back of his shirt, but he said nothing. *What's he going to do, hunt on the plane ride?* Hawken thought. *No good can come from hunting with a man with this kind of ego.*

The dentist had a new rifle that had obviously gone straight from the store and into his luggage, shiny and cold. No hands had worked the bolt or rubbed the stock. The blued steel showed no signs of wear or use. Trammel had no bond with the tool, and therefore, it could not truly belong to him. If he was going to take the life of one of earth's magnificent animals, he should have had a weapon that was a part of him, not a shiny toy. To Trammel, the rifle was just another possession that proclaimed his status, not an extension of him, as it should be. The dentist was not capable of setting up the rifle for hunting. Maybe Motumba would do it for him and then Trammel could leave Africa with a trophy to show his friends and family.

Hawken hated every minute of the safari with the dentist. Brenn Von Snierden was generous and accommodating as usual, but there was tension in the air around camp. As Hawken, Brenn, and Trammel sat drinking around the dinner table on the third night of the safari, the conversation turned to hunting buffalo. Lions and leopards had the reputation of being the most ferocious predators on the plains, but Cape buffalo killed more people than any other animal in Africa, earning them the name "Black Death."

"Hey, Dr. Trammel," Hawken said. He poured himself another whiskey. "Why don't we go for a nice buffalo if we get your lion before the week's end?"

"How much will that cost?" asked the dentist.

"Maybe we can throw it in for free if you can kill it with one shot," Hawken said. "If you don't kill it with the first shot, I don't think you'll be around to worry about the cost."

"My wife would never let me put one of those on the wall. They're too ugly," Trammel said. "And they're not very impressive to me."

"They're magnificent beasts," Brenn said. "So ugly and brutal that they're lovely. They may seem like large black cattle when they are grazing far away on the plains, but they lack any hint of the domestication of their tame cousins. They have an incredible nose—far superior to that of a lion. And the buffalo are constantly sifting through the winds to detect any intrusive smell that raises their attention. You have to be extremely careful of the wind if you want to get close enough for a shot. If you *do* get close, you can see that their hide is like tank armor with wiry black hair. Those tree-trunk legs can move their mass nearly forty miles an hour—when they want to. And that's another problem—you never know when they want to."

Hawken joined in. "They have the meanest, beadiest eyes I've ever seen on an animal and a killer set of polished horns waiting to bury themselves in some slow-running dentist's ass."

"Well, you make it sound very interesting, but I was thinking of shooting something like a zebra. They make great rugs. My wife would love to have one for the library," Dr. Trammel said.

"We can give that a look if we get your lion," Brenn said.

"Great. And since I just took my sleeping pill, I'm going to my tent. It's been a long day, and I want to be ready to go tomorrow. Good night, gentlemen."

"Good night," Hawken said.

Hawken and Brenn left the dining hall and settled into a pair of canvas chairs by the campfire. Hawken brought the bottle of scotch.

"You were a little hard on your client there," Brenn said.

"That man gets to me," Hawken said. "He doesn't deserve to shoot a lion."

"Yes, but without clients like that, there would be no hunting, and we would have no livelihoods."

"Well, that might be, but I'm pulling for the lion tomorrow. In my opinion, there are two kinds of men—the ones who listen to their instincts and the ones who have evolved into dentists. Hunters and dentists. This business of ours is for the hunters, not the dentists."

"But the dentists have the money," Brenn said.

"Yes…and they pay well to *pretend* to be hunters. It's easy to spot them, isn't it?" Hawken asked.

"Yes, it is."

They sat quietly, gazing into the fire until the conversation resumed. "You know, sometimes I hear drumbeats here in Africa," Hawken said. "I swear. Just like some ancient drums in my head driving me toward something that I have no control over."

"Tribal drums can carry a long way on the savannah," Brenn said.

"Maybe…but damn, it's special here. Look at the stars tonight. Is it my imagination, or do the stars sink down closer to the earth here in Africa? Damn, Brenn, it feels like I'm living *in* the stars, not looking at them from a distance. Do you ever think about what heaven is really like?"

"It's Africa, Hawken."

"Maybe. Maybe that's why I wish Trammel wasn't here. I imagine he's sleeping right now and dreaming about his bank account or his accumulation of trinkets. Damn, I hope a lion eats him tomorrow."

"I'm beginning to think that maybe you'll shoot him yourself," Brenn said.

"Not until he pays us. It's not that I have anything against dentists, you know. I just like lions better."

"Do you ever consider that maybe your dentist is a better man than we are?" Brenn asked. "You should think about that. At least your dentist doesn't know that the lion has a soul. And we know that. To him, it's just a thing. So, who's the better man?"

"Don't start getting philosophical on me. What are you saying? You regret sharing all this with clients?" Hawken asked. "I know not everyone sees it the same as we see it here."

"I sometimes feel like a bloody pimp. But it's all going to change someday soon anyway. Too many people. Too much encroachment from civilization. We've got to change with the times, you know," Brenn said. "But I'll fight it to the death."

The men sat silently, staring into the flickering flames. Brenn rose from his chair and retrieved a log. He tossed it into the flames, sending a rising shower of sparks twisting high into the black African sky.

"Are you a golfer?" Hawken asked.

"Yes, I play a bit of golf now and then," Brenn answered. "Keeps me civilized, I suppose."

"Civilized? Not me." Hawken laughed. "I get those same drumbeat feelings in my head when I play golf. I can't figure the connection to the hunting, but it's like going to war. When I lace up my spikes and take up that bag of clubs, it reminds me of a warrior shouldering an armful of weapons and going into battle. I love that sound of the steel spikes when they grind into the pavement and the clubs clank together with the rhythm of the walk. It churns my blood."

"I'm not sure I want to play golf with you," Brenn said.

"I'm not proud of that feeling, but I can't deny it either."

Hawken sat silently, staring at the fire. "Do you ever think about women when you're out here on the plains?"

"Yes, I do," Brenn answered. "I mostly think about the days when my wife Bessie and I hunted together before she died. It's pleasant to have a woman on safaris, actually."

"I can imagine. It's all related somehow—the drumbeats, the hunt, the lions, and the love of a woman," Hawken said. "It's like we were born to be here. Or maybe we were just born here."

Hawken finished his scotch and poured another for himself and Brenn.

"Tell me something about the Hemingway trip, Brenn…"

Just then, Motumba stepped in from the darkness and stood next to the fire. "The wind will be out of the east tomorrow," he said. "We should hunt the western plains."

"The bridge is washed out on the Nokowi River, but I think we can manage a crossing," Brenn said.

And just like that, with a nod of his head, Motumba vanished into the night.

Brenn walked to the woodpile and returned with another log for the fire.

"Do you have a special woman now?" Von Snierden asked.

"I did a while back," Hawken said. "I screwed that one up too, but it was damn good while it lasted. Now I think that I'm just destined to be alone."

"That's no good."

"I do think about that first one sometimes. You know, the one who…" Hawken took a long drink of scotch. "Died." He paused in thought. "Sometimes I go someplace incredible, or see something that no one would believe, and I find myself wishing she was there. Like now, I wish that she was sitting here, right now."

"I can relate to that feeling."

Brenn checked his watch and stood from his chair. "Well, if we are hunting early tomorrow, we need some sleep. Good night, Hawken."

Hawken was always the last one to his tent when on safari, retiring just before the staff secured the camp for the evening. He stayed alone by the fire and stared into the dwindling flames, a canvas tent dimly lit by a flickering lantern awaiting him. The heavy African air smelled like trampled earth and animals. He was as far from home as he could be, but the glowing fire and the heat of the night brought back memories of Sam at the pool by the lake. He could see her hand as she reached for him, he could feel the softness of her kiss. Hawken stirred the fire with a long stick. He withdrew the stick, snapped it in half, and extinguished the thought. Another scotch and he was dreaming of buffalo.

Much to Hawken's dismay, the dentist got his trophy—a magnificent black-maned lion, old enough to be past his prime. The lion would not have lasted another year, but it took Trammel three shots to kill him. Motumba had to track the wounded lion for the better part of the day and finished him off with the final shot. The dentist didn't care. His taxidermist would patch the holes, and the lion would look ferocious in his den. Hawken witnessed the entire disgusting event, recalling the look on the Colonel's face when he first taught Hawken about shooting: "One shot. That's all you've got. Make it pure."

Throughout the lion safari with Trammel, Hawken watched Brenn closely. The elderly gentleman belonged in Africa. Maybe Hawken belonged there, too.

Hawken stayed for a few days after Trammel flew back to the United States, under the pretense of scouting the concession for future clients, but truthfully, he was in no hurry to return home. He and Brenn spent two days hunting plains game for the ranch. They hunted well together. Careful and deliberate. They shot two fine kudu and four gemsbok, which they dressed and packaged for the ranch freezer. The days were long and exhausting, but hunting with Brenn was hunting as it should be. They were the apex predators, and they were hunting for meat, not sport. It was pure, honest, and wild.

Hawken and Brenn spent the last day driving over the savannah and searching for game with their cameras. They photographed giraffes neck-fighting, lions stalking prey, and bright orange sunsets behind the bare branches of baobab trees. They gathered at the campfire in the evening to drink their scotch and talk about the things that men talk about around a fire. They listened to the sounds of creatures in the dark. A pride of lions moved in close to the lodge and roared loudly at night to lay claim to their territory.

"Did you hear that beastly one?" Brenn asked. "The one with the deep roar?"

"Yes. He must be the dominant male," said Hawken.

"I suspect that he is the old one that walks with the limp. Most likely younger males are challenging him. In the dark, it's difficult for the young ones to judge him. That ferocious roar will keep them away for a time, but not too much longer."

The old lion roared again. It was so loud that it shook the trees. It sounded as if he was standing just on the other side of their tents.

"It's a harsh sight to observe when a lion is too old to remain the dominant male," Brenn said. "The younger males will chase him from the pride. From then on, the old man just follows the pride and watches from the outside as he withers away. All the bloody battles and fighting for the pride over the years, and then they abandon him to die."

"Better to go out fighting, I'd say."

"Of course. And many of them do," Brenn said. "Those are the ones we need to hunt here. Just before they begin their decline."

The two men sat listening to the lions roar as they consumed their drinks.

"You had better ease up on that scotch, Hawken. We'll run out of the good stuff."

"The cheap stuff works just as well."

"I suppose it does." Brenn turned his gaze to Hawken. "You haven't had much to say about the Colonel. I was very saddened to hear about his death. I spoke to Maggie at length about it, and she said he remained strong until the end. I would have expected nothing less from him."

"That's true. It's sad to think about all the time we spent together, but he wouldn't want me to grieve. You know the old man was as tough as nails. He taught me so many things, but he never taught me about grieving. He never grieved. Not even when my grandmother died. I'm sure that the old man never shed a tear in his life."

Brenn stirred the fire with a stick. "He was a great man. All that flying he did in the war. And winning the elections to congress all those years. A great man." There was a moment of silence as the men gazed into the fire. "You can't say that about many men. Take my father, for instance. A drunken wife beater who ran off and left me and my mum to fend for ourselves. He didn't set much of an example to follow."

"I'd say you did okay with that upbringing," Hawken said. "Whatever happened to him? Do you know?"

"I went back home and found him. That was Bessie's idea. She was a brilliant woman. Truly she was."

"How did it turn out?"

"Christ, I felt love for him just as if we had spent all our lives skipping through parks and riding ponies. Loved him until the day he died, and then cried like a baby when he was gone."

The lions grew silent, and the two men were well numbed with alcohol.

"I remember quite fondly the time I spent in the States with your grandfather and Roy," said Brenn. "They were both great men. That entire fiefdom that you have there is magnificent. The family houses with their tall white columns, all built around the lake…those beastly oak trees with the Spanish moss hanging down…that white fence that surrounds the whole property. Reminds me of a British estate, with three castles and a lake. It's superb. And your family—magnificent. You know your mother is a strong woman as well. Like the Queen Mum. Incredible lady."

"Yes, I know."

"But Hawken," Brenn drained the scotch from his glass. "I know one thing for sure. There is no Camelot."

"No Camelot?"

"No. All of that nonsense is a bloody fairytale. There are no white knights fighting for honor and truth. There's no perfect succession of kings, queens, and princes. But there is beauty, Hawken. You just have to recognize it."

Hawken poured himself another scotch. A serious pour. Much more than a two-finger gentleman's pour.

"You seem to have something troubling on your mind, Hawken."

"What do you mean?"

"You have the Hemingway eyes—the look he had when he seemed to be remembering something painful. What is it that you're thinking when you stare into that glass?"

"I'm wondering if you have enough ice."

"Seriously. You seem distant. Maybe it's a woman. Did that woman of yours break your heart?"

"Which one?" Hawken asked.

"The mother of your children."

Hawken took another drink. "I guess losing the family broke my heart, Brenn. Yes. The answer to that is yes."

"How do you and the ex get along now?"

"Okay. When we first got divorced, she wouldn't look me in the eye. Now she acts like I never existed. It's okay, you know? She's happy. Looks better every time I see her. She's working out—in great shape. I think she tries to torture me. She'll show up when she's dropping off the kids and maybe one of the buttons will be left open on her blouse. Or she'll lean over to tie the boys' shoes like she's showing me everything I'm missing. But it's my fault."

Brenn smirked with understanding. "And the sons?"

"I miss the boys. It's difficult to maintain a close relationship when you're separated, you know. I feel it slipping, but I need to have something a little more stable before I can be a better father to them," Hawken said. "How about you? Do you ever get lonely out here by yourself?"

"It's been quite some time since my Bessie passed," Brenn said. "She loved it out here. Think about her all the time. I wish I had treated her better, but we had a good life here."

"How did the two of you meet, anyway?"

"I met her on a British Airways flight from Cape Town to Johannesburg many, many years ago. Quite stunning in her flight attendant uniform. I was drunk and disorderly, but she must have seen some potential, because she gave me her telephone number anyway." His eyes glazed over as he continued. "I guess she saved me. She did. I was running the ivory back then and no good to anybody."

"You never found another woman?" Hawken asked.

"I have a friend in Cape Town. Handsome woman, actually. But she hates what I do."

"That's not good," Hawken remarked.

"She's a good woman. Don't be surprised if one day I leave all this and retire to the beach in Cape Town."

"I'll have to see that to believe it. It's difficult for me to imagine you living among the city dwellers."

"If it weren't for all those bloody sharks in the water, I might be there right now," Brenn said.

Hawken laughed. "Perfect. The great white hunter is afraid of sharks."

"Can't swim with a rifle, now, can you?"

"I suppose not."

Africa felt like home to Hawken Turner. Life there was raw. The smells were of earth and the colors vivid. This was where human life began. Maybe even his own life. He did not ask the question, but someday he would. He would return to Africa, but he wasn't ready yet. No, that wasn't it. He was ready to ask the questions, but not ready to endure the consequences when he found the answers he sought.

CHAPTER ELEVEN
The Trip from Hell

As Hawken Turner continued building the hunting and fishing destinations for Lewisville Safaris, one country kept cropping up in discussions—Colombia. He knew it was a dangerous country, but before the drug wars and ensuing political unrest had taken hold, Colombia had been the premier wing-shooting destination in the Western Hemisphere and a country much favored by American hunters. The crop damage from the immense dove population in Colombia was so severe that it accounted for a 30 percent loss to Colombian farmers. Each day in the fertile green valleys surrounding Cali, swarms of doves dropped from the sky to devour the kernels of corn and sorghum seeds as they began to mature for harvest. Losses for Colombian farmers were staggering.

In the United States, there was a limit of twelve doves per day for hunters. Sometimes a hunter in the United States got the limit, sometimes a hunter got less than the limit, and sometimes the hunter hunted all day and got nothing at all. In Colombia, there were no limits, and even the average wing shot was able to shoot hundreds of dove in a single day. The Colombians were more than happy to have Americans spending tourist dollars, and the outfitters provided superb accommodations, lavish meals, and plenty of alcoholic beverages to ensure that the American hunters were comfortable.

When cocaine and marijuana exploded on the drug scene during the seventies, the hunting gave way to more lucrative ventures for the Colombians. As the bloody battle for cocaine distribution consumed the country, violence spread throughout the farming region and brought a rapid close to the hunting operations. Hunting in Colombia simply became too dangerous.

In the early nineties, the government put pressure on the cartels. Colombian citizens had become weary of the drug wars. They tired of seeing innocent people caught in the violence, and a corrupt government unable to stop it. Eventually, the people elected a strong government, and with the help from the US DEA, Pablo and most of the notorious drug cartels were driven out, imprisoned, or killed. Better conditions led Hawken to believe that it might be time to bring back hunting in Colombia.

Hawken had a process for building operations in an unfamiliar destination. He began with finding someone with knowledge of the area—someone he could trust. Once he found that key person, he asked for an introduction to their contacts. Once he established a network, Hawken visited the targeted destinations to arrange the details. It nearly always worked just fine. US travelers were widely viewed as a means for making significant money, and finding people willing to work with him was rarely a problem.

Hawken's neighbor in Lewisville, Frank Gordon, knew about Colombia. Frank was a petroleum engineer who had met Luz, his wife, while working on a project in Cali. An older gentleman, Frank was a character who always had an eye for the ladies. He was more than willing to help when Hawken approached him asking questions about Cali.

"Hawken, you *need* to go to Colombia. Forget that nonsense you hear about the danger. I'm telling you, Colombian women make the best wives," Frank said.

Hawken shook his head. "Well, Frank, that's not what I'm interested in hunting right now."

"Listen. When you see those black-haired beauties with tanned skin walking the streets in Cali, you'll forget all about hunting."

"I'm sure that's true, but I still need to make some money. Do you really think it's safe to go down there now?" he asked.

"You go down there with your good looks and that American passport, and you won't be able to fight the women off. Hell, even when we were married, if Luz left my side for a minute, there would be some hot-looking Colombiana making eyes at me."

"Damn, Frank. You think with your six-inch brain."

"No, it's better than that."

"Well, I'm not going to measure it."

Frank just kept on talking. "I think that drug war must have killed off a bunch of the men down there. There always seems to be more women than men. Maybe two to one, maybe three to one…" Frank thought some more. "Hell, just a lot more."

"Yes, but is it safe down there?"

"Sure. Just take lots of condoms."

"That's not what I'm talking about—I mean safe for the hunting," Hawken said.

"Do you like curvy women or skinny ones?" Frank asked.

"I like all women," Hawken replied.

"Well, those Colombian women are curvy. They have the best-looking asses of any women in the world."

"Is it safe?" Hawken asked again.

"I never have problems down there. Just use your common sense. Stay out of the rough neighborhoods—just like you do in any big city. Don't travel outside the city at night. And when you *do* go outside the city, take an armed escort with you. Don't wear your expensive watch, and don't get too drunk and loud, especially with that Southern drawl of yours. They'll tag you as a rich gringo right away."

"Drunk and loud? You sound like a man with experience in that regard. But I'm sure that Luz keeps you on a pretty short leash down there."

"That's another thing about those Colombian women. They're jealous as hell. And trust me—you don't want one of them mad at you. I tell you what I'll do. I'll talk to Luz. She has a lot of family there in Cali, so I'll get you set up with somebody to take you around down there. Go and check it out for yourself. You need a Colombian woman. Did I mention they can cook?"

Frank spoke with Luz as promised, and she provided Hawken the e-mail address of a family member in Cali. After exchanging a few exploratory messages and a couple of pictures as well, Hawken began working with Luz's cousin, an attractive woman named Patricia. Maybe it was a set up from the start. She was well educated and wrote her e-mails with perfectly punctuated English grammar. She was single, Hawken was alone, and the e-mail communications began probing for romantic possibilities. Exotic woman, exotic country, flirtatious words, touched-up photographs, and Frank's tales of sweet, intelligent women, fueled a plan. Six weeks later, Hawken had a first-class ticket for Colombia in his hand.

"Well, you've sold me on that country of yours," Hawken said when Patricia answered the phone.

"What?"

"I'm coming to Colombia in three weeks. Just for a few days. Maybe head up to Buga and look around at the hunting there."

"I was wondering if you were ever coming here," Patricia said. "Are you staying in Buga?"

"No, I'm planning on staying in Cali. You have a hotel you could recommend?"

"Stay at the Intercontinental. It's very nice, and only a few minutes from my house. It's first class." Patricia hesitated for a moment. "That is, if you want to see me."

"Of course I want to meet you. I need to see the face that belongs to all these e-mails. I'm going to Argentina for business first, and I'll stop in Cali on my way home."

When Hawken hung up the phone, he turned on his computer and took another look at Patricia's picture. The anticipation in her voice gave him reason to believe that she was just as eager to meet as he was, and from that night on, business talk faded into the background and personal conversation took its place. Patricia seemed anxious for their meeting, but she did so with hesitation. One evening when they were chatting on the phone, she sent out a warning.

"I feel a lot of stress today," she said.

"Why is that?"

"My ex-husband found out that you are coming here and that we're going to spend some time together. He's been spying on my e-mails, and he read everything."

"I thought you told me he had a new girlfriend and is living with her? What's the problem?"

"Yes, he has a girlfriend, but he doesn't want me to see anyone. He thinks that I'm disrespecting him if I spend time with another man. I'm the mother of his child, so he thinks I should stay home to respect him. He wants to control me even though we're not married."

"That's unfair," Hawken said.

"I know, but he's still jealous and he doesn't respect me. All the men in this country are crazy like that."

"Maybe it's the beautiful women that make them that way," Hawken said.

"He has more than one girlfriend too," Patricia talked on. "He bought an apartment for this other low-class girl, and bought her new breasts too. Big, big breasts." Her voice was shaking. "He comes from a family of nothing. No education. No manners. A low-class family. But—" she hesitated for a moment—"they made a *lot* of money in coffee."

The mention of making money in "coffee" reminded Hawken of another conversation; Frank told him to be wary of anyone in Colombia claiming to have made their money in "coffee."

"Does this mean that you don't want to see me?" Hawken asked.

"No. I just want him to stay with his girlfriend and leave me alone. I want a life of my own, but he controls me."

Hawken was not deterred by the warning signs.

The trip to Argentina's Rio Torcido Lodge was routine for Hawken but his clients were first-timers. They feasted on the hunting during the day and feasted on fine grass-fed beef and red wine at night. Every aspect of the trip exceeded their expectations. When the out-fitter found a large concentration of pigeons in the fields outside of Cordoba, the group extended their stay for two more days, meaning that Hawken would arrive two days later than Patricia expected.

When Hawken finally left Rio Torcido Lodge, he was running late and barely made his afternoon flight to Cali. The flight was seven and a half hours long with a connection in Bogota. He finished his sixth scotch and glanced out the window when the A320 descended through the clouds and dropped onto the dark runway in Cali. It was near midnight and the airport was quiet. He wondered if Patricia had received the e-mail explaining his delay.

Few passengers on the plane meant a quick pass through immigration. In the baggage zone, Colombian military kept a close watch with automatic weapons slung on their shoulders and a frisky beagle running free as he sniffed at passengers' bags. There had been unrest with the FARC, bombs had exploded in Bogotá, and security was stiffened in the airports. Hawken watched as the beagle worked the room twice, pausing at the feet of each passenger. The dog hopped onto the baggage carousel and began sniffing bags, one by one. He worked the entire length of the conveyor. Then, to Hawken's amusement, the dog went under the rubber flap and into the loading area. When the beagle popped out from under the flap on the other side, he was riding a large duffel bag, pawing at the canvas like a starving badger. The bag was not just any bag—it was Hawken's bag.

Tension gripped the room as soldiers began scanning for the owner of the bag. There was no escape. *What the hell is going on?* Hawken held his palms up in a look of disbelief. He walked over to his bag and brushed the dog aside with his boot. As soon as he reached for his bag, two soldiers grabbed him by the arm and escorted him to a private room where a grim-faced captain ordered him to open the bag.

The first article out of his bag was the hunting jacket he had hastily packed before leaving Argentina. When the jacket hit the concrete floor, the clatter from inside pockets answered all the questions. Hawken had ammunition in his jacket. He locked eyes with the captain and calculated his next move.

When Hawken failed to explain the ammunition in his broken Spanish, the captain took him to a detention center and locked him in a cell. He spent the rest of the evening trying to sleep on a concrete slab with a single blanket. There was nothing in the cell except a stainless steel sink and toilet. The strong antiseptic smell could not hide the odor of criminals that had been there before him.

The following day was something of a nightmare. A stone-faced guard brought a steel bowl filled with pale broth, rice, stale bread, and water. Yellow chicken feet floated on top. Each time he demanded to speak with a lawyer, he received the same answer: "tomorrow."

On the second day of detention, the cell door opened and the guard ushered Hawken to an interrogation room where a scowling captain sat behind a desk picking his teeth with a toothpick. On the desk were two passports: Hawken's current passport, and the one that should not have been there. He had lost that one several months earlier, and the probing Colombians found it hidden away in a forgotten compartment of his luggage. Dual passports added to their suspicions.

Hawken described his business and the hunting in Argentina, and offered a reasonable theory about the second passport. The scowling captain kept scowling.

"I want to call the embassy," Hawken said. "The US embassy. Not tomorrow. Today."

The captain put the passports in a drawer and shifted the toothpick. "Tomorrow."

The following morning, Hawken heard keys at his cell door. The lock turned, the door swung open and a fresh-faced guard spoke.

"Señor Turner, you are free to go."

Welcome to Colombia? That was not the start that Hawken had hoped for. His instincts told him that he should not ignore the bad feeling in his gut, but he had come this far and he wanted to see Patricia.

When he arrived at the Intercontinental, there were three messages waiting for him at the reception desk. Just a name and a phone number on each one. He hurried to his room, tipped the bellhop, and dialed the number. When he spoke his name, the receiver went dead. He called back and it went dead again. Maybe her ex-husband was there.

Hawken showered and made another call to Patricia with the same result. He was not getting anywhere staying in his hotel room, so he decided to walk the streets and find a place to organize his thoughts. It was lunchtime and Cali was hot. Hawken knew hot, humid weather; but he felt like he was swimming in hot soup. A blinding glare radiated from office buildings, concrete, and cars in the street. Sweat was beading on Hawken's lips and his clothes were heavy with humidity. He found a tiny outdoor café and took a seat at a table under the shade of a canopy, his back to the street. The waitress brought a bottled water, and when she left, the hair stood up on the back of his neck. *Bad omens.*

One of his travel rules was never to sit with his back to the door, or—as was the case—to the open street. He turned his head to look behind, recalling that Frank Gordon had once told him it was easy to die in Colombia. Someone hands someone else fifty dollars, a motorcycle pulls up next to you in the street, a gun comes out of a jacket, and your children are left fatherless.

Hawken's shoulders were tight and his neck was stiff. He recalled a salon that he had seen near the hotel advertising haircuts, manicures, and massages. Hawken slapped three dollars on the table and left. The salon was just a short walk from the café.

When he entered the salon, Hawken noted the number of men receiving manicures and pedicures. It was a two-story salon. In the downstairs, eight busy hair stations lined the left side, and eight busy nail stations occupied the right. *Damn, these Colombians value their beauty.* He asked the receptionist about a massage, and she directed him to the second floor. At the top of the stairs, he was greeted by an attractive woman dressed in a white lab coat, white pants, and white soft-soled shoes. She was petite and tan with subtle Mayan features and a pleasant smile.

"*Hola. Cómo estás?*" she asked.

"*Bien. Y tu?*" Hawken asked. "*Habla Inglés?*"

"A little," she replied in English. "I study in the school now. You wish for a massage?"

"Yes, please."

"Are you American?" she asked.

"Yes, I am. My name is Hawken."

"I'm Isabel. Follow me."

Hawken followed her into a small private room with white walls, white floors, white ceilings, and just enough room for two white shelves and a massage table. He noticed that her hands were unsure as she fumbled with the sparse array of ointments on the shelf.

"I'm a little nervous," Hawken said. He tried to ease the tension in the room because *Isabel* seemed nervous.

"No, no. It's okay," she replied. "You relax."

"With clothes or without?" Hawken asked.

"However you like." She did not look at him.

They stood as far apart as the tiny room allowed. Hawken shuffled out of her way anticipating the awkward moment of undressing in front of a strange woman. He tried to avoid sexual thoughts, despite knowing that she was about to have her hands all over his naked body.

Hawken removed all his clothes, handed them to Isabel, and wrapped a towel around his waist. They avoided eye contact as she dimmed the lights and started a tape of soothing music in the portable cassette player on the shelf near the foot of the table. Hawken stretched onto the table while Isabel warmed her hands with lotion and then began caressing his temples with hands that were shaky at first then smooth and rhythmic when they gathered momentum.

She rolled Hawken onto his stomach and began kneading his back, pressing deep into the tissue. His body and mind let go of conscious thought, and Hawken nearly forgot he was naked as he fell into a blissful state of relaxation. When he opened his eyes, he caught a glimpse of contentment in her face. He could not contain his curiosity.

"You have a husband?" he asked.

"No, no husband."

"A boyfriend?"

"No, no boyfriend."

Isabel went back to her work. The hour-long massage seemed to go by in minutes, and Hawken felt rejuvenated when the lights came on and the music stopped. He pulled up his trousers and turned his attention to Isabel.

"Listen—I'm alone here in Cali. Why don't you have dinner with me tonight?" he asked. "Just dinner for company...like friends."

Isabel hesitated for a moment, but did not appear offended. She put away the cassette player and capped the lotions before answering. "I have work until eight tonight," she said.

"Well, how about eight-thirty? I'm staying at the Intercontinental, just down the street. They have a good restaurant there. I can pay your taxi."

"No taxi. I have a motorcycle," she said.

"A motorcycle?" Hawken asked. "Isn't that dangerous here in Cali?"

"Yes, a little," she said. "I had an accident last month." She lowered the waistband of her pants and revealed the scar on her well-toned hip.

"Damn," he said. "It looks okay to me."

Isabel smiled and pulled her pants up.

"So, I see you at eight thirty?"

"Yes, I can be there at eight thirty."

Hawken Turner finally felt relaxed. He regained his thoughts and walked down the stairs toward the door. Surely, dinner would be good, and the company would be a needed distraction from the communication breakdown with Patricia. When he stepped onto the sidewalk, he saw two thugs leaning on a car, waiting for him a block away. It was so obvious that it had to be a dream. The men nodded to each other, began pointing in his direction, and then slid into the car and started in his direction. Hawken didn't wait to see what they wanted. He jumped into the middle of traffic, dodged a delivery truck and a motorcycle, and scampered to the other side of the street, then briskly walked inside the hotel entrance. *Holy shit. Bad things happening.*

Isabel was even lovelier than he remembered when she arrived in the lobby of the hotel dressed in her street clothes. She wore a tasteful application of makeup and lipstick, and her brown hair hung down to her shoulders.

Hawken had chosen a quiet corner of the open-air restaurant, between the hotel lobby and the swimming pool. He rose and held out her chair, placing her napkin across her lap before taking his own seat across the table. If Isabel was not accustomed to fine dining, she did not show it. Her table manners were proper, and their conversation interesting. It seemed to be no time at all before the waiter was bringing dishes of grilled meats, vegetables, and a bottle of red Chilean wine to fill their glasses.

Hawken explained his mission in Colombia and his plan for exploring the hunting possibilities there. As conversation continued, Isabel shared stories of her simple life and family in Cali. Like many of the Colombians he had met, she was ambitious. She worked long hours to pay her living expenses, and she used the extra money from her job to pay for English lessons and accounting courses. The conversation flowed the same as the wine and the food was delicious.

"I wonder if you would do me a favor..." Hawken stopped midsentence. Something had caught the corner of his eye. The object was like a meteor, moving slowly but directly in their direction, destined to collide with a horrific explosion. He recognized the object from the pictures—Patricia.

Hawken had spotted her talking to a receptionist who had pointed her toward the restaurant. And then she was walking their way. Dressed in fashion jeans and a white linen blouse, her silky black hair fluttering down to the middle of her back, she held her head high and walked with the elegance of a woman who had spent years in charm school. *Damn good-looking.*

"What is it?" Isabel asked.

"Nothing."

Patricia stopped at the entrance of the restaurant and scanned the tables. When she found Hawken and Isabel in the corner, at their cozy table, she gracefully spun around and walked away... exactly as she had entered.

Hawken packed his bags and left for the airport the next day in a taxi with no air conditioning and torn seats. He despised cheap taxis, but he had no options. When he passed the valets, Hawken shot them a smile and gave them a two-finger salute. *Screw Colombia.* He felt like a coward, but it was time to go. Except for Isabel and a damn good massage, the only good thing he found in Colombia had been the chicken-foot soup at the jail, and he was not stopping for the recipe.

Hawken boarded the plane and reclined his seat to its lowest position. He ordered a double round of airline scotch as the drone of jet engines churning toward Miami muffled the chatter of passengers. Patricia might have been the one, but he would never know. He did, however know one thing. There was little in Colombia to remind him of Sam. He opened his calendar and crossed *Colombia* from the book. Then he took a drink and turned the page. There were eight days circled and titled in big letters: *CUBA.*

CHAPTER TWELVE

Cuba

I s it the tropical breezes that bathe the island, the beauty of the women, or the sultry combination of African and Spanish cultures that stir the passion of men in Cuba? The invitation to Havana seemed too good to be true, especially given that it had come from Blake Fowler, a man of big stories and questionable character. Blake laid out the plan with significant gaps in detail, but the highlights were enticing enough to draw Hawken's attention. The first part of the plan was to travel to Cancún, Mexico, to meet a friend aboard a fifty-foot Viking sport-fishing boat. From there, they would cruise to Havana to spend a week fishing the famous Hemingway tournament. Due to the US embargo, it was still illegal for Americans to visit Cuba, but that detail only added to the anticipation of adventure.

According to Blake, boats from all over the Caribbean were taking part in the three-day tournament. Most of the anglers would stay aboard their boats moored at the Hemingway Marina, which was the headquarters for the contest, but Blake Fowler, along with a mystery contact, devised a plan to stay inland on a pristine stretch of beach just outside Havana. The plan included a four-bedroom house with a swimming pool. From the stories Hawken had heard about the economy in Cuba, it was difficult to imagine an upscale beach house, but according to Blake, the amenities included a local guide, a car, a full-time maid, and a cook. Embargo or no embargo, Hawken Turner could not resist the temptation to see for himself.

When he and Blake landed at the airport in Cancún, Hawken wasn't surprised that no one was there to meet them outside the airport. Fowler's plans rarely evolved as promised. After standing on the sidewalk for a half hour looking for someone who might be looking for them, they hailed a cab and headed for the marina.

It didn't take long to spot the boat, a handsome Viking fully rigged with outriggers, fighting chair, and an impressive array of electronics designed for long-range fishing. To Hawken's relief, half-drunken Captain Chuck greeted Blake and welcomed him aboard with a slap on the back.

That evening, Hawken, Fowler, Captain Chuck, and two other middle-aged men drank cold Coronas and lied like fishermen long into the night. They shared stories they'd heard about Cuba, the fishing they would find there, and the smooth rum and the fine cigars they'd soon be enjoying.

At first light, they cast the lines, and the Viking idled out of the Cancún marina with the fishing party quieted from the long night of drinking. The skies were clear, but a stiff fifteen-knot wind was blowing from the east and it hit them dead in the face when the boat swung out of the harbor and assumed a heading for Havana. The bow of the Viking pounded wind-whipped waves into salt spray, dampening the mood on the boat as it battled with the sea. The boat swayed, lurched and rolled, and soon everyone aboard moved below decks to escape the beating. Everyone except Hawken and Captain Chuck.

"Ever been in seas this rough, Hawken?" Captain Chuck asked.

"Much worse, actually. My guide for caribou hunts in Alaska invited me to work a crab boat for a week in the off-season. Freezing weather and a steady diet of twenty-foot waves. Makes this look like a picnic."

"Catch any crab?"

"Caught tons of crab. Made a killing," Hawken said. "Ate lots of crab, too."

"Ever been in rough seas in the Gulf?"

"Took a Catalina 42 from Key West to Fort Myers in Hurricane Isabella a couple of years back. Took a pounding on that one."

"Think you can take this one to Havana? I need to stretch out for a while."

"Love to," Hawken said.

Hawken took control of the Viking and stayed the course for Havana. He worked the wheel with every swell to bring the bow in at a soft angle, and then slid down the backside, taking care to minimize the roll of the boat and ease the drop into the trough to spare the pounding heads of the crew below deck. The crossing was long and rough, but the Viking arrived intact.

Despite political tensions between the two countries, the Cubans were obviously happy to see them when they arrived. More Americans meant more money. There seemed to be a gentleman's agreement that nobody, Cuban or American, would mention the embargo. After clearing Cuban customs, they docked the boat in a designated slip among the other fishing boats at the marina.

Based on past experiences with Blake, Hawken was a bit impressed to find their English-speaking guide, Nelson, waiting for them at the dock. It was no wonder. The average salary for a Cuban worker at that time was ten to fifteen dollars a month. Nelson would earn a minimum of fifty dollars a day.

Nelson drove the party directly to the beach house. They passed through the city of Havana in silence, humbled by the sight of crumbling buildings, dangling electrical wires, chipped stucco, and faded paint. When they reached the beach house, the scene changed drastically. The resort consisted of a clean and modern cluster of a dozen vacation homes with swimming pools and privacy gates. The upscale property was out of place in a country riddled with poverty, and the houses were vacant except for the one that was theirs for the week.

Just as promised, they had a stunning view overlooking a white sand beach. The water was clear as gin, and the beach was wide, yet void of sunbathers. A block wall, four feet high, surrounded the two-story house—an odd imitation of an upscale home like the ones owned by rich exiles in Miami. The contemporary vacation resort was a blinding contradiction to the gray mass of decaying buildings in central Havana—only one of the many contradictions they found in Cuba.

Two days of average fishing on a poor tide were uninspiring, and the fishing party began to hang around the marina and beach house drinking beer and Havana Club rum. Nelson drove them to a nearby colonial mansion that had once been the property of a rich diplomat but a state-owned cigar store had moved into the space. They stood inside the humidor, mesmerized by the stacks of premium cigars that were forbidden back home. They tasted coffee and fine rum and cigars before purchasing their selections and returning to the beach. Led by Blake Fowler, the fishing trip was turning into the cocktail trip, and the Viking crew cancelled the next day of fishing in favor of throwing a party at the beach house instead.

Hawken and Nelson chose fresh lobster grilled poolside as the main entrée for the fiesta. Like everything in Cuba, things got done by knowing the right—or wrong—people. Nelson knew the connection for lobster, an American man named Roger, who lived on a yacht docked at the marina near Cojimar. Roger had escaped to Cuba two years earlier with a Toyota Corolla strapped to the deck of a Morgan 55 sailboat and a vague story about some IRS problems in the States. He spent most of his days drinking rum in the air-conditioned cabin of his yacht, watching satellite TV with his latest version of a Cuban girlfriend, a woman Roger had lured in with promises of cooking oil, soap, and American cigarettes.

Hawken and Nelson found Roger at the marina, and after a couple of drinks and an hour of listening to him complain about the lack of basic necessities in Cuba, they bought twenty black-market lobsters for twenty dollars. They probably could have bought them for less, but no one was complaining. Selling lobsters in Cuba was highly illegal, but Roger kept the harbor police on retainer with cigarettes and spare change. No one said a word as they removed the lobsters from the dockside freezer and loaded them into the car.

"Do you want to see Papa's house?" Nelson asked.

"*Your* papa?" Hawken asked.

"No, my friend," said Nelson, laughing. "Papa *Hemingway*. His house is near here. It's a museum now, and everything is kept inside just the way it was when Ernesto left. His boat is there, too. They put it under a building behind the house."

"Sure, I'd like to see that. I thought he lived in the bars downtown," Hawken said.

"He did. But his wife wanted a house. She thought having one would keep him out of the bars—but that didn't work."

"You know, my family knew Hemingway," Hawken said. "Actually, they were pretty good friends, too."

"I don't believe you," Nelson said.

"It's true. They hunted together in Africa. Just once, but they had a mutual friend there, Brenn Von Snierden," Hawken said. "Hemingway's guide."

"Are you telling me the truth?" Nelson asked. "I think you are a lying gringo."

"Yes, it's true. We have photographs at home," Hawken said. "I wish I'd brought them with me. I never knew the Cubans considered him famous."

Nelson's eyes were wide. "He's a *very* famous man here in Cuba. Very, very famous. There's Hemingway everything. Hemingway's daiquiri bar. Hemingway's mojito bar. Hemingway marina. Hemingway motel. Everything he touched is famous here. Even some things he never touched. We love Hemingway. But I still don't believe you."

"Believe what you want," Hawken said. "I've heard that he spent all his time in Cuba drinking and fighting. Doesn't seem like much to love about that. Have you read his books?"

"It's not his books that are so great, it's the way that he lived here. The passion he had for life. We Cubans love that. I'll take you to his house. You'll see what I mean," Nelson said.

As they drove toward the house, the tall buildings of Havana faded into the background and gave way to cinderblock houses with tin roofs and wooden doors.

"Do you remember the statue on the Malecón—a man with a mustache holding a baby in one arm and pointing toward the United States with the other?" Nelson asked.

"Not really."

"That's José Marti," Nelson said. "He was a better writer than Hemingway. He wrote poems and romantic stories about freedom. Do you know him?"

"I've heard of him."

"He's Cuba's national hero. He led the war for independence from Spain. He fought his whole life for independence, and was killed in the first battle. Anyway, he was Hemingway's inspiration for writing."

"That's bullshit."

"No, it's true. Hemingway loved what he said about being a man."

"What's that?"

"Marti said that a man should do three things in his life. He should plant a tree. He should have a son. And he should write a book."

"I imagine Hemingway had those covered."

Nelson parked the car in front of a white stucco house perched high on a lush hill overlooking the sea. "This is it," said Nelson. "Hemingway house. *Finca Vigía*. Lookout Farm."

The two men walked to the front, where Hawken held his camera to his eye but never took the shot. He followed Nelson behind the house to the gardens surrounding an empty swimming pool—the very pool in which, it was rumored, Hemingway swam naked with movie stars when his wife was away. They stopped at an open door at the side of the house and looked into the study at the modest desk and typewriter in the center. Bookshelves, liquor bottles, and a collection of hunting trophies lined the white stucco walls. Tall doorways, large windows, and white tile floors gave an open and breezy feel to the house.

The Cuban government did not allow tourists to walk inside the house, but they kept the doors open so the tourists could see in. A bored state worker guarded each door. Hawken stopped at one of the doors and peered inside at the master bedroom. He saw a photograph above the vanity. The black and white photograph showed Hemingway in Africa with a leopard draped over his shoulders. In the background stood a woman with a familiar face, though her hairstyle was different. Without thinking, Hawken walked past the guard and into the house, camera in hand. Nelson grabbed his arm and yanked him back.

"Are you crazy? You can't go inside. We'll have trouble."

"I want a picture of that picture over the vanity," Hawken said. He pointed at the old black-and-white photograph.

"Give me your camera," Nelson said. "You have to learn how things work in Cuba." Nelson spoke to the guard in Spanish and then turned to Hawken. "Give me a dollar," he said.

Hawken handed him a dollar. Nelson passed it to the guard. The guard took Hawken's camera and snapped a photograph of the photograph. That was how it worked in Cuba.

Nelson led Hawken down the winding path past the green garden and behind the pool. At the end of the path was a shelter, and beneath the shelter was Hemingway's boat, *Pilar*. The boat was well suited to the owner, and just as Hawken had pictured it from Hemingway's stories—finely crafted of varnished mahogany, with sleek lines, a flying bridge and a wooden wheel at the helm with worn pegs where the famous man had once plowed into rolling waves in search of marlin—or German U-boats, as the stories went. There was a single fighting chair centered at the stern. If chairs could speak, no doubt this one had stories to tell.

Hawken looked on in silence before speaking. "Damn, Nelson. Son of a bitch had it made, didn't he? I'd give my left nut to have been out there with him for just one day."

"You drink well enough. I'm sure you would have fit in."

"You need to fish with a man to really know him. That's in the Bible, you know."

"We don't have a bible for Santería." Nelson turned and started back up the path. "Let's go. If you're hungry, we can eat some lunch at La Terraza. It's the restaurant by the sea where Hemingway used to eat. And drink, of course."

"How's the food?" Hawken asked.

"Shitty, like most of the food in Cuba, but we can't eat lobster every day," Nelson said.

"Okay. Let's go—but let's get a beer first."

Nelson stopped the car in front of a roadside bar at the edge of the village, and the two men ordered beers. A cool breeze was blowing off the ocean, and the thatch roof provided shade from the sun. Music drifted in from a loud stereo in a nearby house, blended with the voices of men and women doing chores and tending gardens, children playing, chickens crowing, and dogs barking. Like Africa, Cuba was beginning to feel like home.

After finishing their beers, they drove to La Terraza. Inside the restaurant, Hawken settled into a large wooden chair next to the window with a view of the harbor. The scene was familiar. The fishermen, the harbor, the smell of coffee in the restaurant—it was *The Old Man and the Sea* in life. Hawken looked down on the beach where the small boat had finally landed with the skeleton of the great marlin picked clean by sharks. *The Old Man and the Sea* was the only Hemingway book Hawken had ever read. He was not a student of Hemingway's writing, but he remembered the despair captured in the tale of the old fisherman. Hemingway probably sat by that very window listening to the tales of fishermen as the great story came together in his head. He would not have been far from the white house on the hill and it would not have taken him long before placing a sheet of paper in the carriage of his Royal typewriter and spewing words from his soul.

A calico cat appeared from nowhere and jumped into the seat of a chair at an empty table next to Hawken and Nelson. The cat held his tail high and looked to them for some scrap of food from the table.

"Look at the balls on that cat," Hawken said.

"He's a Cuban cat," Nelson remarked. "Big balls."

"Maybe he's one of Hemingway's cats."

"Sure he is," Nelson said. "Why don't you bring some of your rich clients down here, and we'll sell them one of Hemingway's cats as a souvenir. I'm sure that cat won't mind living in the United States."

"If we name him 'Papa,' maybe we can get a little more money for him," Hawken said. "Or Ernesto."

Hawken and Nelson took turns stroking the cat.

A waiter set down large plates of overfried chicken and fried potatoes.

"How difficult could it have been to be Hemingway?" Hawken asked.

He and Nelson tasted their food.

"I mean…what did he do that was so great? Maybe he gets his heart broken by some beautiful woman, someone he can't forget, so he marries a bunch of other women, hoping to find her all over again. He starts drinking, pisses off everybody in Paris, so he moves here, drinks more, and pisses off more people. He goes fishing because drinking is a requirement for fishing. He fights every living thing he can find. If he can't catch it, he shoots it. Then…then he writes about it, and people buy his writing. Hell, he probably didn't even have to think about it. Just wrote everything down as it happened, and readers thought there was hidden meaning in his words because they didn't understand him." Hawken took a drink from his beer. "When he runs out of things to shoot and catch, and finally figures out that he's all alone, he shoots himself. The end. I'm going to buy myself a typewriter when I get home."

"You want to end up like Hemingway?" Nelson asked.

"No, but I'm sure he didn't want to end up that way either," Hawken said. "Let's hurry and eat so we can get those lobsters back to the house. Remember, we have to get beer and rum, too. Grab the cat if you want."

"Sure—but first, let's go into Havana. I want to show you where Hemingway did his best work," Nelson said.

"I thought he did most all his writing at the house."

"He did. But he did his best drinking in town."

Nelson drove into Havana and turned onto a narrow street in Old Havana, Calle Obispo, and parked in front of the Floridita. "This was his favorite bar."

The Floridita had a half-dozen tables and a long bar, which ran perpendicular to the street. Rich wooden walls, red velvet curtains, and a floor made from black-and-white checkered tiles added class to the joint. Long-stemmed fans hung from the ceiling and creaked as they slowly turned the air. The staff wore black trousers and vests with black bow ties, adding a sense of sophistication to the run-down smoky bar. A drinking man's bar.

"This is the home of the daiquiri. Hemingway's drink," Nelson said. "And that's where he always stood." Nelson pointed to the corner nearest the street where a bronze bust of Hemingway stood leaning on the bar, as if he would always be there.

"You have to drink a daiquiri here. You haven't been to Cuba unless you have a daiquiri at the Floridita."

They ordered two lime daiquiris, costing four dollars each, nearly a week's wages for the average Cuban. Hawken paid for both and looked about the bar. Faded photographs scattered about the bar showed Hemingway with Gary Cooper, Hemingway with dignitaries, and Hemingway with gangsters. Another showed Hemingway with Fidel, standing close together, hands clasped, each man wearing a look of uncertainty.

"Finish that drink and we'll go to the place where Hemingway drank his mojitos," said Nelson.

They stepped outside the cool bar into the hot Havana sun and started down Obispo on foot. When they reached the hotel Ambos Mundos, Nelson pointed inside.

"There's an empty room there that's kept as a tribute to Hemingway—the room where he slept when he had too much to drink. His wife hated this hotel because he was always drunk here. That's the reason she insisted they buy the house in Cojimar."

"Which wife? He was married four times, you know."

"I don't know."

"If you are going to be a top guide when the Americans start coming, you need to know that. It's important to American people."

La Bodeguita del Medio was a garage-sized hole-in-the-wall bar with saloon doors and tall glasses lined up on the wooden bar with lime and sugar waiting for rum, soda, and a sprig of mint: the perfect mojito at the home of the mojito. A water-stained, handwritten note on a tattered sheet of yellowed paper hung over the bar. On it, Hemingway had scrawled, *My mojito in La Bodeguita del Medio and my daiquiri in la Floridita.*

Nelson and Hawken quickly drank two mojitos each and left for the beach house with lobster, rum, and beer. Before entering the house, Hawken walked down to the beachside bar just a few hundred yards away and spoke to the leader of the five-piece band playing guitars, trumpets, and maracas. He offered them twenty dollars to come and play at the party. The band packed up and left so fast that they nearly beat Hawken to the house. It didn't matter that they left because there were only three Italian tourists lying on the beach listening to the band. And they were not tipping.

The band set up by the pool and began to play lively music, singing along with their instruments. Within seconds, angry-faced security guards appeared at the front gate shouting in loud voices, interrupting the music.

"*No fiesta! No fiesta!*"

The drunken Americans were getting hard to handle, so Nelson walked to the gate to speak with the guards. He had a concerned look on his face. It was difficult to determine if the guards were private security or regular Cuban police, but they had chattering radios, pistols strapped to their sides, and stern expressions on their faces. The Americans watched from the house as Nelson began waiving his arms and shouting back at the guards. There were fingers pointing in all directions. Five minutes of shouting and angry posturing and Nelson returned to the house.

"Have you got a couple of beers for these guys?" Nelson asked.

"Sure." Hawken reached into the cooler and pulled out as many beers as his arms could hold. He followed Nelson to the gate.

Nelson handed a beer to each officer. "*Fiesta?*" he asked.

"*Sí, fiesta.*" The guards put away their radios, leaned against the wall, and drank their beers. Confrontation dissolved.

The music continued and the guards spent the remainder of the evening watching the party and drinking their beer. Whenever the guards ran out of beer, Hawken returned to the fence with fresh cold ones and an occasional chicken leg from the grill. The Americans dined on lobster and grilled chicken. They drank rum, and smoked cigars while the band played until well past midnight. The band left drunk and happy with twenty dollars and beers in their hands.

Papa had found something many years before. Life was good in Cuba.

On the fourth night in Cuba, Hawken, Blake, and Nelson decided it was time to leave the house and drink out on the town. Nelson, who was deliriously happy with his sudden influx of American dollars, insisted they go to a disco named The Blind Crab. Although the men considered themselves a bit old for "disco," they trusted Nelson's recommendation.

It took quite some time to scour off the accumulated sweat and salt from a hard crossing, four days of partying, and two days of fishing. After hot showers, everyone dressed in clean clothes, washed and pressed by the housemaid. Everything was clean and smelled fresh except the car, which reeked of bait, sweaty fishermen, liquor, and beer. The stench was nearly unbearable despite the men's generous dousing of cologne.

"Damn, Nelson," Hawken said. He held his nose high and took a sniff at the air. "Now this car smells more like a whorehouse than a bait bucket."

"No. You're wrong," Nelson said. "It smells more like bait now. You'll see what I mean."

The chrome-and-glass disco entrance was attached to the wing of a dilapidated hotel on the waterfront. A large crowd of girls gathered around the front. A steady stream of dented Fords, Chevys, and Plymouths from the 1950s brought an endless line of more girls dressed like aspiring stars at a Hollywood premiere. The lack of men entering the club was curious, but many things in Cuba were curious to the Americans.

Inside the club, they found a thumping nightclub scene with mirrors, flashing lights, and modern music. The bar was crowded and the small dance floor was packed with girls and men dancing. More girls dancing with girls than dancing with men. Hawken and his friends bought drinks at the bar and stood back with Nelson to observe the scene. Before long, six gorgeous girls surrounded them. The girls spoke little English and the American men spoke very little Spanish. Hawken turned to Nelson. "Nelson…are these girls hookers?"

"No, amigo," Nelson answered. "You just all of a sudden got real handsome."

The men enjoyed a good laugh over Nelson's joke, and then settled in for some serious drinking. Hawken stood near the dance floor with a Cuba libre in each hand as he surveyed the club's sexy clientele pulsating to the music.

"Nelson, this place is loaded with good-looking women. Maybe I should look for a wife here," Hawken said. He spoke with sarcasm, but Nelson accepted the challenge.

"Go ahead. Which one do you want? I'm sure that you can have any one of them for a wife."

"Are they *all* hookers?" Hawken asked.

"Of course not. Everybody comes to the disco to dance. Here is the same as any place in the world, but in Cuba, there aren't so many places where people can dress nice and dance to good music like this. Everybody comes. What do you want? A doctor? A scientist? But it might cost you."

"A doctor. No, a nun. A sexy nun."

"Okay. Wait here and I'll bring you a sexy nun for a wife."

Hawken was only joking, but Nelson disappeared into the crowd before he could stop him. When Nelson returned twenty minutes and two Cuba libres later, he was accompanied by three stunning girls in their early twenties. American tourists were rare in Havana, and the girls seemed intrigued. They looked Hawken over with approving eyes as Nelson introduced each one of them.

"This is Osiris, Yudy, and Gabriela."

"*Hola*," Hawken said as he took each one's hand with a greeting. The women began speaking with Nelson in rapid Spanish, which Hawken could not follow.

"Which one do you like?" Nelson asked.

"I like the one with the blue eyes," Hawken said.

"There are two with blue eyes. Which one?"

"The one on the left?" Hawken said.

"No. You want this one." Nelson pulled Gabriela from the pack and brought her to Hawken's side.

The rest of the evening was a blur of flashing lights, pounding disco beats, too many Cuba libres to count, and lots of dancing on the crowded dance floor. The night went by quickly, and the sky was turning to daylight when Hawken, Blake, and Nelson left the disco, exhausted and sufficiently drunk. As they walked toward the car, Nelson handed a slip of paper to Hawken.

"Here's your future wife's phone number. It rings at the neighbor's house."

Hawken Turner took a liking to Nelson, and the two formed a fast friendship. He treated Nelson as a friend rather than a hired guide, and refrained from insulting the poverty and dilapidated socialist infrastructure that was rotting away in Havana. He saw the crumbling remnants of a once-pristine country, but he also saw that Nelson was proud of Cuba and carried with him a blend of love and regret. He noticed that Nelson patted young boys on the head and said hello to old women in the streets, and Hawken liked that. He was not going to verbalize his own dismal perceptions to a friend who was living the only life that he knew.

When Nelson invited Hawken to stay another week and visit his family's home on the outskirts of Havana, Hawken readily accepted. Getting back to the United States on his own was complicated, but Nelson knew the requirements and after a full day of talking to the man who sent them to the man who sent them to another man, Hawken had a flight back to the United States with a backdoor connection through the Bahamas. The route was simple, the story he would have to tell customs was not.

Hawken felt like he was the last American on the island when he waved good-bye to his friends and watched the Viking churn out of Hemingway Marina and turn westward toward Cancún. He had enjoyed their company, but he was glad to see them go. Nelson drove directly from the marina to his home on the outskirts.

His house was like many others in Cuba—a mortar-and-stucco structure with steel rebar protruding from the top floor, giving the impression that it was under construction, though it had been that way for many years. Mismatched tile in random colors and haphazard arrangements covered the floors and counters. The neighborhood houses stood so close that Nelson could stand in his house and shake the hand of his neighbor through open windows. The front door was always open, inviting an endless flow of friends, family, and neighbors.

Nelson let it be known he was bringing an American guest and curious onlookers were waiting inside to see the rare site, a gringo in Cuba—and a friend at that. It was soon evident that the one who most anticipated the visit was Nelson's younger sister.

When Gabriela from the disco entered the living room crowded with family and friends, Hawken had to look twice. "It's you."

"Hi," she said, and gave Hawken a kiss on the cheek.

Her skin was damp, and she smelled of strong soap. She wore her freshly brushed hair pulled into a neat ponytail and tied in the back with a light-blue ribbon that matched her eyes. She was a natural beauty with tanned skin and a shy smile—even more beautiful than the night Hawken had first seen her in the disco.

Hawken had not planned on having a third person tag along when he and Nelson toured the rest of the island, but from that day forward, Gabriela was always with Nelson, and Nelson was always with Hawken. She spoke sparingly and shyly with Hawken, hanging in the background while Nelson took Hawken from one end of the island to the other. She was sweet and considerate and appeared to pay much attention to Hawken, but she was too young for him to think of her as a girlfriend. Few people in Cuba would have disapproved of that, but she was Nelson's sister. Hawken had to respect Nelson—even when Gabriela's charms caught his eye.

The week flew by for the threesome while Nelson pointed out historical and *turista* sites. They saw the beaches of Cayo Coco, the palm-studded hills and valleys of Santa Clara, the infamous Bay of Pigs, and tobacco plantations in Pinar del Río.

When the trip was over, Nelson drove Hawken to Havana's José Marti Airport to board his flight to Nassau. Gabriela went with them. Outside the airport, Nelson smiled broadly and hugged Hawken hard when he received two hundred dollars for the extra week of guiding. Gabriela's face was not as happy.

"You don't like me," she said, wearing a look of disappointment.

"*Sí!* Of course I do. You're a beautiful girl. Very *young* and beautiful. And—you're Nelson's sister. I have to respect Nelson."

"It's no problem," Gabriela said. She rolled her eyes.

"Yes, it's a problem."

Hawken moved quickly through check-in and paid his exit fee to the bored woman sitting behind the counter. Gabriela stood with him, silently, as neither had more to say. She excused herself to find Nelson, and just before Hawken entered the security booth, there was a tap on his shoulder. He turned to find Nelson holding a small photograph from his wallet—a lovely picture of Gabriela with her shy smile, standing outside her modest home. Nelson placed the picture in Hawken's hand and slapped him on the shoulder.

Maybe it was Cuba. Maybe it was Gabriela. Or maybe it was the blended sweetness of them both, but Hawken Turner was reluctant to leave. He looked back, saw Gabriela standing in the background, and knew he had to return. *The rules are different in Cuba.*

CHAPTER THIRTEEN
Return to Cuba

When Hawken Turner returned to the United States, a strange darkness came over him. He lay awake every night staring at the ceiling and trying to figure out why. He drank more and shaved less. He stopped calling his boys. His work began to suffer. He knew that his behavior was hurting him, but he could not stop it. Maybe it was his destiny. Maybe it was his heritage. Maybe he knew that he was running out of options to start his life again.

He often thought about Gabriela. The emotions that he felt for her and the things that he saw in Cuba kept swirling in his head. There was something mesmerizing about Cuba—and Gabriela as well. His life in the United States had become a blank existence. The once satisfying conversation with happy-hour friends at his favorite bar and the occasional cocktail parties seemed frivolous now and without purpose. He had regained a few friends after the divorce, but talk about stock portfolios, spectacular golf shots, and nagging mothers-in-law didn't interest him anymore. During the sleepless nights, he thought of Cuba and the warm, humid breezes rustling through palm fronds, and the rhythms of salsa flowing from open windows and doors. He thought of waking in the morning to chickens crowing and dogs barking in the streets. He thought of the laughing Cubans, people who seemed to know happiness even when the world around them suffered. The island was calling to him and the tide was drawing him back.

When Hawken landed in Havana, Gabriela greeted him outside the airport terminal with a strong hug and a broad smile. She waded through the tightly packed crowd and took him by the elbow as Nelson gathered and loaded the bags into the trunk. Gabriela slid into the backseat next to Hawken and placed her hand on his knee.

"I study the English now," she announced. She spoke decent English before, but was too shy to try much.

"Good. Can you explain to me Einstein's theory of relativity?" Hawken asked.

"Tomorrow," she answered.

Hawken had flown from Costa Rica where he was guiding a group of clients on a billfishing trip to the west coast. He was tired after four days of hard fishing, but buoyed by the thought of seven days in Cuba.

Nelson had rented a private house in Havana so they could stay together—Hawken, Nelson, and Gabriela. Normally, Hawken preferred the convenience of a hotel with maid service, laundry service, and bar and such, but the government did not allow Cubans to stay in tourist hotels, and a house was more convenient if he wanted his guide with him at all times. His guide and Gabriela.

When they arrived at the small but efficient two-bedroom house, Nelson directed Hawken to the largest of the bedrooms and presented it to him with a broad sweep of his arm. Gabriela followed him into the room with her orange suitcase that was scratched and dented. One latch was closed and the other was broken. Before Hawken could question the sleeping arrangements, Gabriela dropped her suitcase in the corner and placed Hawken's duffel on the bed. Most of the clothes he had brought from Costa Rica were wrinkled and many required cleaning.

Gabriela sorted through his clothes, showing each article to him. "Clean?"

"Yes."

"Clean?"

"No, dirty."

"Clean?"

"Yes."

She folded the clean clothes neatly and put them away in drawers. She piled the soiled clothes in the corner to be cared for later. She appeared pleased as she straightened the room and organized their belongings.

They planned a festive dinner that evening to celebrate Hawken's return to Cuba. Nelson had some "business" to attend to, so Hawken and Gabriela went alone to a fine *paladar* that served fish and lobster purchased on the black market. Privately owned and mostly family run restaurants, *paladares* were the best places to dine in Cuba, as their owners had the freedom to operate one of the few private businesses allowed by the government. Many of the top chefs left the government restaurants to work in *paladares*, where they could share tourist dollars and tips.

Gabriela was a light drinker, but that evening she was celebrating Hawken's return, and she soon drank herself into a mild state of intoxication. The mojitos were strong, the lobster excellent, and when the cooking was done, the *paladar* owners joined in the celebration. They played loud salsa music and everyone danced, young and old, in the tiny restaurant until late in the night.

Cubans often joke about the way Americans shield an imaginary space around their bodies to avoid close contact with others. Gabriela showed Hawken the Cuban way when she sat in his lap with her arms around his neck during the taxi ride from the restaurant. They did not speak of romance, but romance hung in the air. The night was hot, steamy, and sexy. Inhibitions did not exist. Hawken tried to hide his desire, but the tightness in his trousers must have given it away, because seconds after entering the house, the shy Cuban girl pulled him onto the bed, threw her blouse to the floor, and gave Hawken Turner everything he wanted in that moment of passion.

Hawken awakened early the next morning to commotion in the bathroom. It was dark outside but he could hear chickens beginning to crow, and when chickens were crowing, dawn was coming. He looked over and saw the empty pillow next to him as he began to piece together the memories of the evening. There was a light in the bathroom and shadows moving about inside. Hawken cracked the door to investigate the commotion, and there was Gabriela. She was standing over the sink with his underwear in one hand and a bar of soap in the other. The rest of his clothes covered the bathroom, hand washed and hanging to dry. She turned and smiled at him with contentment. *What the hell is she doing?*

"I wash the clothes now," Gabriela said.

"Thank you."

Even if he should, Hawken felt no guilt for sleeping with Gabriela. There were no rules and no promises. If he was using her, he did not care. This was Cuba, and the Cubans saw it the other way—maybe she was using him. No matter, there was some pleasing going on. Pleasing him pleased her, and pleasing her pleased him.

After two days of romantic dinners, salsa music, and sex in Havana, Hawken informed Gabriela of his plan. "Nelson is busy with that man from Spain, so you are my new guide."

"Guide?"

"Yes, guide. You're a lot better looking than Nelson. And your skills are better. So, you are my new guide and I have some work for you to do. How much will I have to pay you?" Hawken asked.

"I'm not worried. You'll want to pay me lots and lots of dollars."

"I see. All right, so your last job was painting fingernails and cutting hair. How much did they pay you there? One dollar a day?"

Gabriela smiled and looked toward the ceiling. "Sometimes I worked for the other stylist, too. She paid me to do her work so that she could sell her paintings to tourists. Two dollars a day sometimes."

"Okay, I'll pay you two dollars a day," Hawken said. "And all the sex that you want."

"You're a kind man, Mr. Hawken."

"I found out about a place where I can shoot doves near Ciego de Ávila. I need your help to make the arrangements. Do you know where that is?"

"I know. It's far to the east."

"That's why I'm renting a car."

"What kind of birds are you hunting there?"

"Dove. You know...*paloma*."

"Do you eat those kinds of birds?"

"Hell, yes. They're good to eat. You'll see for yourself."

Hawken's plan for this trip to Cuba was to try the hunting and explore more of the island. He wanted to learn as much as he could about Cuba, as he was sure that it would soon open to American tourists, and he wanted to have the competitive advantage of experience and knowledge. He rented a red Suzuki jeep in Havana and set out with Gabriela for Ciego de Ávila. Long before he went there, Hawken had heard stories of the great dove hunting in Ciego, and it was exactly the type of business opportunity he was looking for.

When Hawken and Gabriela drove into Ciego, a man in the street directed them to a small concrete house painted tan with bright red accents, with a gardener on his hands and knees in the front yard, cutting the lush green grass with scissors. Rose and Lopez, the couple who owned the house, greeted them as if they had all known each other forever—the Cuban way. Hawken unloaded the bags and stored them in the back bedroom while Gabriela chatted with Rose and drank a coffee. They sat around the kitchen table talking like long-lost friends.

Hawken diverted Gabriela long enough for her to call the hunting guide and thirty minutes later, they heard a rumbling noise and a loud horn honking in front of the house. A Russian military truck was parked outside, its diesel engine hammering on the cylinders and black smoke spewing from the exhaust.

"What the hell is that?" Hawken asked.

"It's the men," said Gabriela. "The hunting men."

"You've got to be kidding."

The beastly green vehicle was the size of a dump truck, and the inside was large enough for twenty people. There were five Cuban men on the inside. Three men wore green military uniforms, and the other two wore faded camouflage jackets. It would have been an intimidating sight for any American had not all the Cubans looked so cheerful.

Hawken stopped at the driver's door where green paint, three shades too light to cover, attempted to hide the Russian star. Inside the truck was a bird dog, a respectable-looking shorthair pointer tied to the bench seat with a tattered leash.

"Good-looking dog," Hawken said. "Are all these guys hunting with us?" Hawken asked.

"Yes, of course," the driver said. "But you're the only one shooting. We've only got one gun."

The afternoon of dove hunting in Cuba was exceptional. The truck stopped at a freshly harvested rice field with bits of rice scattered in the rich dark soil. The stubble left in the field, just four inches high, provided no cover for hunters, but no cover was needed. Hawken sat on a hand-carved stool in the middle of the five-acre field. Gabriela joined him there while the other Cubans stood at the edge and watched Hawken shoot.

The shooting was not furiously fast, but slow and steady— suitable for the sunny hot day. He shot a battered Italian Beretta, left behind by a Russian officer when he and the rest of the Russians pulled out and left the Cubans with a financial mess. The worn gun was a good fit, and Hawken soon began knocking down birds with regular frequency. The observing Cubans admired his skill as they watched intently, cheering and clapping each time he shot one down. The farther the shot, the louder they cheered.

One of the downed birds fell close to Gabriela, and she walked over to get a closer look. She was hesitant to touch it, but she grasped the bird by the tip of the wing and held it dangling from her outstretched arm.

"I could never shoot one of these," she said.

"Do you want me to stop?" Hawken asked.

"No."

"I've had enough. I can stop now," Hawken said.

"No. You'll be very popular tonight in Ciego with these birds to eat."

"Really?" he asked.

"Yes, and I'll be even more popular because you're my boyfriend."

He stopped hunting and turned to her. "Boyfriend?"

"Yes, boyfriend."

"I'm not your boyfriend," Hawken said. "Don't make that mistake. You're a beautiful girl, and I like your company, but I'm not your boyfriend."

"Okay…Mr. Hawken."

Hawken only hunted one day in Ciego, but he and Gabriela chose to stay longer. Those were among the most peaceful days of Hawken's life. Every day was sunny, and they drove the countryside with the top down, sunglasses on, and the wind in their hair. There were no road signs and no directions. Every turn in the road took them someplace new. There was no traffic other than the occasional horse-drawn wagon piled high with sugarcane stalks. They found a narrow dirt road and followed it to a pristine beach northwest of Ciego with white sand and blue water where they cooled their bodies in the middle of the day. The beach was empty and there were no footprints in the sand except their own. In the evenings, after they returned from their beach, Hawken waited on the lumpy mattress as Gabriela showered her body and then joined him in the small bed with damp hair and the smell of soap on her skin.

There were no fine restaurants, decent cinemas, or fancy shopping malls in Cuba during that time. The island was still in its "special period," with rolling blackouts during the day and often into the nights as the electricity came and went. Making love had surpassed baseball as the favorite Cuban pastime, but Hawken Turner, a lover of baseball, did not complain. When he was with Gabriela, Hawken thought less, drank less, and shaved his face clean every day.

On the fourth afternoon at the house, they returned to the beach and again it was theirs alone. Hawken found it hard to believe that tourists had not discovered their "secret" beach. The snow-like ribbon of white sand, blue water, and swaying palm trees extended for miles in each direction. They spread towels on the sand sat close to the sea with a light breeze rippling the surface of the water. It was well past noon, and the sun moved out over the water taking with it the strongest rays of heat and leaving a coolness to the air.

Hawken read a book about José Marti and studied a map of the island that he had found in one of the hotel gift shops. He kept a few beers buried under a wet towel and he lined the empty bottles in the sand when he finished each one. Gabriela had a spiral notebook with lined paper and a yellow pencil that she used to make lovely drawings of sunsets, empty towels on the beach, and tilted bottles of beer nestled in the sand. She turned the pages of the notebook as she drew picture after picture, then went back to the beginning and drew on the other side. When she wandered into the surf to cool her body, Hawken's eyes rose from the book and admired God's work as she splashed cool water on her neck and breasts.

Hawken learned something about the Cuban economy that afternoon. Just beyond the far end of the beach was a rocky point where they had found a small wooden shack. The palm-roof shack served as a restaurant for the mostly non-existent tourists. One man served as chef, proprietor, and waiter, offering up lobster and cold beer. There was no apparent reason for the shack but this was Cuba and there it was. The man's name was Carlos, and every day he came to the shack around noon dressed in torn shorts, flip-flops, and faded T-shirts. Carlos was cheerful and cooked the lobster to perfection in a dented frying pan heated over a petroleum burner made from rusted scrap metal obviously plucked from the garbage.

"I feel sorry for Carlos," Hawken said as he and Gabriela returned to their towels after a couple of lobster tails and cold beer at the shack.

"Why do you feel sorry for Carlos?"

"His restaurant has so few clients, and he looks poor. But I guess he's happy. I'll never understand why he wears all that gel in his hair though. For the gulls?"

Gabriela laughed. "He's a rich man."

"Why do you say that?"

"That's his car parked over there. Anyone in Cuba with a car is rich. I'm sure he has many girlfriends, too."

"He makes a lot of money from tips?"

"Maybe, maybe not. But it doesn't matter. He sells his own lobsters. He has a friend who catches the lobsters for him, and Carlos sells them to tourists for lots of money."

"The lobsters he cooks at the restaurant?"

"Yes."

"And the government lets him do this?" Hawken asked.

"They don't know. He sells maybe fifty lobsters a month for himself and two for Fidel."

"So he sells his *own* lobsters to tourists?" Hawken asked.

"Yes, *turistas*," she answered. "Like you."

"So Carlos is setting the price for my lobster?" he asked.

"*Yes*, Carlos makes the price."

"And I'm paying the gringo price?" Hawken asked.

"Of course."

"I'll be damned. You Cuban communists make very good capitalists. Damn."

"This is Cuba," she said.

"Yes, I know."

With so many young Cuban men competing for Gabriela's attention, Hawken Turner was not the logical choice for her, but he was the one she slept with. He was thirty-nine and she was barely twenty. He was nearly twice her age, but there were no power plays with the sex. There were no inhibitions, and there were no questions. She seduced him with innocence, yet she knew him as no woman had before. He was a gentleman before and a gentleman after, but during sex, it was primal, passionate, and natural. They made love at bedtime, in the morning, and sometimes in between. It happened on the beach, in the bed, and in the shower. Man-woman-sex. No talk of love. No need for rules. It just happened.

With each new day, Hawken became more curious about Gabriela, and curiosity proved to be the catalyst that changed their relationship. He wanted to know her better, and knowing her better led to caring. Then caring led to that place between love and sex, and living somewhere between love and sex was a pretty good place to be for Hawken Turner.

"You can have any young, handsome man that you want. Why don't you have a boyfriend here?" Hawken asked.

They were lying in the lumpy bed, flushed from morning sex. Gabriela looked him in the eye and replied matter-of-factly, "I don't want a young, handsome boy. I want a man like you."

Hawken laughed to himself and pondered the implications. "Okay. But I see lots of Cuban men here—good dancers, funny guys, smart—" He shrugged his shoulders.

"Not one faithful man on the whole island." She waved her arm in a rainbow motion to be sure that I understood she meant the *whole* island.

"Have you ever been in love?" he asked. He was certain that she was not "in love" with him—at least not at the moment.

"Yes…and married too." She rubbed her ring finger with her thumb indicating that there was once a wedding ring. Hawken was surprised but said nothing.

"I don't want to love like that again," Gabriela said.

There was no look of pain, or remorse, just the determined expression that told him she was content to live without love.

When the day came for them to leave Ciego, Hawken felt a type of sadness that he never felt at home. He loved Ciego and the beach and the modest house and Carlos, who was now his friend. Lopez gave him a warm handshake and Rose had tears in her eyes when she said good-bye and watched the couple drive away. Gabriela put her sunglasses on, propped her bare feet on the dash, and began turning the radio dial until she found a song that she liked and joined in with the singing. The morning sun was chasing the coolness from the air, and the road was empty when they left the tiny town behind and headed for Havana.

The awkward moment came on the last morning in the rented house in Havana. While Hawken showered and shaved, Gabriela meticulously packed his bag and placed it on the bed. Hawken checked the contents, zipped it closed and turned to thank her. Gabriela stood with her hand extended and palm turned upward, her face holding a forced smile. Hawken had played enough poker in his life to judge a player's hand by the look on their face. Nothing. She had nothing. The seconds went by like minutes, but she held her smile without blinking. In the carefree days of the previous week, Hawken had nearly forgotten an important detail—there was a financial component to their relationship. Lust, love, respect, and friendship all fell behind the need to survive in a country where there was so little. Hawken reached into his wallet, and placed two one-hundred-dollar bills into her hand. He had been caught by surprise, but now he was pleased, very pleased. A simple relationship based on needs—his needs and her needs. Neither of them needed love, ever again, and that suited Hawken Turner just fine.

On the way to the airport, he stopped at the only department store in Havana that carried goods barely suitable for Western consumers. He parked the jeep and led Gabriela inside to the hardware section. The three-story building was just a grand shell of a spacious prerevolution store, with tall ceilings, tile floors, and a meager scattering of hard goods. Hawken stopped at a kitchen stove and began inspecting the quality. He opened and shut the door several times. He looked at the electrical wiring and heating coils on the surface.

"What do you think?" he asked.

"It's very nice, but do you need a stove?"

"No, but you do," Hawken replied.

"What do you mean? We have a stove at my house," she said.

"No, you don't. You have a rusted fuel container, a rubber hose, and a broken burner. That's not a stove, that's a bomb. I've worried about that since the first time I saw it. The fuel is exposed, the hose is old, and there's going to be a fire. I'm buying this stove for you."

The expression on Gabriela's face was not happiness. It was fear. Fear that she was hearing a lie. Fear that it was some cruel joke. But it was true. Hawken bought the stove and paid the store for delivery.

When they reached the airport terminal, Gabriela stood in the check-in line holding tight to Hawken's arm. When he acquired his boarding pass, he put away his passport, and turned to say good-bye.

"Why did you tell me in Ciego that you're not my boyfriend?" Gabriela asked.

"Because some day you will want something and somebody different," he said.

"How do you know?"

"I just know."

"Will you come back to see me?"

Hawken Turner hesitated and looked into her uncertain eyes. "Of course I will."

CHAPTER FOURTEEN
Andrew Conner

H awken Turner grew to love Cuba, or maybe he was in love with someone in Cuba. Whatever the reason, he continued to go there. With every ensuing trip back to the island, he felt more at home there. Cuba was good to him. Gabriela was good to him.

On one of Hawken's return trips to Cuba, he met a man named Andrew Conner. Even though they would eventually become good friends, Hawken never knew exactly what Andrew did for work, or what he was doing in Cuba. He first spotted Andrew speaking Russian with a cover-girl platinum blonde in a crowded airport bar in Nassau, where Hawken was waiting for his flight to Havana. The woman wore red lipstick and glitter blue eye shadow, and had squeezed her lusciously curvy body into white, cropped slacks. She smoked thin cigarettes one after the other. Andrew Conner sat on the stool next to her. The more rum Andrew drank, the more fluent his Russian language became. When the Russian woman left her seat to find a bathroom, Andrew turned his attention to Hawken.

"Are you on the Havana flight?" Andrew asked.

"Yes, how about you?"

"Me too."

"I couldn't help but notice you speak Russian," Hawken said.

"Yeah. I live in Saint Petersburg six months out of the year. I have some apartments and real estate there."

"So what are you going to Havana for?" Hawken asked.

"Just going down to look around, see the place for myself, you know? What are you doing down there? Looks like we'll be the only Americans on the plane." Andrew surveyed the boarding area and the collection of passengers, which was three-fourths Cuban, a handful of Bahamians, the Russian blonde, and the two Americans.

"Same. Just looking around."

"First time down there?" Andrew asked.

Hawken was a bit wary of the questions since the US government still did not allow its citizens to travel there, but instincts told him that Andrew was trustworthy. "I've been down a couple of times before."

The two men finished their drinks when the boarding call came over the loudspeaker. Andrew had been drinking for quite some time. Hawken had not been there long, but he too had been drinking hard in anticipation of the hour-long flight on Cubana de Aviación—the airline from hell. Cuba did not publish the safety records for Cubana flights, but it was widely accepted throughout the travel world that it was the world's most dangerous airline in existence. Hawken liked planes with names like Boeing, McDonnell Douglas, and Airbus, but today he and Andrew and the mystery woman from Russia were flying on a Yak. A Soviet Yak. A handed-down, worn out Yakovlev Yak-40 bought from Russia instead of going to the scrap yard...or maybe the Russians just gave it to Cuba.

Walking from the terminal to the waiting Yak provided an up-close look at the decrepit aircraft, with its peeling paint, dented fuselage, and steel cables visible through the worn rubber tires. The door was like the entrance to a space capsule. Passengers had to bend low in order to enter without hitting their heads. The blue plastic interior reminded Hawken of an aging carnival ride that had been taken apart and put back together more times than should be allowed by law. The ambiance receded further when fog began rising from a crack in the flooring. Hawken surmised—no, he hoped—it was just a result of humidity rising from the air compressor and not something more ominous.

In contrast to the old and beaten appearance of the jet were the cheerful, young, and well groomed flight attendants dressed in carefully pressed red polyester uniforms that seemed a bit frayed but clung tightly to each of their toned physiques. Each of the attendants wore hair neatly tucked behind their heads in ponytails with a small amount of gel to keep it in place. As soon as Hawken and Andrew took their seats, an attendant greeted them with cellophane wrapped candies served from a red plastic lunch tray.

Two young Cuban men took the seats directly in front of them. One of the Cubans took a liter of rum from a paper bag, and the other poured Coca-Cola into plastic cups. The first man topped off each Coke with a generous pour of rum. The Cubans tasted their drinks and nodded approvingly before turning around and offering a drink to Hawken. He declined the offer, but Andrew Conner accepted without hesitation. *What the hell?* Hawken thought, and joined the party.

"So, what do you do in the States?" Andrew asked, as they settled in with potent rum and Cokes.

"I have a travel company. We guide hunting and fishing parties all over the world."

"That sounds like a great job. Ever do anything in Russia?" Andrew asked.

"A little. There's some boar and bear hunting on the Volga outside Moscow. Great brown bear hunting to the east in Kamchatka. The problem with the Kamchatka trip is that once you get to Moscow, you've got another nine-hour flight to the east, then a four-hour helicopter flight to bear country. You fly all the way across Russia just to end up in a place that's next to Alaska. It's a tough trip for most people."

"How's the hunting near Moscow?" Andrew asked.

"It's okay. I need to find better outfitters there. The contacts I have are great guys, but if you go on a nine-day hunt, you have eight days of drinking and one day of hunting. Then they want to do something crazy like kill the bear with a knife. Up close, you know."

"Yes. That's the Russians. You a single man?" Andrew asked.

"Divorced."

"You should get a Russian girlfriend."

"I've been seeing this girl in Cuba—you have a Russian girlfriend?"

"Of course. Russian women are incredible. I'm sure you've seen them."

"Sure. Some very pretty women there."

"Saint Petersburg's the best. And not only are they good-looking, but cultured, too. Extremely cultured. I swear, every one of them can sing, dance, recite poetry, or write a book. It's impossible to keep up with them when you talk about culture." Andrew took a drink from his rum and Coke. "Is it serious with the girl in Cuba?"

"I'm not sure," Hawken said. "It's tough to figure exactly what the Cubans are thinking. Just going with the flow right now."

Andrew Conner reached into his wallet and brought out a faded business card. The card belonged to a Mexican official at the Mexican consulate in Havana. "If you ever want to take her to the States, call this man. And tell him that I sent you."

"It's pretty much impossible for a Cuban to enter the States legally right now," Hawken said.

"Call the man if you ever decide to try," Conner said.

The flight to Havana was a haze of loud conversation, anxious anticipation, and lots of rum. It seemed the plane had barely groaned up off the ground in Nassau when the Yak bounced onto the runway and lumbered to the terminal in Havana sparking a round of unanimous cheering from the passengers.

Once in Havana, Andrew Conner joined Hawken every evening, and they went out on the town drinking in seedy bars, listening to music, and smoking cigars. Of course, Gabriela went with them, though she was not fond of bar life. She waited patiently for Andrew to leave Cuba, but the night before his departure, Conner got drunk and lost his passport. Hawken, Andrew, and Gabriela searched every bar and hotel they'd patronized the night before, but there was no passport to be found. That left Andrew with no passport and no money.

"Hawken, do you think I could borrow some money?" Andrew asked. He asked so shamelessly that Hawken was sure that Conner would pay him back someday or somehow.

"Sure. I can loan you a little. Gabriela won't be happy, though."

"Why's that?" Andrew asked.

"I promised I'd help her out with a few things for her family. You know the problems here in Cuba. I'm worried about your passport. Do we even *have* an embassy here?"

"Yeah, but they don't call it an embassy. They call it the American Interest Section. It's right down on the Malecón. Across the street from that new pavilion Fidel built to make the anti-Imperialist speeches so the Americans can hear him."

"What are you going to tell them you were doing here?"

"I'll think of something."

Andrew seemed apprehensive about visiting the Interest Section, but he had no choice. He sobered up, put on a clean shirt, and made up a story about dropping his passport in a river when he was baptizing Christian converts in the countryside. He received his passport two days later, and no one was happier than Gabriela to see Andrew Conner leave Cuba.

Hawken never considered an exclusive relationship with Gabriela. He was observant enough of Cuban culture to know that she did not sit home every night to watch state television, with its only channel dominated by Fidel's ranting speeches. Even that channel came and went with the blackouts. The poor infrastructure actually bolstered social activity as Cubans gathered in the streets at night to drink, dance, and laugh with their friends. Couples walked hand in hand throughout Cuba, and Hawken was sure that Gabriela went out with other men. But he never asked.

As soon as Conner left Havana, Hawken rented a car and drove with Gabriela to their hidden beach near Ciego. Again, the empty beach was theirs alone, and except for Carlos and his shack far off in the distance, they were like two lovers shipwrecked on a desert island. Nothing ever happened there, but something was changing. The wind blowing onshore from far beyond the horizon carried a message, calling him with the call of a distant siren. He shared the beach and the bed with a beautiful woman, but something was missing...something far, far away.

As he sat on the beach facing the timeless sea, he thought of Hemingway at the helm of his beloved boat, *Pilar*, there many years before Hawken ever found it. He looked far past the breaking waves and imagined Papa—binoculars in one hand, gin in the other—the boat bucking and rolling as he scanned the horizon for German U-boats. Hemingway had breathed that air just as Hawken breathed it again. He smelled the salt of the sea and watched the birds soaring overhead stopping periodically to dip low and dive into the sea. Hawken mind began to wander while he watched the rows of waves rise up from the horizon and fling themselves at the shore, only to retreat into the sea to try again. Maybe it was time to leave Cuba.

The United States held stubbornly to the Cuban embargo, and it made no sense to keep looking for business opportunity on the forbidden island. Gabriela was sure to be disappointed, but Hawken knew she would never leave and he had to tell her it was over. It would not be totally unexpected. She was Cuban, and she was a survivor. She would miss the financial assistance, but she would be okay. He broke the news to her as they said their good-byes at the airport.

"I'm not coming back to Cuba again," Hawken said.

Gabriela's face melted with sadness and confusion. "I don't understand," she said.

"I'm not coming back."

"You don't like it here in Cuba?" she asked.

"I do. But there is no business for me here. I don't know why I'm here."

"What about me?" she asked.

"You'll find a nice husband here," Hawken said. "Start a family. You'll be fine."

Gabriela rolled her eyes. She had told Hawken many times before that she had no intention of marrying a Cuban man and settling down with a family in Cuba.

Hawken continued. "And I want a family in my own country. I want to try and live again with my sons as a family. Maybe I'll find a wife, too."

"I don't mind if you have a wife there," Gabriela said.

Hawken laughed out loud at the idea. When he found his soul mate, he had no intention of having a mistress—in Cuba or anywhere else. "No. If I have a wife, I can't see you anymore for sure."

"So, I'll never see you again?"

"You want to marry me and move to the United States?" he asked.

Hawken knew the answer. Nine out of ten Cuban girls would jump at the chance to go, but Gabriela was different. She had never left home, and she was as Cuban as the vintage cars and fine cigars. She adored her family, and her family was there to stay. She was never going to leave Cuba.

CHAPTER FIFTEEN

Embaraza

Nearly a year after his last trip to Cuba, Hawken received an e-mail message from Nelson telling him that he had discovered a new location for fishing in a river estuary largely untouched by fishermen. With a tip from a local fishing guide, Nelson had found the hidden river deep in the Zapata Swamp, and the fishery was bursting with plentiful schools of tarpon and snook. Hawken had tried to forget Cuba, and the embargo was still in place, but the dream of fishing the perfect river was irresistible.

On the third day of March, just after noon, Hawken landed at the airport in Havana, and Nelson stood waiting to greet him. Hawken looked around the airport for Gabriela, but she was not there. Nelson was fidgety as they loaded the bags in the car and left for Jagüey Grande. He was more serious than usual, as if he had something to say. Hawken started to question his demeanor, but he knew that Nelson would tell him when the time was right.

The dirt road leading into the swamp was full of muddy puddles and deep ruts, making the drive slow and tedious. An hour later, when they arrived at the end of the trail, their guide Felipe was waiting for them. Felipe's boat was only slightly larger than a canoe, with a square bow, flat bottom, and small outboard motor. It took thirty minutes of talking, pointing, and planning before they were able to push the boat from the bank and head downriver.

The dark river was quiet, with narrow bends and mangroves encroaching from the banks—just the kind of river Hawken loved to fish. The river had no name and few men had ever fished there. Only the slapping of the engine and the occasional screeching of egrets and cormorants startled from the trees broke the peacefulness of the journey. When the boat came to rest and the wake dissipated into the swamp, Felipe nodded. It was time to fish.

Hawken's first cast was perfect. The lure flew from the reel and plopped onto the water just beside a fallen tree, breaking the stillness of the river. Hawken twitched the lure once, then again, and the water exploded as a silver tarpon went airborne, the hook glinting in its jaw. After a spectacular ten-minute fight, Hawken landed the tarpon—a catch-and-release trophy fish in any other country, but this was Cuba, and the tarpon was food. Felipe struck the tarpon on the head with a wooden bat and placed the fish in the bottom of the boat.

Life could not have been better for Hawken Turner. No work, no worries, and the fishing continued until the sun hung low over the mangroves. He stayed at a private house with Nelson for two more days of fishing in the river. Each day produced spectacular fishing during the day and restful evenings in the small house where they slept and had their breakfast. He missed Gabriela and was happy when she called him on the third day. They spoke of nothing important over the phone, but there was uneasiness in Gabriela's voice when they arranged to meet before Hawken left.

Hawken met Gabriela at a Havana restaurant on his last night in Cuba. She was scrubbed and dressed in her best clothes with curled hair and painted nails from the salon. She glowed in the soft lights of the candle-lit restaurant as they sat close and touched hands as if each was pondering their former relationship—whatever that had been. Their conversation was light and centered on children and family, the small talk of two people avoiding an issue and waiting for the right time to speak.

After their dinner, when the taxi brought them to the door of Hawken's hotel, Gabriela leaned in and spoke to their driver, "Wait five minutes."

She followed Hawken into his hotel, stopping short of the elevator since both of them knew that hotels did not allow tourists into their rooms with Cuban girls. Hawken kissed her on the cheek, but she did not go.

"I want to go live with you in the United States." She did not waver but looked Hawken straight in the eye.

"What?"

"I want to go with you to live in your country," she repeated.

"Why do you want to do that? You're happy here in Cuba, aren't you?"

"*Embaraza,*" she blurted out in Spanish.

Hawken's Spanish was far from perfect, but he knew the meaning of that word—pregnant. The smile went away from his face.

"*What?*"

"*Embaraza.*" She rubbed her stomach.

Hawken studied her belly, looking for any sign of a bulge. He knew the baby could not be his.

"You're pregnant *now?*"

"*Sí.*"

"You're sure?"

"*Sí.*"

"You want to have the baby?" he asked, knowing that abortion was an acceptable option for most Cubans.

"It's too late to stop."

"Who's the father?"

"Not important," she said.

"*Yes*, important. Who is he, and what does he think?"

She rolled her eyes and made a hissing sound to indicate that the father was *not* important. Hawken looked at her without speaking as the scenarios raced through his head. Her eyes fixed on his, obviously anxious for his answer. She would not be happy in the United States—he was sure of that. And how would he explain it to his family and friends—a pregnant woman coming to the United States to live with him—if in fact she *could* come? And... he was well aware that she was not *the one* for him.

"Not possible." He said it firmly and definitively, but it took all he had to keep from reaching out to her. She began shaking and tears formed in her eyes and then rolled down her cheeks and splattered on the floor. She was a strong woman, a Taurus just as he was. She had seemed capable of storing her emotions and selectively letting them out as she chose, but this was uncontrollable weeping. She seemed ashamed of her tears and she hid her face as she turned quickly and retreated to the taxi. Hawken stood speechless in the doorway as the '54 Chevy gushed a cloud of exhaust and drove away into the night. *Damn it.* He loved her. She was not the one, but he loved her.

CHAPTER SIXTEEN
The Visa

Hawken Turner lost sight of his purpose. He started to drift. Visits with his sons became further and further apart, his family life fading. He spent more time drinking alone. He slept poorly at night and woke early in the mornings as if driven by an urgent need to do something, but not knowing what. He made coffee every morning and waited impatiently with a mug in his hand as it filled the pot drip by drip. Coffee fueled the drumbeats that drove him toward the unknown. With fuel in his hand, he walked onto the porch and waited for the answer. And the answer finally came.

Sometimes a man has to trust his instincts, and that was exactly what Hawken decided to do. It was supposed to take three months to get a K-1 fiancée visa for Gabriela to come to the United States. Endless red tape and countless Cuban palms to grease resulted in a process that took much longer than that. Gabriela's baby was born during the early stages of the visa application. Although unsure of the exact nature of their relationship, Hawken made a commitment, and if Gabriela was coming to the United States with a newborn, he needed to be the father that she needed.

He wanted to be present during the birth, but Gabriela went into labor early, and Hawken didn't arrive until two days after she gave birth to a six-pound daughter she named Sofía.

When he walked into the hospital, Hawken found no reception desk at the front door, just people coming and going as if it were a city park. Hawken walked down the hallway until he found an open office. A surprised middle-aged woman with ugly glasses pointed him to the maternity ward after looking up from her tattered magazine. On his way to the room, he passed two women in nightgowns leaning over the drinking fountain, brushing their teeth in the hallway. Rusty wheelchairs parked in the halls held blank-faced patients waiting for someone, or something. The heavy smell of antiseptic filled the air. Paint was chipping from the walls. Medical care might be free in Cuba, but Hawken was saddened at the condition of the hospital.

When he found her room and peered inside, Gabriela beamed with happiness. He did his best to ignore the dismal conditions at the hospital, smiling as he stood at her bedside, taking her hand in his. Hawken surveyed the room and recognized many of Gabriela's friends and family. There was no Cuban father to be seen.

The room was the size of a typical American hospital room, only this one contained four rusted beds jammed together. One mother and one baby occupied each bed. Hawken had seen better beds abandoned on the side of the road in Lewisville, waiting to be picked up and hauled away by the sanitation department. Strips of tape covered the windows for protection—as a hurricane had torn through Havana two weeks earlier, and many of the windows were broken and remained in disrepair. Exposed wiring protruded from holes in the stucco walls awaiting nonexistent monitors and medical machines. There was one wooden table with a stack of dingy towels. *A hospital room, or a prison cell?*

Hawken remained in Havana for two weeks. He stayed with Gabriela for most of that time. They were never alone since the room was crowded with mothers, babies, and a bustling parade of joyful friends and family. Still, no Cuban father to be seen.

In the evenings, when Hawken left the hospital, he drove to the Hotel Nacional and sat on the terrace drinking rum, smoking cigars and pondering his future. It was all or nothing for Hawken, and he had made his decision. He left Gabriela and Sofía in Cuba—he had no choice at the time, but he would be back to get them. When he boarded the flight for Nassau, he showed flight attendants and fellow passengers the photographs of Gabriela and her precious baby. Just as any proud father would do.

After waiting nine months for the visa approval, Gabriela and Sofía were finally on their way to Lewisville. Hawken paced back and forth while he waited by the baggage carousels at the Tallahassee airport. He held a dozen red roses and a helium-filled Disney balloon that bounced behind him as he paced. He had not been able to reach Gabriela for two days and her plane was two hours late. As the last of the passengers walked down the corridor, Hawken finally spotted Gabriela. She looked surprisingly relaxed, pushing a stroller piled high with warm blankets.

"Where's Sofía?" Hawken asked. He kissed her on the cheek and gave her a quick hug.

"She's here." Gabriela peeled off the blankets, exposing the nine-month-old baby dressed in a heavy polyester jacket. "It's so cold here," she said.

"Cold? My God, it's seventy degrees outside. You haven't seen cold. This is April. We got down to the twenties last month."

They gathered Gabriela's orange suitcase from the carousel, loaded the truck, and started for home. Hawken pointed out things that Gabriela had never seen: a McDonalds, a shopping mall, a Ford dealership filled with shiny new cars, and the interstate highway with speeding cars and no hitchhikers like seen on the highways in Cuba. Gabriela observed with wide eyes but sat quietly as if wondering if it was all a dream. She had seen pictures of Hawken's house, but seeing it as her own must have been overwhelming for Gabriela. She had never been inside a house like that, much less ever lived in one. He watched intently when she wrapped Sofía tightly with blankets and walked to the door.

Hawken had done his best to prepare his home for her arrival. He borrowed or bought everything he thought Sofía would need, including a crib, a rocking chair like the one Gabriela had in Cuba, a wind-up swing, baby bottles, and lots of Disney toys. He had done well, but Gabriela began rearranging the house as soon as she walked through the door.

Hawken took Sofía in his arms and followed behind as Gabriela swarmed over the house, moving furniture, looking in drawers, and putting things in order. It was far different from the carefree days in Cuba when they had sunned themselves on the beach and drank beer in the afternoons.

Gabriela never looked toward Hawken while she worked at her tasks, and when she finished in the kitchen and den, she took the sleeping Sofía from Hawken's arms and placed her in the crib. She unpacked her suitcase, neatly folded Sofía's clothes and put them away in drawers, and began placing pictures of her family on the chest.

Hawken moved to the porch trying not to seem selfish, but yearning for Gabriela's attention. Finally, he gave up and retired to the bedroom and lay down in his empty king-size bed. When he closed his eyes and started to sleep, the door creaked open and Gabriela tiptoed through the bedroom and into the bathroom. He heard running water and mouth-swishing sounds coming from behind the closed door. When she finished brushing her teeth, she removed her clothes, slipped a nightgown over her naked body, and eased into the bed next to Hawken.

Gabriela lay on her back and moved her arms up and down the sheets as if measuring the spaciousness of the bed. She did the same with her legs. Finally, she sat up in bed, removed her gown, and slid next to Hawken. She wrapped her leg around his thighs, reached around his chest, and drew her breasts across his back as she leaned her head close to his ear and whispered, "I have something for you."

It was difficult to imagine the emotions Gabriela must have been feeling as she adjusted to her new life in a strange country. Hawken knew that she was determined to make a good life. Her happiness had nothing to do with her feelings for him. He knew she would make herself happy if living in the United States made life easier for her family in Cuba, and presented a better future for Sofía. Hawken envied her sense of simplicity. He knew that she didn't believe in soul mates or true love—or at least she did not pursue those ideas for herself—but she did believe in family, and that was her purpose in life.

Hawken feared that Gabriela would not last the allotted time allowed by the K-1 visa to determine the future for them as a couple. The visa allowed three months in the United States. After that, the foreign fiancée had to marry or leave for good. Hawken had warned her of the challenges of life in the United States. He explained how his country's culture was far less welcoming than Cuba's, and how it would be difficult for her to make friends. He described how everyone liked their own space, and how they kept themselves distant—physically and emotionally—from neighbors and people in the street. He told her how families often became scattered and rarely spent every day together like in Cuba. He knew it would be a difficult three months for Gabriela. Unfortunately, they did not get that long to decide.

"Hawken, is it true that you're living with your Cuban girlfriend and baby?" asked George Kirby, Hawken's attorney. He had been working for Hawken to file for a legal change of custody for the three boys. They were okay in Nashville, but they were missing their father as much as he missed them. They wanted to move back home. The situation was tense with his ex-wife, and they were working with their respective attorneys to prepare for the legal challenge. Hawken knew that she would have something to say if she knew about a live-in Cubana and her young child.

"Yes, it's true."

"How long is she there for?" George asked.

"I'm really not sure."

"My God," Kirby said. "We were almost done with the petition."

"I know."

"Well—you have three options. You can send her back to Cuba, you can forget about your sons coming to live with you, or you can marry her." His attorney sounded very perturbed.

"Okay," Hawken said.

"Okay what?"

"Okay, I'll do one of the three," said Hawken.

"Let me know which one you decide."

"Okay, George."

When young couples on the island of Cuba get married, they receive a gift from the Cuban government of housing and furniture. Many couples marry for that reason, only to later divide the furniture and split soon after marriage. That was a new custom in Cuba, brought on by the "special period," when the need for survival outweighed the luxury of marrying for love. It was possible that Hawken and Gabriela were together for a similar reason, but only the future could answer that question.

Two days after speaking with his attorney, Hawken arrived home from work just before dark and was greeted by the rich aroma of dinner simmering on the stove. Gabriela met him just inside the door with a kiss and a smile, looking pretty in her jeans and a simple T-shirt. She wore little or no makeup, and her hair was brushed and tied in a ponytail with beautiful pink ribbon. Hawken noted a hint of perfume as he gathered Sofía from her arms and kissed her cheek.

"I have a present for you," Hawken said. He handed Gabriela the small square box from the jewelry store.

"Oh my God." Gabriela opened the box, and her mouth fell open when she saw the diamond solitaire ring set in white gold. Any confusion, wonder, or puzzlement was vanquished as Gabriela held the ring as if she had never seen anything so lovely. She was speechless and she quickly slipped the band on her slender finger.

"Do you want to get married?" Hawken asked.

Gabriela was still smiling. "I thought we had three months to decide," she said.

"My lawyer says that we have to get married now if I want the boys to live with me. It's a complicated situation in this country. The judge won't allow them to live here if we're not married. We have to marry now, or that can't happen."

Gabriela hesitated only a moment before answering.

"Okay." She held the ring to the light and twisted it back and forth to see it sparkle.

Marriage was not a complicated issue for Cubans. If things worked out well after marriage, they stayed together. If things were not good after marriage, they divorced. It was not "'til death do us part." Gabriela apparently did not need to give it much thought.

"We can drive to Alabama tomorrow and get married in the courthouse. They don't need a blood test, and I have all the documents we need. You can be Mrs. Turner before dinner."

"I'll have a husband tomorrow?" she asked.

"Yes, a *handsome* husband."

"And you'll have a sexy wife." She kissed him on the lips and let the kiss linger in confirmation that she was pleased to be kissing her future husband.

It was only after they were married that Hawken realized that she would have liked something better than the thirty-minute Alabama courthouse wedding. It was difficult to treat her like a princess with no wedding dress, champagne toasts, or bride's maids. Two plain clothed clerks, a stuffy office, and quick "I do's" were less than special. Hawken deeply regretted that arrangement, but he did not regret the marriage.

Due to cultural differences, married life with Gabriela had its difficulties, but on the whole, it was pretty damn good. The house was clean, the food was good, and there were sounds of life inside that had been missing for a long time. Perhaps the marriage was based on domestic necessities, but laughter and playfulness filled their lives.

Gabriela spent most of her time taking care of the house and nurturing Sofía, but she never failed to turn her attention to Hawken once Sofía was asleep. Like brushing her teeth, making love was a habit she never ignored. "I have something for you" was Gabriela's saying when she arrived in the bed. Sometimes the sex was spontaneous and passionate, sometimes it bordered on routine, and sometimes it reminded them of the days spent dreaming on their secret beach in Cuba.

Despite growing affection, after six months of marriage, Hawken could see the longing for Cuba in Gabriela's eyes. She was still a visitor in a strange land, and suffered from loneliness brought about by separation from the family she had left behind. He could sense her sadness and sometimes he could see the tears that she tried to hide.

With relentless complications and a lack of communications between Cuba and the US, it took months of preparing documents and forms to allow Gabriela to visit her homeland. Endless denials and countless rounds of interviews began to take a toll. When Gabriela finally had the precious documents in her hand, she booked the first available flight to Havana.

She stayed in Cuba for three weeks. Hawken was happy for her when she left, and happy for himself when she came back... happy until she started the grueling process again—just four days later. Stubborn as she was, there was no changing her mind once she had decided.

"I know you're not happy, but I *have* to go back," Gabriela said. "We have a big party planned for Sofia's second birthday. Do you want to tell my family they can't see her on her birthday?"

"Of course not, but there's a law that says you can't go."

"They told me in Cuba I can," she said.

"Yes, by falsifying documents. I'm not going to do that for a party. It's a big problem if you are caught. Do you want to live in Cuba for the rest of your life? Really? Tell me. Do you want to? If you go, you might not be able to come back, Gabriela. You have to think about that."

"I want to come back here. I live here," she said. "It was possible before."

"The only thing certain in Cuba is the fact that there will be problems in Cuba."

"I have to go."

"If you go, you're not coming back," Hawken said. "I can't go through this every time you have an excuse to go back. It will never end."

"I'm sorry," she said.

Four months later, Gabriela packed her bags for Cuba. On her last night at home, after putting Sofia to bed, she slipped on her nightgown and slowly brushed her hair. She then turned out the lights and crawled into bed next to her disgruntled husband. "I have something for you," She said.

CHAPTER SEVENTEEN
The Card

Hawken had his first drink of MacLachlan when Brenn Von Snierden introduced him to the single-malt scotch in Africa. The strong whiskey smelled of the earth, and the taste spoke of history and heritage. It was a good drink for Africa. The scotch blended well with safari life and the company of the men around the campfire. There, Hawken drank from a heavy glass with a single piece of ice. No water—just whiskey and one jagged piece of ice. It never tasted the same again. But that did not stop him from trying.

Gabriela had been gone for over a month, and Hawken missed her. She told him of her plans to stay with her family in Cuba for good. He missed his boys. And he missed others whom he tried to forget. MacLachlan was still his drink, and one hot summer night, he had something important to do, and he wanted the perfect drink in his hand when he did it.

Hawken walked into his house, set down his briefcase, and went straight to the liquor cabinet. He reached in and brought out the bottle. He found his favorite drinking glass on the top shelf. The glass was a good one for scotch, rounded and short and perfectly fitted to his hand, with a heavy base nearly an inch thick.

Hawken dropped a single chunk of ice into two fingers of whiskey. He had learned early on that the size and shape of the ice made a difference. It was a simple drink, but there were layers of taste when he savored it slowly. The first sip was strong and bitter if not yet chilled by the ice. The last sip was the tease, when the scotch was diluted, creating a desire to pour another. The middle of the drink was where the elusive perfection existed. Arrive at the middle too soon, and the drink was raw. Arrive too late, and the whiskey had lost its bite.

With whiskey in hand, Hawken walked to the study and sat at his desk. He sipped the scotch. *Too stiff.* He opened the bottom drawer of the credenza and took the faded yellow envelope from inside where it had lain untouched for years like an unexploded mortar on a forgotten battlefield. He had never opened the dreaded card. He propped his feet on the desk and held the card to his nose. *You're going to read it tonight. You have to…if you are ever going to close the book.*

Hawken turned the envelope over twice, and then carefully opened the sealed flap. He removed the card and held it in front of his eyes. He set it down, took another drink of scotch. *Almost perfect.* He picked up the card again. There was a cartoon figure of a cat on the front that asked, *"Are you free Saturday night?"* When he opened the card, the inside read, *"If not, I will go as high as $2.95."* Sam had circled the word *"Free,"* and had written a note that Hawken finally read, slowly, again and again, until it was burned into his memory:

> *I got this card just because I kind of liked it and thought it was sort of appropriate, And even if it isn't, so what!*
> *Love ya,*
> *Sam*

The card was Sam…so Sam. Over the years, Hawken had managed to lose every photograph, note, card, and other reminder of Sam—except this one. It was a simple cartoon card in a yellow envelope, but it was all he had left of her. She had mailed the card the very day that she died. Hawken lifted the glass slowly and took another drink of scotch. *Too late.* Another missed opportunity for the perfect drink. Like everything in his life, he could not grasp and hold the moment when it was good.

Hawken looked across the room and focused his eyes on the Winchester rifle standing inside the mahogany gun cabinet with glass doors and brass hardware. He walked to the cabinet, unlatched the doors, and lifted the gun. He thought of the men who had owned the rifle before him and the memories they had shared. The Colonel. Chat. He sat back at the desk and held the rifle between his legs with the stock resting on the floor. He raised his glass and took a long, slow drink of diluted scotch. He took the card in his hand, looked once more at the signature, and returned it to the drawer. He held the barrel of the Winchester with both hands, rested his chin on the muzzle, and closed his eyes. *What was she thinking?*

A week later, Hawken was on a flight to Havana. He had no plan, but he had a mission. He had let Gabriela go without a fight, and he wanted her back. If it were possible, he would find a way. He was not convinced that she prepared to stay in Cuba. She had been there long enough to know what she truly wanted, and Hawken Turner was on his way to find her.

His heart was pounding when he made the call from his hotel room in Havana. Four families shared a single phone in Gabriela's neighborhood, and an elderly woman speaking rapid

Spanish answered the call. She lived two houses down from Gabriela's family. The old woman said something about going next door, and left Hawken waiting for ten minutes. Finally, an English-speaking man came to the phone and gave Hawken the news.

"She's in Spain."

"What?"

"Gabriela has gone to Spain."

"*España?*"

"Sí, *España*—Spain."

"When is she coming back?" Hawken asked.

"I don't know."

"Did she go alone?" Hawken asked.

"I don't know."

"Where is Nelson?"

"Gone."

"Gone where?"

The phone went dead.

That was Cuba. The mysteries. The answers he would never find. The way the island embraced him at times, and treated him cruelly at others. His flight out did not leave for another four days.

Hawken spent two miserable days walking the streets of Havana. The warm, tropical breezes and floating rhythms of salsa music were replaced by oppressive heat, torturous humidity, and loud horns blaring from dilapidated cars as they bounced down the streets followed by toxic fumes. It was not the return to Cuba that Hawken Turner had hoped for. Even the architecture seemed changed. Finely crafted historic buildings in the city center turned into ugly blocks of decaying concrete. The sweet sounds of life in the streets had transformed into abrasive noise.

He had no place to go, so he stayed in the hotel bar, drinking rum and pondering his future. His friend Luís was working the bar and serving his drinks with polite conversation. Next to the bar, Maira was working the reception desk, thumbing the pages of the guest log to relieve her boredom. The front door was open for breezes, and an attractive young woman caught Hawken's eye when she walked up to the desk and greeted Maira with a hug and a kiss on the cheek. The women whispered and giggled and Hawken returned to his drink. When he looked up, the two women were standing in front of him. Maira spoke first.

"Hawken, this is my friend Jessie."

The young woman extended her hand and smiled at Hawken.

"Hi, I'm your new girlfriend," she said.

Cuba was incredible. You lose a wife one day, and you have a girlfriend the next. There was temptation in the offer, but Hawken shook his head and declined with a laugh. He had learned something about caring for a woman from another culture, and though he knew he would never have all the answers, he was not doing that again. He was going home. At least, that was his plan.

"That's a wonderful thought, but I'm only in Havana for one more night," Hawken said. "I'm going to Cienfuegos tomorrow." It was a lie, but he was not in the mood for company.

"Are you going alone?" she asked.

"That's the plan."

"I can go with you," she said.

"What did you say your name was?" Hawken asked.

"Jessie."

Hawken was still trying to figure out what had happened with Gabriela, and he was not interested in Jessie. Still, with her light brown hair, tight figure, and infectious smile, she was not taking "no" for an answer.

"Do you know Gabriela?" Hawken asked.

"No, but I heard the news. And I know she's gone to Spain. Today's your lucky day." Jessie took a seat next to him at the bar.

"Are you sure about that?" Hawken asked.

"Yes, I'm very sure. Why don't you take me to dinner tonight?"

"And what about Cienfuegos?" Hawken asked.

"We'll talk about that tonight," she replied. "You're all alone here in Havana, and you need some company."

Hawken paused and turned to Jessie. "What the hell. Maybe that's true. How about nine o'clock? Meet me here at the hotel, and we'll walk to someplace near here."

"Okay, baby," she said. She smiled and kissed him on the cheek before leaving.

Luís wiped the bar clean and waited for Hawken to speak.

"So what do you think?" Hawken asked.

"She's a beautiful girl. You can never have any regrets with a beautiful girl. But then again, I'm Cuban, you know."

CHAPTER EIGHTEEN
Jessie

Hawken Turner was an intelligent man. He knew when he was making a bad decision. But sometimes he just could not stop himself. Changing his plans and spending a couple of days in Cienfuegos with Jessie was not going to answer any questions, but Jessie was too charming to ignore. She was a university graduate with a law degree—a noble profession, but there was little reward in Cuba for a lawyer who worked for the state. She was easy to talk to, and even easier to look at. And there was no uncertainty in her offer.

Hawken rented a car in Havana and drove with her to the southern coast of Cuba. They were like two refugees, unsure of the next move, but comforted by each other's company. They rented a house and shared a bed in Cienfuegos, but lingering thoughts of Gabriela purged Hawken's desire for sex.

They were sitting on the terrace one evening, looking out to sea, when Hawken asked ask about her life in Cuba. "If you have your law degree, why aren't you working now?"

"It's a long story," she began. "I wanted to be a lawyer to help people. That's what I thought lawyers did. But I found out that was a lie. Lawyers here only work for the government, and they do the things that the government wants them to do. I tried to help one of my neighbors, but the government didn't want me to help him and they took my certificate. It was all over a pig."

"Over a pig?"

"Exactly—over a pig. My neighbor had pigs at his house he was feeding for the government. His family didn't have food, so he killed a pig. The pig was at his house, but it wasn't for him. So the government put him in prison."

"And they took your certificate?"

"Yes."

"Sorry to hear that. What do you do for work now?"

"Nothing. Nothing important. Sometimes I sell clothes and shoes. I have an aunt in Ecuador and she sends a package every two, or three months and I sell them in the street. But not for much money because they're Chinese clothes. Cheap. Very cheap."

"Do you make enough money to live on?"

"It doesn't cost much money to live in Cuba if you like eating rice and beans."

"I like rice and beans," Hawken said. "What do you do for fun?"

"Fun?"

"Fun."

"Not much. I sit outside my house and talk to the neighbors. Walk the street to see friends, and sometimes I watch the TV. The Cuban TV."

Hawken laughed. "I've seen Cuban TV."

"Oh yes, they have the state programs all day—but on Saturday, they have one movie on Saturday. I never miss TV on Saturday."

"One movie?"

"Yes, one movie."

"You're a lucky girl."

"So lucky."

After three days of lying on the beach and wandering the sleepy streets of Cienfuegos, their escape came to an end and it was time to leave. For the first time since they had met, Hawken noticed the depth of her beauty when she tossed her bag into the backseat of the car. Her tanned skin was golden brown and glowed in the morning light. Her brown hair was lightened by the sun and twisted into untamed locks by the salt and wind from the humid breezes blowing in from the sea. She was as wild and natural as the drifting birds and swaying palms. Her eyes met his. Jessie held the car door open and stopped before sitting inside.

"I want to go to Varadero," she said.

"Varadero? It's too touristy," he said. "It reminds me of Miami Beach. Besides, I need to go home."

"I've never been there, and I want to see it," she said.

"But Cubans aren't allowed in Varadero."

"I know, but maybe we'll get lucky. It's not fair that the most beautiful beach in Cuba is only for the tourists. Did you ever go there with Gabriela?"

"Yes, but we couldn't stay for the night. Even the private *casas* don't allow Cubans to stay the night there," he said.

"That's okay. I only want to swim in the water. And see the hotels."

"Well…what the hell, *mi amor*. If that's all you want to do, let's go—I'll show you Varadero."

The town of Varadero was like a mirage on the island of rampant poverty. The seven-mile stretch of powder-white beach and diamond-clear water was lined with megaresorts serving daiquiris and mojitos to sunburned tourists from Canada, Italy, and England. A stiff breeze from the north pushed the waters into white-crested waves folding onto clean, manicured sand. Wooden lounges sat beneath green umbrellas, and palm-roofed *palapa* bars dotted the beach. It was the kind of place where people who sit behind desks every day came to become someone else. It was pretty, but it was not Hemingway's Cuba.

When they got there, they drove the length of Varadero, looking at the grand hotel entrances on the beach side of the road and open-air restaurants on the other. They found an open beach, and Hawken pulled the car onto an empty service road between two parking lots.

"Here," he said.

"Here what?" Jessie asked.

"Here's where we swim."

"Where do I put on my swimsuit?" she asked.

"In the car."

"Okay."

Jessie retrieved her bikini from the bag in the backseat and began removing her clothes without hesitation. Hawken found his swimsuit and did the same.

They walked to the water's edge, crashed through the breakers, and swam to the sandbar where the waves were gentle and the water was shallow. Jessie swam close to him, put her arms around his neck, and wrapped her tan legs tightly around his waist and began kissing him.

"I want to swim naked," she said.

"There are still people here on the beach."

"You're no fun. Where will we shower before we go?"

"Wait here."

Hawken swam to the shore and retrieved a bar of soap and bottle of shampoo from his luggage. When he returned to the sandbar, they washed their hair and scrubbed their bodies with soap in the warm salt sea. When they were done, they sat on the sand and let their bodies dry as the big orange sun sank low and slowly melted into the sea. It was a day that left no room for wandering thoughts of sadness.

It was almost dark when they returned to the car and started down the busy street for Havana. While Hawken backed the car to turn around, Jessie removed her damp bathing suit and wrapped a towel around her naked body. When Hawken pulled onto the main road crowded with tourists, her towel fell open, exposing her breasts. With no hint of modesty, Jessie took her hands and began massaging her breasts.

"Damn," Hawken said.

"I love to touch my body." She threw her head back and closed her eyes.

"You're crazy," Hawken said. "Don't you care if people see you?"

"No, I don't care." She seemed oblivious to the passing cars and people on the sidewalk. "I feel safe with you, Hawken," she said. "I feel free. Do you know what that's like for a Cuban woman, to feel free?"

"No."

"It feels good."

"It won't feel good when the police see you."

"I don't care." She smiled and looked outside at the people on the sidewalk and the cars as they passed.

Hawken drove carefully as heavy traffic in the center of the strip slowed their pace. The cars were lined close together, and the sidewalks were filled with tourists. They passed a middle-aged man on the sidewalk, and his mouth fell open when he peered inside and saw the topless woman.

"Look at that man," Jessie said.

"Maybe I should ask if he needs a ride," said Hawken.

"Yes, a good idea. I think he'll like that."

"He would have a heart attack, I'm sure."

The cars thinned when they reached the outskirts of Varadero, and they were soon alone on the two-lane road winding along the coast. The hills were dotted with distant lights from scattered houses, each one lit by a single light, faintly flickering in the twilight. Jessie put her hands behind her head, closed her eyes and began singing a Spanish love song. The towel was still open down to her waist. Her voice was low and beautiful and she sang from her soul. She tilted her head and looked at Hawken from the corners of her eyes. There was an invitation in her look. The car drove on into the night, and inside the car, the temperature was rising and the air was thick. It was another hour and a half to Havana. Hawken had his hands on the wheel and his eyes on the road, but the bulge in his pants was driving the car. He turned onto an abandoned road and slid to a stop.

"Do you want me?" Jessie asked in a whisper.

"Get over here," he said.

In the daylight hours, in the eyes of the sun, they were strangers—yet on this abandoned road, under the tropical moon, in the black shadows of tall palms, they were more. An hour later, when he started the car and pulled onto the highway leading back to Havana, Hawken Turner began to wonder if the unlikely union was just the beginning of something that he never saw coming.

Hawken spent the last night in the Hotel Nacional before leaving Cuba. Jessie joined him at the hotel to say good-bye. The walked out onto the terrace and stood by the cannons overlooking the sea. The breeze from the sea was warm and the lights were low. They held hands and talked about nothing. A Cuban quartet sang love songs in the background.

Jessie told the story of the father she could not remember, a man who had left her and her mother behind during the Mariel boatlift. They had thought they would be going with her father, but he took another woman instead. He settled in Miami and became a prosperous businessman, with tomato farms in Florida and Virginia. He offered to send money to them, but Jessie's mother never accepted a dime.

Hawken and Jessie talked about beautiful dreams, hopes for the future, and the certainty that they would see each other again. Jessie squeezed his hand, and her eyes grew misty. She covered her face to hide her tears.

"Hawken, I'm dying in this shit country."

CHAPTER NINETEEN
The Plan

Hawken Turner had learned something from his marriage to Gabriela. He discovered that it was hard to love a woman from a foreign country—especially Cuba. He would have been wise to never return. It was like trying to make seed with two souls planted in different gardens. But when he thought of Cuba, he could not resist the prevailing winds blowing him in that direction. He remembered the streets that were filled with people hanging onto life and living every minute. Just inside open doors, cheerful ladies cleaned tile floors with a bucket and mop, the smell of cooking drifting from tiny kitchens. Children laughed and played in doorways as vintage cars lumbered by, honking their horns and splashing through potholes. There were no fragments in the soul of Cuba—it was many hearts beating as one. And…most important to Hawken, there was nothing in Cuba to remind him of Sam.

Then came Jessie. The year following his initial encounter with Jessie, Hawken traveled every two months to see her. They were happy together, but spoke frequently about her suppressed misery and dreams that seemed out of reach. There was only one solution. *Damn Cuba. Damn it, damn it, damn it.*

In early December, on a cold rainy night at home, Hawken searched his wallet and found the business card given to him by Andrew Conner. He stared at the card while he chose his words, then picked up the phone and called the man at the Mexican embassy in Havana.

The Mexican seemed to have been waiting for his call and readily accepted Andrew Conner's referral. The plan was simple, but dangerous. The Mexican could deliver an invitation for Jessie to visit Mexico. The visa would be bogus, but he had a contact in Cuba to provide validation and issue an exit permit to leave—for a price. That was the dangerous part, as there could be no permanent record. The permit could only appear on the day of travel and then erased from existence before the following day. The visa would only get her to Mexico City. Once there, she would travel to the border, cross to the US side, and seek political asylum—generally given freely to Cubans.

After weeks spent working out the details, they initiated the plan. Hawken was back in the United States, but kept in touch by phone. He was careful not to say too much in fear that someone might be listening to the calls. They waited anxiously for the Mexican to process the papers, and the days passed slowly while hope hung in the balance for the eight weeks it would take to complete the documents.

Hawken never stopped to think about his own risks, but he knew that Jessie faced prison if the authorities discovered their plan. Regardless of the opportunities she was seeking, leaving

home would not be easy. It would not be a journey without consequences, but she had made her decision.

Hawken tried to ease her fears whenever they spoke on the phone.
"What's the first thing you want to do when you get here?" he
asked.

"Make love to you in your country," she said.

"I want you to see the grocery stores here. And the cinemas.
You'll love the cinemas. And I'm going to teach you to fish."

"I need to visit my aunt and uncle in Miami. Can you imagine
the looks on their faces when I knock on their door?" Jessie asked.

"Your father too?"

"No, not him."

Hawken acknowledged that she might live in Miami like so
many Cubans. This was okay with him. She was a smart woman
with skills for a good job and fruitful future—a future that was
not possible for her in Cuba. He remembered her tears the night
in Havana, when he had told her that he would help her. There
were many opportunities for failure within the plan, but they both
agreed it was worth the risk.

Hawken was at home when he got the urgent call from Jessie. She
was crying into the phone, and he could barely understand her
words.

"The man from Mexico is gone," she sobbed. "The governments had a big fight, and all the Mexicans have left Cuba. The
embassy is closed here, and nothing is possible. Not now." Jessie
was speaking half English and half Spanish. The phone went
dead, but she called back five minutes later.

"Hawken…I feel like I'm on a long road now, and there's nothing at the end of my road. I'll never get out of this country."

It was true. Before the Mexican visa was issued, a handful of Cubans seeking political asylum had crashed the gate at the Mexican embassy in Havana. The embassy refused to put them out, and that led to a conflict between the two governments. The Mexican ambassadors were expelled, the embassy closed, and the hopes of obtaining a visa for Jessie drifted away like a feather in the wind.

The sound of Jessie's uncontrollable crying haunted Hawken Turner, but there was no alternate plan. He lay awake at night knowing how cruel it was to offer freedom, then tear it away at the last moment. Yet just when he had nearly given up hope, Hawken got the call. The plan was back on. The Cuban government had made up with the Mexicans, the Mexican contact was back in Cuba, money was paid, and Jessie had a temporary visa to Mexico in her hand. The first part was complete, but the Cuban part of the plan was unsure and dangerous.

Jessie had one day's notice when everything was in place. She was told to go to the airport with her family and the money. She would check in and present her papers to the immigration officer before entering the boarding area. If her papers were verified, she would leave and her family would hand the money to the unnamed man standing with them. If the papers were discovered to be false, there would be hell to pay.

Hawken Turner wore a sober look on his face when he boarded his flight for Mexico. The plan was for him to arrive in Mexico City at approximately the same time as Jessie. He did not want her wandering around Mexico with false documents. Not alone, anyway. To get the timing right, however, Hawken had to depart Tallahassee before Jessie left Havana. *If* she left Havana. *If* she was not in prison. *If* she went to the airport at all. Hawken would not know until he got to Mexico.

When Hawken's flight landed in Mexico City, he claimed his bag and wandered through the airport looking for Jessie. She was nowhere in sight. He found a corner of the building where he sat on his bag and leaned against the wall so he could watch the passengers from all over the world as flights arrived and lines formed. No Jessie. He walked over to the nearby bar and ordered a cold beer.

"Hawken!"

It was Jessie. He had turned his back for only a second, and there she stood. He saw sweat beading on her brow, and Hawken felt tears running down his back when he grabbed her and hugged her tightly.

"I was so scared, Hawken. My body was shaking when I was in immigration. I was fighting to keep from crying. I had to think of you to keep from thinking of my mother because she was crying when I looked back. You can't imagine."

"I'm sure you were scared. But we're not done yet. Try to be calm, okay?"

"Okay, but I can't tell you what I feel right now." She wiped her eyes as she began to sob. "Let's go to the hotel and get a drink. I don't want to think right now."

"Hell, yeah. That's the best idea I've heard all day."

Hawken took her by the hand and they crossed the busy street to the Marriott just across from the airport. They checked in and went to the room, where they emptied the minibar and talked late into the night. Jessie recounted every second of the day and described her fear when passing through the layers of security in the airport. It was not the right time for Hawken to remind her that the worst was yet to come.

On the following day, they went back to the airport and boarded a flight to Monterrey to be closer to the US border. The flight was uneventful as there was no immigration check or customs to pass. The most challenging segment of the plan would come during the three-hour drive from Monterrey to the US border. The roads through Northern Mexico were like a gauntlet lined with human traffickers, drug smugglers, and Mexican military checkpoints. And trouble always seemed to congregate at the border.

Hawken kept Jessie out of sight as much as possible in Monterrey. They checked into the Holiday Inn and went straight to their room. He needed to find a driver to take them to the border, and the fact that Jessie was there with illegal papers made them vulnerable. Hawken did his best to relax, but he kept thinking of Jessie and the life she would face in Cuba if she were caught, or possibly a much worse fate there in Mexico.

He spent two days studying the pulse of Monterrey. He walked the streets and took notice of the inhabitants—how they were dressed, the look in their eyes, what they were doing, how they moved—trying to get a sense of which of them could be trusted and which could not. He made small talk in broken Spanish with strangers in shops and bars, searching for an opportunity to find a driver who could lead them to the border.

After two days, Hawken found the perfect man for the job. He had befriended one of the doormen at the hotel who suggested a man named Sergio, no last name—none needed. Sergio, in his early twenties, worked part-time as a taxi driver when his uncle was not driving the taxi. He was clean-cut and looked like an engineering student with a neat haircut and black-rimmed glasses. Hawken explained to Sergio that a friend would be accompanying him, and that the friend's papers were not legal, but he was careful not to mention that his friend was a woman. Sergio seemed to understand the unspoken words, and was amenable to the mission as soon as Hawken offered to double the initial price from $150 to $300. Sergio was familiar with the roads and knew of a route with only one military checkpoint. Hawken expected the checkpoints, and he was prepared for trouble with a pocket full of dollars.

The two-lane road stretched for miles. Straight as a rifle shot and empty of cars. It lay baking in the hot sun on barren landscape dotted with cactus and mesquite. Two buzzards circled high in the sky, tilting their wings and riding the updrafts from distant mountains to the west. *Son of a bitching buzzards.* After four hours of driving, the taxi topped a rise in the highway, and in the valley of fate before them was the military checkpoint Hawken had been dreading.

Sergio slowed the car. "There it is," he said.

Jessie sat in the backseat as Sergio had suggested. Hawken sat in the front passenger seat. He turned to look at Jessie as she stuffed her Cuban passport down the back of her pants.

"Hawken, I don't know about this. I'm scared," she said. Her voice was cracking with nervousness, and her eyes filled with fear.

"It's too late to turn back now," Hawken said. He reached into the backseat and took her hand. "It's your lucky day. Remember that."

"I know."

Nobody spoke as they started toward the roadblock ahead. Perhaps it had been a mistake for Jessie to leave the safety of her government-controlled, futureless country and seek a better life in the land of milk and honey. That was the way that the Cubans envisioned the United States—milk and honey. Maybe it was not milk and honey, but it *was* a hell of a lot better for an ambitious woman like Jessie. There was just this one obstacle left in her way. She was stepping into the minefield, with Cuba behind her, and the United States in front. One wrong step and her young life would be ruined.

"Everybody relax," Hawken said. "Pleasant smiles and no sweating."

They rolled into the checkpoint and Sergio rolled his window down and handed over his papers to the soldier. The soldier had approached the car alone, leaving three or four others at the guard-house. They were heavily armed, with M16 rifles hanging from their shoulders.

Good. He's alone. If he asks for Jessie's papers, I'll have a better chance at bribing him.

The soldier thumbed every page of the car's registration and license and then looked into the taxi at Sergio. There was a single bead of sweat on Sergio's right temple. Hawken propped his elbow on the open window, concealing his angst with a guise of boredom. Jessie looked out the window to shield her face from the soldier.

The soldier returned the papers to Sergio, and with a wave of his hand, ordered the crossing raised for the taxi to pass. With each change of gears, the taxi regained momentum on the freedom highway and the occupants breathed another sigh of relief. They had run the gauntlet.

When they reached the border just after the siesta hour, the brutal sun was still high overhead. The dusty streets of Matamoros were busy with people and cars. Sergio did not drive directly to the bridge, trying to avoid suspicion from watchful eyes on the Mexican side. He drove along the Rio Grande River that made up the border, the thin ribbons of trickling water and trash-laden sandbars that divided the two countries. The eroded banks were steep, with thorny bushes sprouting from sand and clay. The river was barely hanging to life, beaten by hot sun and little rain.

Sergio stopped the car two blocks from the bridge. From their vantage point, they could see the flow of pedestrians on foot and the long line of cars waiting to cross. Sergio pointed the way to Jessie. She was prepared and showed no fear. She took her small bag, filled with all the possessions she owned in the world, and walked quickly toward the bridge. She did not look back. Ahead lay a faded yellow line painted across the center of a narrow rusty bridge. On one side of the line was the United States of America; on the other side was Mexico. One side was freedom, the other was despair.

Sergio and Hawken watched from the car. Jessie was more fortunate than the Mexicans walking beside her. She was Cuban, and if she put one foot on the US side, she could be welcomed as a political refugee. It was still a dangerous plan. When she approached the bridge, a large truck pulled beside the taxi and blocked their view. When the truck moved away, Jessie was gone.

Hawken paid Sergio $300, and they hugged each other like two lost brothers. Their brief encounter had built a bond of respect, and they parted with a mutual sense of relief and accomplishment. Hawken waved good-bye, and waited a few minutes before walking across the bridge. With his American passport in his shirt pocket, he was humbled, as he had never before fully realized the power of the document he carried with him.

Hawken spent three anxious days in the Brownsville Holiday Inn waiting for the call from Jessie saying that she was okay. He had planned carefully, making sure that she had the name of and number of the hotel so she could call as soon as possible. Hawken was stretched out on the hotel bed watching television and fearing every dark scenario when the phone rang.

"Hey, baby!" Jessie sounded elated.

"Where the hell are you?" he asked.

"I'm here in prison."

"In prison?"

"Yes, in the immigration prison."

"Are you getting out?"

"They said that maybe I can leave in one week or so," she said. "They need to give me documents so I can stay in this country. It's complicated, but it's okay. There are two other Cubans here."

"Is it bad there?" Hawken asked. He had known that the border patrol would send her to detention, yet he was troubled that she called it a prison.

"No, it's good. We're eating hotdogs and playing Ping-Pong. It's like a resort here."

Hawken laughed at her description of lavish accommodations. "Okay. I'm going back to Lewisville. You have my number?"

"Yes, I'll call you, Hawken. I miss you."

"I miss you too, okay? I'll send you a plane ticket to get from Brownsville to Tallahassee when you get the papers. There's nothing I can do here until you get out. Call me when you know when you'll be released."

Finally, after three more days, they released Jessie from detention and she flew to Tallahassee. When she arrived at Hawken's home in Lewisville, she took one look at the five-bedroom home and her mood brightened like a child at Christmas. She gazed at the large tract of land surrounding the picturesque lake and bordered by the long white fence. She entered the door, and her mouth fell open when she saw large rooms designated for every purpose. She had seen a few houses like that in Cuba, but in her country, at least four families would live there.

After two weeks of adjusting to her new life, Jessie began to make changes in Hawken's home. Her relatives in Miami had told her about Wal-Mart, and she wanted to see one for herself. When the entered the superstore, she walked down each aisle, touching the merchandise on each side. At the end of the aisle, she turned around and walked in the opposite direction, touching the merchandise again. She said nothing until finally she stopped.

"I want to buy some color for the house," she said. "Your house is dull and dark. We need more color."

"Okay, but just a little."

A little color turned out to be an amazing array of silk plants, striped towels, flowered curtains, and two cans of red paint. Hawken's house was Cubanized, but Jessie was happy, and that made him happy also. Hawken's friends, and especially his mother, were more apprehensive than happy.

Maggie Turner looked around the house at vases filled with green-and-purple floral arrangements made of plastic and sparkling with glitter. "You really don't care what people think, do you?"

"Not really," Hawken answered.

Even if he did care, the long explanation was too difficult to attempt. Anyway, it gave the people of Lewisville something new to talk about. His male friends took one look at Jessie and congratulated him with sly smiles. They saw Jessie as a conquest, much like the trophies he brought back from hunting safaris on foreign soil. His female friends glared at him and gossiped about the middle-aged man sharing a house with yet another voluptuous woman half his age. At least this one came without a baby—a baby that everyone had assumed was his own when Gabriela was there.

Maggie Turner was not pleased. "Well, it's embarrassing to me," she said.

"Sorry." There was nothing else he could bring himself to say.

"How long is she here for?"

"We're taking it day by day."

"You can't keep doing things like this, Hawken. You need to get back to church and pay some attention to God," Maggie said.

"I tried paying attention to God," he said. "But God doesn't pay attention to me."

"Are you going to marry her?" Maggie asked.

"I don't know yet. I imagine she'll end up living with her family in Miami. But you'll like her when you get to know her."

"What am I going to say when I go to my Sunday school class?"

"I have never known Maggie Turner to give a rat's ass what other people think."

"I still don't like it. I swear, Hawken. Sometimes you amaze me."

Hawken saw Jessie as unripened fruit. She was young and Hawken knew that the heart reaches out when life is cruel. And Jessie's life had been cruel. In the back of his mind, Hawken had always considered that his home was only a temporary stop for Jessie.

But despite growing tensions, it appeared that Jessie was preparing to stay. She had no problem making herself comfortable. Jessie was bullheaded and determined to bring Cuba to his house rather than adjust to the American way. Hawken had seen it before, and he was not optimistic about the results. He began spending more time alone sitting on the porch with a stiff scotch, facing the lake and remembering the days when his world was perfect. He wanted to fish with his boys and dreamed of a day when they would live together again. Just like before, living with Jessie would be an obstacle, and the news from his lawyer did not ease the concern.

"Hawken, did you have a run-in with the law lately?" It was George Kirby on the phone.

"Not that I'm aware of, George. Have you heard something?"

"Your ex-wife has called her attorney, and they want to limit your visitation."

"What?"

"She says that you got a DUI with your sons in the car last month. She's moving to have your visitation limited."

"Oh hell, George. That was *not* a DUI. I rolled through a red light. Barely. And they saw a bottle under the front seat. I was *not* drinking."

"Did you get a ticket?" George asked.

"I got a warning about the light, and they wrote me a ticket for having an 'open container.' How in the hell did she find out about that? Don't you see what they're trying to do? They're trying to keep me from ever getting custody. Damn it, George, I bet that's Stan's idea. If that son of a bitch keeps me from seeing my kids, I'll go up there and kill him. I swear."

"You need to be careful what you say. And you need to be careful what you do. This incident might be the last straw for you.

She's making you look bad, and she doesn't need any more help from you. So, there's nothing else I need to know about, is there?" George asked.

No…just another young Cuban living here with me, Hawken thought. But he said nothing.

Tensions began to grow and eventually reached the boiling point just when Jessie was planning to visit her aunts, uncles, and cousins in Miami.

"I have your plane ticket to go to Miami," he said. She was still in bed, not yet fully awake.

"Are you sure you can't go with me?"

"I'm sure."

"Okay. What day did you make the return?"

"It's only one way."

"One way? What are you saying, Hawken?"

"I think you should stay in Miami for a while."

"For how long? A week?"

"No, a long time. Until you know this country better. You'll be happy there."

"I like it here," she said. "With you."

Tears began to form in Jessie's eyes, just as Hawken had feared. He cared deeply for her and did not want to hurt her. He was not sure if he would ever love her the way he had loved Sam, but there was one thing he was sure of—something inside was telling him that they needed time apart. Keeping her in Lewisville would only prolong the uncertainty of a life together.

"Life is complicated here, and the culture is different. There are lots of Cubans down in Miami. You'll have family there and lots of friends."

"I like this culture, and I don't know my family there in Miami."

"It's not going to work here unless you go," Hawken said.

"I know there are problems sometimes, but I can change."

"No, you can't. And you aren't the problem, anyway. I don't want you to change."

"Then what *is* the problem?"

"We need to take things slow. Don't you see? We'll never know if we were meant to be together if you don't leave. Trust me."

When Hawken left the room, she was crying. He did not want to listen to her arguments. He knew what he had to do, and that was it. She had to go.

They went directly to the airport with barely enough time to catch the flight, and no time to suffer through a long good-bye. She tried to fight him to the end, but Hawken knew what had to be done.

He had seen it before in airports—uncontrollable crying, people baring their souls in front of everyone as they parted ways, leaving the gawkers to wonder what tragedy might be taking place. He tried to avoid that kind of display, but Jessie was crying and Hawken was nearly crying himself when they broke their hug and she melted into the security line, dragging her lone suitcase behind her as if it weighed a thousand pounds. He would not let her see a crack in his decision or any weakness in his resolve. It was her love for him that had forced his decision.

Hawken was both relieved and sad as he exited the airport, leaving behind the crowds of skycaps and travelers with push-carts loaded with bags. He felt sorry for Jessie, picturing her sitting alone at her departure gate with tears running down her face while she waited to board her flight. Maybe she didn't know how much he cared for her, or how he hoped they would be reunited. It didn't matter, Jessie never came back.

CHAPTER TWENTY
Cocktail Party

Hawken Turner soon discovered answers to his questions about Gabriela and her move to Spain. He had been asleep for two hours when the phone awakened him in the middle of the night. It was Gabriela, and she sounded cheerful.

"*Hola*, Hawken! How are you doing?" she asked.

"I'm asleep. What happened to you? Where are you?"

"I'm in Miami," she said. "With my mother."

Hawken sat up in bed. "I heard you were in Spain."

"Yes. It's very complicated. I went to Spain so my mother could get a visa and come here, too. We had to live there for six months before we could go for the visa. It was terrible. We were unsure, and all we could do was wait."

"My God," Hawken said.

"It's been a long time, and I want to come and see you," she said.

"What for?" Hawken asked. He was still half asleep. "Do you want to come here and live?"

"I don't know. I'm happy now in Miami. My mother is *very* happy," she said. "It's a good place here, with all the Cubans. My mother is visiting friends every day."

"I can imagine," Hawken said.

"I want to come to Lewisville for a visit," she said.

"You left without saying anything."

"I know. I tried to call, but the telephone in Cuba—you know. And I didn't know what to tell you."

Hawken rubbed his eyes and paused. He had all but forgotten about Gabriela but he was happy she had called. "Do you have something for me?"

Gabriela laughed into the phone. "*Sí.*"

Hawken laughed with her. "I don't know, Gabriela. It's been so long. Let me sleep tonight. I'll call you in the morning. Okay?"

"Okay, Hawken."

There was not much that was complicated about Gabriela. Hawken thought about the visit and sent a plane ticket to her in Miami. When she arrived, it was like two old lovers who had fought a war and lost. There were smiles, there was laughter, and there was a hint of the freedom they once shared on the white sand beach in Cuba. But there was no talk of a future together.

A week after Gabriela returned to Miami, Hawken received an invitation to an afternoon barbecue at a friend's house. He arrived at the two-story colonial home and made his way through the house to a shaded backyard with majestic oaks dangling Spanish moss and an open-air, outdoor kitchen overlooking a swimming pool. Guests gathered around the pool picking at hors d'oeuvres and sipping cocktails. A large black barbecue grill stood on the freshly cut lawn with thin blue smoke curling from the stack. Typical mid-summer entertainment in a splendid Deep South setting.

Hawken was present, but he was out of place. Those were his friends, but he no longer belonged there among them. He had arrived alone, and he would leave alone. He made himself a drink, and his thoughts drifted to Gabriela and how lovely she would look at the party, but she didn't belong there, either. Hawken was sure of that. His thoughts drifted to the one who *would* have belonged there. A tap on his shoulder interrupted his thoughts.

"Hey, Hawken, how are you?" Alicia asked. They exchanged friendly cheek kisses.

Hawken liked Alicia. A true Southern belle with dark curly hair and a mischievous smile, she had the look of a woman who had found the secret to happiness. She projected confidence and the sense of peace that Hawken desired for his own life. She was older and married to a nice man who was also Hawken's friend, so there were no romantic insinuations, but they had developed a certain connection and enjoyed flirtatious conversation.

"I almost called you the other day," she said, taking a sip from her gin and tonic. "I thought of the perfect woman for you."

"And…?" Hawken asked.

"Then I thought, I shouldn't do that to her," she said. She was smiling, but Hawken could sense a hint of truth behind her smile.

"What do you mean?"

"Well…you know."

"Know what?"

"All these girlfriends you've had. I don't want her added to the list."

"That's all rumor, nothing based on facts, Alicia," he said.

"Are you trying to tell me you're not a player, Hawken?"

"A player? Where did you get that?" He was smiling, but there was surprise in his eyes. "That hurts."

"Well…you *do* have a lot of girlfriends."

"I don't have a lot of girlfriends. It only looks that way," he said.

"Let's see…there's the ex-wife. Then Melissa, the Colombian girl, then the Cuban wife—aren't you still married?—and then another Cuban. And maybe a couple of domestic girlfriends?"

"That's funny. The Colombian never developed into anything. And no domestic girls…recently. Besides, you know that I only want what you have," he said. "It takes some time to find something like that." Hawken took a drink from his scotch. "A player?"

Alicia paused for a moment as she studied Hawken's face. She dropped her jaw and sighed.

"I'm sorry, Hawken. I thought I was paying you a compliment."

"Hey, it's okay. Don't worry about it. It's probably true anyway," he said. "I'm going to get another drink. You want something?"

"I'm sorry."

"Forget about it."

When everyone at the party was full of food and drink, the sun began to set, and the guests began to leave, Hawken thought back to Alicia's words. Maybe she was right—he was nothing but a *player*. Maybe it was too late for love. Maybe it was time for Hawken Turner to stop looking.

CHAPTER TWENTY ONE
Russia

In the fall of 1995, Hawken Turner lost the court case for custody of his sons. No South Georgia judge was going to take young children from a fit mother, and especially if the father traveled as much as Hawken. The loss left him drowning in a life of take-out dinners, fishing alone, and drinking on the porch. When an invitation to a hunting and fishing exposition in Saint Petersburg arrived in the mail, Hawken thought of Andrew Conner and his love for Russia. He remembered Conner's tales describing the beauty, sophistication, and, most of all, the availability of Russian women. There had to be a reason why all those "Russian bride" services existed, even if they were greatly exaggerated. If short, bald, pudgy American men like the ones featured in advertisements could find slender, intelligent Russian brides, as the dating services claimed, then a good-looking, successful man like himself should have no problem finding one. The thought of wading through hundreds of photographs of women willing to meet him was intriguing. He opened his computer and browsed the Internet where he found dating sites with stunning Russian women looking for husbands. Surely, he would find her there. All he had to do was go and shop...*What the hell are you thinking? Purge that thought.*

Andrew Conner was pleased when Hawken telephoned him and asked for assistance. There were untamed hunting and fishing opportunities in Russia, and Conner gladly offered his help with arrangements for the exposition. By the following day, Conner had reserved a newly renovated apartment in the center of Saint Petersburg and a personal guide named Elena, who would be waiting for Hawken upon arrival.

"Don't worry about a thing," Andrew said. "Just dress warm. Get yourself here, and Elena will take care of everything."

When Hawken spotted Elena in the Saint Petersburg airport holding a sign with his name, he knew that he was going to like her. She was a tall, blond, forty-something woman who carried herself with a confident demeanor. The moment Hawken sat in her car, it was as if he had been there a thousand times before. Elena drove him to his apartment, and after arranging to meet at a nearby coffeehouse early the next morning, she left him for a good night's sleep. It was a good start. Elena was just the type of woman he liked working with and she seemed more than willing to provide him everything he would need. Hawken was pleased with the accommodations.

The long flight had moved across the earth in one direction while the sun moved in the other, causing Hawken to thrash about on the hard mattress as he lay in bed yearning for sleep. Finally, he gave up on sleep, took a cold shower, and dressed in warm clothes—thermal underwear, two pairs of socks, heavy pants, a long-sleeved shirt, a sweater, a wool coat, a wool overcoat, a warm hat, and a scarf.

The cold Russian air chilled his face when he stepped onto the icy sidewalk and followed the frozen Fontanka River toward the city center. He walked north for one block, turned away from the river, and began using the back alleys to find the coffeehouse where he and Elena were planning to meet the next day. The streets were dark and quiet except for the occasional echo from barking dogs hidden in the distant shadows.

As Hawken neared one of the fortress-style apartment buildings, an attractive woman stepped from a doorway carrying a small child—a girl, maybe five years old or so. They locked eyes for a brief moment when the flushed glow of the woman's face was caught in the corner streetlight and stood out from a thousand shades of black and gray on the frozen street. The dogs stopped barking and the street became eerily quiet. The silence was broken by muffled whispers of the woman and child and the crunching sound of Hawken's winter shoes when the rubber soles searched for traction in the snow and ice.

Hawken could not take his eyes off the woman as she adjusted the child's coat and scarf before tying her own and stepping into the street. When she glanced in his direction, their eyes met again, and just like the first time he had seen Sam, Hawken Turner felt a pulse in his soul. The woman had three choices when reaching the street: she could turn to the right, she could walk straight ahead, or she could turn left and join Hawken as he walked toward the city center. She turned left as if she were meant to join him.

There were no cars in sight and mounds of dirty snow spilled from the sidewalk. Hawken, the woman, and the child met in the center of the icy street, despite each waiting for the other to go first. Converging closely amid tall square buildings on the backstreets felt awkward, nevertheless they walked shoulder to shoulder toward the city center. They walked in perfect unison like soldiers marching in parade formation. Hawken yearned to look at the woman's face, but he feared he might startle her. They walked on, both looking straight ahead, side by side. When he could no longer resist, he turned to her. She met his eyes, and both quickly turned away. They kept walking in silence.

She had that look in her eyes, the same sweet smile that he knew so well, as though they knew each other in an instant. He was close enough to feel the curiosity, sadness, sweetness, and mystery. Hawken stared straight ahead, aching to speak to her. He struggled to remember some proper Russian greetings, but his mind was clouded from lack of sleep and the pounding of his heart. The daughter was holding her mother's hand and walking on her left. Hawken was on the right and he brushed her shoulder when he slipped on a patch of frozen snow. The child leaned her head behind her mother and looked with curiosity at the man walking beside them.

They walked carefully but surely in perfect cadence. When one slowed, the other slowed. When one walked faster, the other walked faster. Each icy obstacle or looming pothole caused them to veer off in unison. Hawken turned to look at the woman again, and she looked back, as if expecting him to speak. They held the look longer and looked into each other's eyes in silence and waiting. They were joined like a family, and with each perfectly matched step, awkwardness slowly faded into acceptance.

After ten minutes of walking, they reached the intersection with the main street, Nevsky Prospekt, bathed in streetlights and alive with crowds of pedestrians. The three strangers stopped simultaneously. Hawken stood nervously, searching his vocabulary for Russian words to speak, but words never came. All three faced the busy street while tension was building. The silence continued. He felt the woman glance at him from the corners of her eyes. Finally, Hawken spotted the coffeehouse on the corner across Nevsky. Perfect, he could use his hands and eyes to issue an invitation for coffee. When he turned to begin his game of charades, the woman was gone.

Elena was an enterprising woman. She made a good living as a guide and interpreter. She had grown up living in the heart of communist rule in Russia, and she did well adapting to the budding capitalist economy. Survivor that she was, she was doing fine for herself in a financial sense. Hawken and Elena became fast friends, and their time together did not end when their workday was done. They concluded their days drinking vodka in a club, or going for sushi, chatting like two old friends. Elena treated Hawken as a brother, and showed him her Russia, dispensing detailed history and personal stories of the life there in the city.

One evening, as Hawken and Elena walked the cold streets to warm themselves in the coffeehouse, the two friends began discussing personal relationships and international romance.

"You told me that you have a boyfriend," Hawken said. "Why don't you ever spend any time with him?"

"Why do you think I don't spend time with him?" Elena asked.

"You're always with me. From early morning until after dinner. What's your boyfriend doing all this time?"

"He lives in England," she said.

"England?" Hawken pondered her answer. "Don't Russian women like Russian men?"

"Russian women do like Russian men. The nice men here are brilliant, but many of them live like peasants. There are many rich

Russian men, but the rich ones—they are the ones who have guns and no appreciation of a good woman or the arts. They have the money, but they are crude and dangerous. It's not a good choice for a Russian woman. The stupid girls go with the guns, but *real* Russian women despise these types."

"I see."

"You're a nice man. I'll find you a woman here in Russia."

"How do you know I'm a nice man?"

Elena looked over at him. Her eyes scanned his profile from head to feet as they continued walking together. "I know," she said.

Hawken laughed. "It's an incredible situation for me. I'm a nice man in all the foreign countries and an asshole in my own."

"Why are you an asshole in your own country?"

"I don't know. Maybe I'm a different man in other countries, or maybe the women in my country are smarter than other places, but I think it has something to do with divorcing an angel."

"Why did you divorce an angel?" Elena asked.

"Now you're asking personal questions."

"Okay, no more personal questions, asshole. But you don't know the Russian women. Maybe you'll change your ways if you know a Russian woman. I'll take you to the introduction agency that I sometimes work for. They have many women who want to meet American men."

"Beautiful women or ugly women?" he asked.

"Both kinds. It's the same as a car—an ugly one will be cheap for you, and a beautiful one will be expensive. Which one do you want?" Elena asked.

"I would take the ugly car and a beautiful woman."

"It'll be easier to find you an ugly woman and a beautiful car," Elena said, clearly putting a plan together. "But I'll see what I can do."

"You really work for a mail-order bride company?" Hawken asked.

"*Introduction agency*. I suppose it's the same thing. There are many stupid women there, but good ones, too. I want to take you there," she said. "We can go tomorrow if you want."

Hawken had sworn to remain single for the rest of his life, but he could not stop thinking of the woman in the street from that first night, and the one-in-a-million chance he would ever see her again. Maybe the heart was ready.

"Okay. I'll go and pluck my beautiful Russian wife tomorrow."

"Yes. And then we'll look for your ugly car."

The next day, Hawken and Elena went to the small café that was now their regular starting point, and drank coffee. When they had enough coffee to feel warm inside, they walked out into the cold and started down the back alleys for the agency. Elena walked briskly as they passed block after block of anonymous buildings without signage of any sort. After ten minutes of walking, she walked to a gray door with ten coats of worn paint and pressed the grimy intercom.

Hawken had not slept well the previous evening. His mind kept returning to the woman and child he had seen in the street. Maybe she was one of these women looking for a better life. Maybe by some miracle he would find her picture there. Maybe he would have a second chance at the opportunity that had dissolved into the crowd on that cold, dark night.

Inside the agency, three young women were busy editing profiles and organizing catalogs. Their desks were covered with photos and biographies of women chasing a fairytale dream. They seemed happy to see Elena and greeted her like a good friend.

The women barely acknowledged Hawken's presence in the room, speaking in Russian, and pulling catalogues from the shelves. Elena handed the catalogues to Hawken, then continued chatting with her Russian friends while he thumbed through countless pages looking for his soul mate. He scanned every picture in every catalog, looking for the face from the street and hoping he would recognize her. The pages were filled with gorgeous women, but he did not find the one he was looking for.

When Hawken was done, Elena presented the manager with five profiles of women he had chosen. Nothing touched his soul, but he didn't want to disappoint Elena. After some short, meaningless conversation, the manager began calling each woman and setting various dates for coffee, tea, or drinks after work. Hawken was tentative about the possibilities, but he waited politely while Elena and the manager arranged his segue into a "live happily ever after" fantasy. When the appointments were set, Elena grabbed the manager's notes, said her good-byes, and started for the door.

"Come on. We have to hurry. We're meeting your new wife for coffee in fifteen minutes. Then we're meeting another future wife for lunch. Let's go."

The dates with the women from the agency were strange. Maybe it was the Russian culture, or maybe the women had become jaded from previous disappointments, but each of his dates lacked any spark of any kind. They were cold. The looks on the women's faces were cold, the conversation was cold, and even the gloomy

Russian weather was cold. Hawken began to compare the Russian women to the ones he had met in Latin America. If he were in the same situation in Cuba, the women would be scantily clothed, sitting close, and reaching for his hand with uninhibited affection.

Russian-agency dating appeared useless for Hawken Turner, but the last of the five women did interest him somewhat—mostly from a physical perspective. He met Ludmila for coffee during a break from her job as an engineer. She was slim and pretty, spoke little English, and spent most of her time talking with Elena. Elena liked her, and Elena's opinion was important to Hawken.

Elena stopped in the middle of conversation and turned to Hawken. "You should ask this woman to dinner tonight," she said in English. She was direct, as usual, and spoke as if the woman was not there.

"That sounds good. You'll go with us, won't you?" Hawken asked.

"Yes, of course." Elena went back to speaking Russian with Ludmila. They were obviously making plans, and only occasionally looked over at Hawken as if they were evaluating a prize steer.

"Okay, Hawken. She's got to go now, but we'll meet tonight at a nice restaurant. They have a folk dancing show there, and she's excited," Elena said.

"Folk dancing?" Hawken asked.

"Sure. It's a treat for a Russian woman like her."

"She doesn't look happy."

"Of course she's happy. Come on, we're going to see Pushkin's apartment now."

The restaurant that Elena had chosen was located beside one of the canals running through the center of Saint Petersburg. Hawken and Elena were waiting outside when Ludmila turned the corner off Nevsky Prospect and started toward them.

"She looks good in those clothes," Elena said. "What do you think?"

"Yes."

"Is that all you have to say?" Elena asked.

"Okay, she looks like a model," Hawken said. "She has luscious legs. Even taller in those high-heeled shoes. Skirt below the knee is a perfect length. Her flowing hair looks like she's been to the salon. Nice. I like those auburn bangs. And that lip gloss she's wearing."

"What are you, a model scout?" Elena asked. "She's an average Russian girl."

"Are you jealous?" Hawken asked.

"No. But I'm sure that she has only one stylish dress. And those are her only shoes too. I'm sure of it."

Hawken saw Ludmila's smile for the first time as they were greeted by the restaurant maître d'. They were seated at a bulky table in front of a small stage with many lights. The restaurant was dark, and reminded Hawken of a high-class strip club without the strippers. There were candles on the tables and an abundance of staff standing around, even though there were few patrons and several empty tables.

Hawken was just another decoration at the table of three while the two women admired the menu and made pleasing sounds each time they found a delicious selection. They read the entire menu from front to back and spoke only Russian.

Elena did the ordering, taking several minutes of Russian conversation with the waiter and Ludmila. Hawken was soon aware of the reason it took so long. The waiter began numerous trips to the table bringing endless dishes of caviar, smoked salmon, freshly baked breads, and, of course, vodka. Good Russian vodka. And lots of it.

When the folk dancing started, it was a different sort than Hawken had imagined. Eight Russian women with long legs and bright smiles crowded the stage as they swirled and kicked in perfect unison. Each dancer held her head the same as the other. Each one kicked at the perfect height and held her arms in perfect position. They had talent that Hawken had never expected. They took short breaks between scenes and returned to the stage wearing different costumes ranging from sexy fur-lined skirts to modest traditional clothing from the countryside. The dancers were nearly identical in size, shape, and beauty. As the show neared the end, Hawken looked around and felt sadness that only a handful of patrons were in the restaurant to enjoy their production.

They ordered another round of vodka and Hawken posed an idea. "I'd like to see a typical Russian home while I'm here," he said.

"You have to go outside the city to see a home," Elena said.

"Well, where do you live?" Hawken asked.

"I live in an apartment," Elena said. "But it's far from the center."

"That's what I mean. I want to see an apartment. Like where the typical Russian lives."

"Why do you want to see that?" she asked.

"I'm curious. That's all."

Elena began speaking with Ludmila in Russian. The conversation went on for a few moments, and then they turned to Hawken.

"You can go with Ludmila to see her apartment tonight. She lives closer to the center, and you can go with her in a taxi."

Recorded music began blaring in the restaurant, and an elderly couple stepped onto the small parquet dance floor. Hawken held his hand for Ludmila, and they joined the couple for a slow dance. He held her at a distance at first, then their feet found the rhythm, and he reached his arm around her waist and drew her in closer as their bodies moved to the music in perfect time.

Outside the restaurant, Hawken and Ludmila said goodbye to Elena and climbed into a taxi as she walked away. Hawken slid close to Ludmila and put his arm around her shoulder. His idea and request had been innocent at the time, but several rounds of vodka fueled a growing temptation. He made no attempt to hide his admiration while he looked down at her long legs and high-heeled shoes. He pulled her closer, and he felt as though he had been there before. His thoughts drifted to pretty Gabriela—and pretty Jessie, too.

The taxi lurched on toward Ludmila's apartment and Hawken began thinking of the woman in the street. The one with the child from his first night. He remembered how it felt to be near her and to walk by her side. He looked at Ludmila's pretty face from the corners of his eyes. He didn't feel the same.

Ten minutes later, Hawken and Ludmila arrived at a gray monolithic apartment in the suburbs. The stylish woman was overdressed for such place. They slowly picked their way over a muddy walkway constructed of broken wood pallets strewn hap-hazardly in the sludge of dirt and melted snow. Hawken held her hand to keep her from slipping into the mud.

A small, black elevator, just inside the building, had a bent metal door and an interior that smelled of urine. The elevator shrieked, the lights blinked, and then it lurched upward to the seventh floor. *Should have taken the stairs*, Hawken noted.

Ludmila unlocked and opened the unpainted plywood door, revealing a room that reminded Hawken of a shabby motel. The walls, painted pea-green, were faded by the years. Sheer white draperies infused with two shades of dingy hung from a sagging curtain rod covering the only window in the apartment. Everything sagged. The sofa sagged, the two chairs sagged, the floor sagged, the shelves sagged. Everything except Ludmila.

She took her slender hands and curled her hair behind her ear. She bent over to take the teakettle from beneath the kitchen cabinet and her blouse rose above the waist of her skirt, exposing her alabaster skin and the gentle curve of her waist. Hawken held the view for a moment before looking away. A feeling of decadence came over him. He crossed his arms and backed away from her.

"It's very nice," he said. He made a sweeping motion around the apartment with his arm and nodded his head with approval.

"Yes?" she asked.

"Yes."

"Thank you," she said in broken English.

They sat nervously on the sagging sofa and drank their tea. They made small talk with simple words that were part Russian and part English. Tension hung in the air. Hawken drank his tea as fast as he could, hoping he would not succumb to his desire to take her in his arms and kiss her. When he was done with his tea, he set the empty cup on the table and rose to his feet.

"I need to go," Hawken said. He tapped his watch twice.

"Ah, yes."

Hawken put his hands together, held them to the side of his face, and closed his eyes to indicate that he was tired. He gathered his coat and scarf, acting quickly before he could change his mind. When he stepped out of the apartment, Ludmila joined him in the elevator, and they lurched downward to the bottom floor. He kissed her on the cheek, stepped out of the smelly black box, and looked back once more as the elevator started upward. He tied his scarf around his neck, buttoned the top of his wool coat, and walked out into the cold darkness.

Thirty minutes later, the cab arrived at his apartment door, but Hawken did not enter. Instead, he went searching for the doorway where he had seen the woman. He walked two blocks north, then three blocks west—nothing familiar. He walked two blocks east and one block south—nothing familiar. He walked four blocks west and three blocks north—nothing. Maybe it was all a dream.

Hawken was glad to see Elena when they met for coffee the next morning. He ordered a coffee. Elena ordered cappuccino and lit a skinny cigarette. Hawken gave a mottled account of the previous evening, and she listened without saying a word. He gave few details, but Elena seemed to know the story before it was told.

"I have a friend I think you'll like," she said.

"I think I should get back to working here. We should go by the hunting exhibition again and forget about these Russian women,"

"Don't be negative. Most of those women in the agency are stupid. Not many of them have any education. I think they lie about their education. They're just looking for money. You'll like my friend."

"I think Ludmila is very nice, and I don't think she's desperate," he said.

"You've never been poor before," she said.

"I've seen poor."

"Yes, but you've never lived it."

"And how poor is your friend?"

Elena took a puff on her cigarette. "She has a good job. I'll call her, and we'll go out to a club tonight. You can see for yourself."

"I'd like to go to a club, and I'll meet your friend. But nothing serious, okay?"

"Of course not. Just for fun."

The busy streets filled with people dressed in warm clothes were interesting to Hawken, and he was fond of Elena. The whirlwind of work and social discoveries kept him from thinking of his empty house and estranged family back home. He was in Saint Petersburg, and he felt alive. He barely had time to reason as he was moving fast in a blur of unfamiliar faces, brutal weather, rich history, and, of course, an endless supply of vodka.

When Hawken met Elena and her friend outside the club that evening, Elena made the introduction. "This is Natasha," she said.

Natasha was smiling sweetly, dressed in a faux-leather mini skirt and tight sweater. She spoke very little English, but that didn't matter because any conversation would have been drowned out by the pounding techno music. Once they were inside, they shoved their way through the sea of patrons to order drinks at the bar.

Luckily, they found an empty table in the middle of the chaos. The dance floor was crowded with new-money Russians and Russians trying to look like new money. There was no shortage of attractive women, and the place was heaven for young men, all of whom dressed in black from head to toe. The women were tall and thin, dressed in stylish clothes tailored to fit bodies, most of them nearly six feet tall and void of any trace of fat.

Hawken never saw Elena talking to the waiter, but soon their table was crowded with bottles of vodka, sushi, and a hookah pipe. Three of Elena's friends joined them at the table, making it five Russian women and Hawken. There was dancing, drinking, smoking, and eating for what seemed like a short time, but when they left the club and stepped onto Nevsky, pastel colors of pink and lavender were rising in the eastern sky. They were all drunk.

"We have to stay at your apartment tonight," Elena said.

The other three girls had left sometime during the night, leaving only him, Elena, and Natasha standing on the sidewalk buttoning their heavy coats to brace against the cold.

"They raise the bridges late at night. Natasha and I can't get to our apartments from here. We stay with you, or we sleep in the street."

"Well—I can't have you sleeping in the street," Hawken said. "There are two bedrooms in my apartment and three people. Who's sleeping with me?" Hawken locked arms with both drunken women as they laughed and began walking toward his apartment.

"Natasha is sleeping with you. It would be unprofessional of me," Elena said.

Natasha laughed as she rolled her neck like a woman who spent all day bent over a computer screen.

"Great. I'll give you an American massage, and then we sleep," Hawken said.

"Only massage and sleep," Natasha replied. She held his arm as she adjusted the strap on her Chinese stilettos.

With the dark sky giving way to daylight, Hawken walked the six blocks back to his apartment holding a drunken Russian woman on each arm. They entered the apartment, and Elena opened each door until she found the empty bedroom and collapsed on the bed. Natasha followed Hawken into his room and turned to remind him: "Only massage and sleep."

"Okay. Massage and sleep only."

Natasha turned her back to him in an unspoken request for him to unzip her skirt. The skirt fell to the floor, exposing her Soviet underclothes, with their abundance of clasps and straps. She fell face first onto the center of the bed.

"Massage," she said.

Hawken summoned all the soberness he could find and began kneading her feminine back and shoulders with remarkable care for a drunken man. Finally, he fell into a deep sleep when he was done. When he awoke, the women were gone.

Elena telephoned him later that afternoon, and they met in the coffeehouse.

"You certainly made an impression on my friend Natasha," she said.

"You approve, or you disapprove?" Hawken asked.

"I'm not going to tell you what to do. But she wants to see you again."

"I'd like that too. I had a great time with her—the parts that I remember. Too bad I only have two more days here," he said. "Why don't we go to dinner tonight?"

"Maybe the two of you should go alone."

"Her English is not so good, and I don't want to say anything that's misunderstood. But tell me, she's a charming woman, so why doesn't she have a boyfriend?" Hawken asked.

"She has some men interested in her, but none she is serious about," Elena answered.

"She has a daughter, right?"

"Yes."

"What about her ex-husband?" Hawken asked. "She's divorced, right?"

"No, he died. It was really sad. They had some arguments when her daughter was young. I think maybe Natasha had something with another man. Or maybe he had something with another woman. But he moved out of the apartment and went to live with a friend. He started drinking heavily, and one month later, he was in a terrible car accident that left him paralyzed. When he got out of the hospital, he put a gun to his head and blew out his brains. It was so sad for her daughter. It was sad for Natasha, too. I think she feels guilty about this now."

"That's terrible."

"Yes. Her daughter is a small girl. Not strong, but good at the ballet."

"How old is she?"

"About fifteen, I think."

"Damn. That's sad about her father," Hawken said.

Elena reached into her purse and lit a cigarette.

"What are we doing today?" she asked.

"I saw an Air France office on Nevsky, down toward the Hermitage. Can we go there?"

"Yes. We can go there."

"I'm thinking of changing my ticket. I have a connecting flight in Paris, and I'd like to spend a couple of days there."

"Ah, Paris...my dream. You're so lucky," Elena said.

"I've never had any desire to stop there. Not really my kind of place...but I want to go just once to be sure."

They walked another few steps.

"I'm thinking of getting a ticket for Natasha too. Do you think she'd like to go with me?"

Elena stopped dead in her tracks.

"You can't tease a Russian woman about something like that. Are you serious?"

"Yes, why not?"

"She would sell her daughter to go with you to Paris."

"Then maybe that's not a good idea."

Elena took a puff from her cigarette. "Maybe I should go too. You can have two Russian women in Paris."

"Sorry…that's not an option."

"You Americans are so prudish." She took his arm and began walking. "Come and we'll see about the ticket. We shouldn't tell Natasha that you had that thought."

He spent his first day in Paris walking the boulevards and getting a feel for the timeless city. He bought a street map in a shop near the Champs-Élysées and carried it to the Eiffel Tower, where he sat on a bench in the gardens and gathered his thoughts. He opened the map and studied it, just as he would study a plot of land he intended to hunt. He traced the route he intended follow and judged the time it would take to walk the trail. He chose to follow the river as much as he could and he memorized the grid of the streets and the location of Métro stops where he would board. He was a wilderness man at heart, but he felt connected to this city. He would not get lost there.

At the end of the first day, when the sun went down and the lights came on in the city, he rode the Métro to the station closest to his hotel. The station was fifteen minutes by foot from his suburban hotel. Trees, small apartment buildings and iron fences lined the streets. It was wintertime, and sweet smells filled the air. He passed corner bistros serving coffee, bakeries baking bread, and small markets selling fresh fruit. Hawken liked the suburbs. He walked the sidewalk like a man who had lived there his entire life.

When he arrived at the hotel, he nodded to the receptionist then rode the tiny elevator to room 356 on the third floor. He took off his shoes, relaxed on the bed, and watched French television, but he was not tired. From his window, he could see the Eiffel Tower standing tall above the surrounding city. He thought of Natasha and how romantic it would be to have a warm body next to him, yet he knew she was not the replacement for the one he wanted. He thought back to the days when his life was perfect and he wished that his life was perfect now. If only Sam was...

He slept until late in the morning the next day and then left the hotel for lunch. People in the street were carrying paper bags with fresh baguettes protruding from the tops. *A simple meal in a sophisticated city*, Hawken thought. On his way to the Métro, he stopped at a neighborhood market and purchased a wedge of white cheese with blue veins, a crusty baguette, and a bottle of Bordeaux. He rode the Métro to the center and found a sunny place by the river where he ate his lunch and watched low-slung boats with square windows drifting downstream. When he was finished, he walked to the Louvre.

Hawken wandered the museum slowly and stayed back from crowds when they gathered by popular paintings. He only gave a glance into rooms filled with smooth statues and huge paintings that did not hold his interest. When he came to the *Mona Lisa,* he stopped. He was ahead of the crowds and alone there in the hall and he stood close enough to feel the emotion of the image. The

Mona Lisa was smaller than Hawken imagined, but…greater. Like millions before him, Hawken was drawn to her eyes and moved by her smile, and he tried to imagine how the flesh and blood had been so perfectly captured with tinted oils brushed onto poplar plank. He felt a strange quiver in his knees and it was difficult to break away. But he had things to do.

Hawken left the Louvre and walked the streets of the Left Bank, then crossed over to the right. When he entered Place Vendôme, pigeons scattered from the cobblestone square. On the other side of the square was Hôtel Ritz Paris, with its four canopies tastefully lit by yellow lanterns. Sleek, black limousines were shuttling guests to and from the hotel. It was Paris at its best. The black limousines looked purposely matched with the tan building's crafted ironwork and black window frames.

He climbed the marble steps to the heavy framed-glass doors under one of the four awnings with the distinctive script forming the name Ritz in cursive black letters. He felt bathed in elegance as he walked through the lobby of tall ceilings and golden chandeliers to the small bar, where he stood looking at its rich interior studded with black-and-white photos of famous patrons. It was early in the day and the bar was nearly empty. He sat on a leather stool and looked to the corner at the bronze bust of a man whose face said he rightfully belonged there. Hawken studied the bust for several minutes without looking away. *Hello, Mr. Hemingway, I'm Maggie Turner's son.*

He was startled by a voice behind the bar. "What's your pleasure today?" the bartender asked.

The bartender wore a neat white jacket and black bowtie. He spoke in a pleasant tone with a French accent while he polished a wine glass with a white cloth.

"What did Hemingway drink here?"

"Bloody Mary."

"I'll have a beer. Any beer."

The bartender poured him a beer and continued with polite conversation as he tilted the glass in the light to admire his work. "History says that the Bloody Mary was invented for Hemingway at this bar."

"I'm not surprised. Bars all over the world invented drinks just for him. Imagine that," Hawken said. "Ever been to Cuba?"

"No, but I'd like to go someday."

"Are you a married man?"

"Yes, I have a wife and a son of six years."

"Don't go."

"I'll take that under consideration."

Hawken turned back to the bronze bust and studied the face while the bartender polished three more glasses.

"He had lots of lady friends, you know," the bartender said.

"Yeah, I know. Too bad he didn't know about 'catch and release' back then," Hawken said.

"Catch and release?"

"Yes—that's when a fisherman catches a trophy, but lets it go because he has no intention of seeing it on the dinner table."

The bartender put away the glass, then cast his eyes on the bust. "So many women. Do you think he was a good-looking man?"

"I think he is like the *Mona Lisa*," Hawken said. "You can see what you want to see."

Hawken turned back to the bust. He studied the face, weathered by time, war and drink. He saw a man who did not forget things. A man with a look in his eye that suggested that he knew a secret. A man who killed, drank, and denied love, all the while searching for something that he would never find. A man much like himself.

The nine-hour flight home from Paris was void of constructive thought for Hawken. The Air France 340 seemed to hang in the air forever, caught in the empty space between continents and disconnected from earth as it shimmered in the sunlight. He tried to focus on the responsibilities waiting for him to the west, but his mind would not engage. *I'll have another scotch.*

The plane landed in Atlanta for a long layover. Hawken found a generic seat in a generic concourse in another generic airport, watching the waves of anonymous passengers move back and forth from concourse to concourse. He had member access to the VIP lounges where bankers and businessmen plugged into laptops and drank heavily, but he preferred the quiet corner with his back to the wall. He faced the doors or gates so he could watch the people. And sometimes—he caught himself watching for Sam.

Other passengers were leaving home, or returning home, but this was home for Hawken Turner—the perpetual state of mind that mirrored the airport section called 'in transit'. He was going from one place to another, but for the moment, the place was nowhere. He journeyed farther and farther away, hoping that one day he would leave the memories behind once and for all. But no, he carried the memories with him, and he brought the memories back. No matter how far he went, or how careless he acted, Hawken Turner was never going to lose that baggage.

When Hawken pulled the truck into his driveway in the late afternoon, the tranquil setting of his lakefront home was not as comforting as it once had been. He was tired, but he couldn't sleep. He took a heavy glass, poured himself a scotch, gathered his laptop, and settled into the cushioned chair on the porch. He opened his computer and waited for the connection.

He used one finger to type her name—*Sam Patterson*. A few pages of unknown references appeared. Not her. He typed *Samantha Patterson Lewisville*. A few more pages, but still nothing. He typed *Samantha Patterson suicide*. Nothing. He put the laptop aside, walked into the house, and brought the half-empty bottle of whiskey to the porch.

Hawken spent the next hour and a half drinking and searching. Nothing. It was as if she had never existed. No history, no image, nothing at all. He wanted to see her face again. The image in his head was blurred, and years of exile had distorted the memory. Everyone he knew had some reference on the Internet, but not Sam. He felt pity for her. Old friends had forgotten her. They had gone about their lives, married, raised their children, and built their careers. Her parents were dead, having lived the remainder of their lives tainted with the emptiness left by her death. Hawken was the only one who remembered her, and all he had for confirmation of her existence was an old yellow card buried deep in his desk drawer.

How could someone so lovely become so insignificant? There was no one to ask.

CHAPTER TWENTY TWO
Return to Africa

It seemed to Hawken Turner that time was running out if he wanted to find his place in life. He still loved the outdoors, but he was losing the passion for his work. There was little to take its place. His boys were getting older, growing up without him, and the distance between them was increasing. Hawken had found more than his share of opportunities to live the life that he wanted, but every time he found a sliver of peace in his soul, something bad happened.

There were two women whom Hawken had admired during his adolescence—one was Sam, and the other was his mother. Six months after Hawken returned from Russia, Maggie Turner died. She lasted a mere three months after the cancer diagnosis. She was a strong woman who had showed Hawken the best love a mother could provide. They had their disagreements, but she loved him unconditionally. She was the last of the family that raised him, and the loneliness after her death weighed heavily on Hawken. There was no father to guide him and no grandfather to fill the void. Chat was dead, his boys were gone, and there was no one left. But

Hawken was a survivor and he knew a place where survival meant life. He knew he could find refuge in Africa.

The opportunity came in the early summer, when he received a call at his office. Hawken recognized the voice on the other end as Dr. Harvey Peterson, a well-known heart surgeon from the Thomasville area, and one of Hawken's best safari clients. Peterson favored whitetail deer hunting in Canada, but he had a wife and three young daughters, and it was time for a family vacation.

"Hawken, it's Harvey Peterson. I have my wife here, and I want her to speak with you about Africa," Peterson said. There was a pause while he handed off the phone to his wife. Peterson's subtlety let Hawken know that, regardless of the wife's wishes, the family would be going to Africa.

"Hello, Hawken, this is Doris."

"Hello, Mrs. Peterson. How are you doing?"

"I'm doing great, but Harvey has this idea that he wants us to go to Africa next month, and I'm not so sure about it. Don't you know of something like a nice family vacation in Europe some-where? Maybe Paris, or a villa in Italy? Something that I know the girls and I would enjoy?"

"Of course, I have lots of Europe plans, but you know Harvey when he makes up his mind. He's been asking me about a family trip to Africa for quite some time."

"I know. But I think he wants to go there so he can find a place to go back and hunt by himself. I think he should just go alone. I mean…what would the girls do in *Africa*?" She said the word the way she might say *trailer park*.

"I think you might have the wrong impression of Africa," Hawken said. "There are some great packages that are very well suited to families. Have you looked at any brochures on the luxury tented safaris?"

"Yes, and they look so—rustic. I'm not sure if we're ready for something that adventurous," Mrs. Peterson said.

"It's not the rugged experience you might imagine. Think Meryl Streep and Robert Redford in *Out of Africa.*"

"I loved that movie"

"Imagine sleeping in canvas tents lit with gas lanterns and filled with hand-carved furniture and fine carpets. It's surprisingly romantic. You can sit by the warm bonfire at night and listen to the animals in the distance, and wake up every morning to a delicious breakfast before embarking on a game drive in an open-top Range Rover. The food is amazing. The scenery is fantastic. And I can't describe with words how thrilling it is to see these wild animals in their natural environment. I really think you and the girls will love it."

"Yes, that does sound rather romantic…but a canvas tent— that's very close quarters with Harvey. You know how he is on vacations. The girls and I would need our space. And we want some places to go shopping."

Hawken surmised that Dr. Peterson must have left the room. "Yes, I know how Harvey can be."

"Hawken, you work with Harvey so well. He respects you, and I've been thinking about this trip. If he has made up his mind that we are going to Africa, will you at least come with us? I'll pay you. I'll pay for your trip and your time. Harvey needs a man on this trip with him."

"I don't usually go on the nonhunting trips, Mrs. Peterson. To be honest, I'm not sure that I can add any value to your trip, but let me give that some consideration. I'll have to check my calendar, but—"

"Please?"

"I'll see if it's possible. No promises," said Hawken.

Doris Peterson was a sweetheart, and Dr. Peterson was an ass. Hawken knew exactly why Doris wanted him to go. Hawken could handle all the bad attitude and the complaints that seemed to be endless when Harvey Peterson was on vacation. Hawken often wondered why the doctor traveled at all since nothing ever lived up to his impossible standards. Traveling made him miserable. But Hawken was fond of Doris, who was an angel and the polar opposite of her pompous husband. She would be a pleasant companion to travel with for sure. If Doris Peterson wanted Hawken to go with her family, he would make it happen. Besides, Hawken was longing for Africa. Nothing else made sense to him or gave him the sense that he belonged there. No place like Africa.

Hawken had a month to arrange the details for the trip to Africa. He would extend his trip with the Petersons and spend a few days scouting and hunting with Brenn Von Snierden. But no trophy hunting. Not the typical safari hunt. He had something else in mind.

Before leaving for Africa, Hawken called Von Snierden from the United States to make sure that it would be okay to stay with him for a few days after the family tour was over.

"Hey, Brenn, it's Hawken Turner. Did you receive that box of cigars I sent you from Cuba?"

"Bloody right I did. I smoked one of the Cohibas last night."

"Well, save a couple for me. I'm coming to Africa. Have you been seeing any good buffalo?"

"Buffalo?" Brenn asked. "Sure, I have a new concession, and it's teeming with trophy bulls. Are you bringing clients with you?" he asked.

"No, it's me alone. But I want to do some hunting."

"Magnificent. It will be great to see you again. I'm sure we can find a good bull for you. When will you be here?"

"I'm dropping my clients in Johannesburg on the twenty-third. I was planning to stay with you for a few days after that. If it's okay with you."

"Stupendous. I'll make the arrangements. The new regulations have slowed the hunting business to a trickle, so I'm sure I'll have an opening. It will be good to see you again. I thought you had given up on Africa."

"I'm almost over that hunt with the dentist."

"Yes, that was something of a disaster. Do you have any clients for me?"

"There's some interest, but everyone's waiting for the prices to drop. We can complain about that over a good scotch when I get there."

"Bloody right we will."

"I'll call you when I get to Africa," Hawken said.

"Okay, Hawken. I'll have a scotch waiting for you."

The photographic safari with Hawken's clients went well as expected. Hawken and Dr. Peterson spent most of their time pointing out animals that they would like to shoot, while Doris and the girls snapped a thousand pictures of lumbering lions, yawning hippos, and majestic giraffes. It was amusing to Hawken how difficult it was for the girls to awake the first morning in camp, with sad faces and eyes full of sleep. On the second day of the vacation, they were waiting by the fire, raced through breakfast, and then stood at the Rover until the staff arrived.

At the end of the vacation, Hawken said good-bye to the Peterson family as they parted company in the Johannesburg airport. Doris was nearly in tears when she hugged him and thanked him for his help, telling him repeatedly that it had been the best family vacation ever.

Once the family vanished through the security lines, he made his way outside the airport, and found Motumba waiting by the Range Rover. Hawken slapped Motumba on the back, and the two men loaded his bag and drove four dusty hours to the camp with fresh provisions and the promise of a warm reunion.

When they arrived at the camp, Brenn Von Snierden was indeed waiting for Hawken with a scotch in his hand, as promised. After a dinner of grilled kudu fillet and fresh vegetables from the garden, the two men settled by the campfire for a drink and a chat.

"Are you getting along okay after your mother's passing, Hawken? That Maggie was one hell of a woman."

"Yes, I'm doing fine. It was hard at first, but it's better now. You know, Brenn…it's terrible when you lose someone and never get the chance to say good-bye. At least I was able to tell her good-bye."

"You're fortunate for that."

"I am, but there was look in her eye—just before she passed— like she had something to say. She was squeezing my hand and moving her lips. But the words never came. She just died."

"I'm sorry to hear that. It must have been difficult. You look like bloody hell, by the way. You don't shave your face anymore?"

"Nothing here in the bush to shave for, is there?"

"No, but I don't want you scaring the animals."

"If they start complaining, I'll shave."

After a moment of silence, Brenn changed the subject. "I see you brought a rifle with you this time."

"Yes. I brought my muzzle-loader."

"A muzzle-loader? You want a primitive weapon hunt? That's a tad on the risky side if you want to hunt buffalo."

"Maybe, but I know what I'm doing. It's a good gun, Brenn. Never failed me yet."

"You can do that if you want, but I'll have two backups with you. Two good trackers. And me, of course. Though I don't shoot as well as I used to. Bloody eyes are knackered now. Your family would never forgive me if I let anything happen to you. Christ, why don't you shoot the Holland?"

"I don't want the Holland, and I don't want backup, Brenn. I want to hunt alone. And besides, there's not much family left."

Brenn looked up from his whiskey with a wrinkle in his brow. "Double rifle or a single?"

"It's a single."

"That's almost suicide, Hawken. You know the buffalo."

"Yes, I know."

"I have to send someone, you know. Those beasts killed over two hundred people in Africa last year. It seems as though they kill more each year. I'll send Motumba with you."

"I want Motumba and the trackers to stay back, Brenn. When we spot the one I want, I'm going alone."

Von Snierden changed his tone to one that sounded more like a father than a hunting friend. "You're a fool to try and prove your bravery this way. Do you think you'll be more of a man if you can spit in the eye of an animal called Black Death?"

"No, Brenn. It's not about the bravery," Hawken replied. "It's more about redemption. I want to feel it. I want to feel the fear."

"What redemption?"

"It's difficult to explain. It's just what I think about."

"You're mad."

"Maybe so, but I want to do it this way."

The two men sat silently for some time, until Hawken changed the subject. "You should see all the new technology hunters are using now in the States. They're breeding some incredible white-tails for trophies and charging exorbitant fees to hunt one. Even selling breeding stock to enhance the herds now. They have feeding programs to increase antler mass, and lots of outfitters are using high fences to keep them from wandering off property. It's like shooting cattle. Everybody has game cameras, too. That's the new thing. They can almost name the deer they want to shoot."

"I hope Africa never comes to that," Brenn said.

"Me, too. And you should see the television shows now with hunters squealing like schoolgirls when they take an animal. They're ruining it."

"I see that you're drinking heavily tonight," Brenn noted. "You should be steady for tomorrow's hunt."

"Don't worry. I'll be steady tomorrow," Hawken said. "That is—if you're going to allow me to hunt like I want."

"I'll let you find your redemption if that's what you want. Bloody fool."

The hunting party hunted hard the first day of the safari. They glassed the plains and hills and drove for hours in the hot sun. They spotted a few buffalo, but not the bull that Hawken was looking for. Their luck turned on the second day when they spotted a lone bull far off in a dry riverbed. He was massive, nearly twelve feet long, his curved black horns glistening in the morning sun. They closed the distance in the Range Rover, going as far as they could before tall brush and pitted terrain forced them to stop. Hawken gathered his gun, stepped from the Rover, and started into the bush to pick up the trail. Just before disappearing from sight, he turned back to the men in the Rover.

"Don't bother sending Motumba with the rifle. I took the cartridges," Hawken said. He turned back, parted the grasses, and vanished from sight.

Hawken found fresh spoor at the place where they had spotted the bull and quickly picked up the trail, following the huge hoof prints as they veered off the riverbed and continued through dense, head-high grasses. He followed the trail another two hundred yards, carefully peering into the brush for any sign that the bull might be aware of his encroachment. He listened at his back, wary that the bull might double back. Hawken paid close attention to the wind, knowing it could carry his scent in the bull's direction. Fortunately, the wind was in his favor.

He walked deeper into the grass and stopped suddenly when alerted by the whirring sound of oxpeckers fleeing from their perch on the back of the bull. He could barely make out the bulk of the animal even though it laid only twelve paces away, resting beneath a bushwillow. Maybe it was the startled oxpeckers, or perhaps a momentary shift of the wind, but the massive bull bellowed a guttural grunt and rose to his feet, facing Hawken through the wisps of tall grass. Hawken had never been so close to a bull in the wild, so close he could hear the beast breathing and smell the odor of chewed grass. From a distance, the bull had appeared as smooth as a polished boulder, but up close Hawken could see the torn ear, wire hair, and battle scars gouged into black hide by winless lions.

Hawken didn't remember raising the rifle, but the weapon found his shoulder. He centered the sight squarely between the angry black eyes. He cocked the hammer, finger on the trigger. The next move belonged to the bull.

It was a deadly game of dare as they stared into each other's eyes. Neither flinched. The buffalo's flared nostrils worked the wind. Seconds turned to minutes. Hawken held the rifle steady as a bead of sweat dripped from his forehead and rolled down his nose. Another minute went by as man and beast waited. Then it happened—the tall grasses bent toward the beast as the cruel wind shifted direction. Without warning, the bull snorted and ducked his head. Hawken froze. He didn't know if the bull was charging or fleeing. Pounding hooves and angry snorts faded into the distance. Black Death had blinked first. Hawken Turner exhaled slowly and lowered his gun.

Brenn Von Snierden and Motumba were waiting when Hawken returned to the hunting party. "We could see you from the Rover," Brenn said. "Why didn't you take him?"

"I was waiting," Hawken said.

"Waiting for what?"

Hawken said nothing.

"Are you done with the buffalo now?"

"Yeah. I'm done."

"Bloody good. Christ, I thought he had you when he ducked his head."

"He did."

"Damn fool. No more of this pissing about. We'll hunt plains game tomorrow," Brenn said. "I've had few hunters lately, and we need bush meat for the staff."

"Sounds like a good idea," said Hawken. "Let's go get a drink."

It was a dark, moonless night on the African continent. Two men sat by the fire as yellow sparks spiraled high into the sky. Hawken imagined how isolated and insignificant the site would appear from the heavens. A tiny speck of light surrounded by an endless sea of black. He refilled their drinks and settled into a mood that was somber and reflective. Brenn had started drinking earlier and was already well past sober.

"I have no inkling of what happened today, but I don't approve of what you did," Brenn said. "Are you back on track with the living now?"

"I suppose so."

"You know what I was thinking when I was watching you from the Rover today?"

"No. What were you thinking?" Hawken took a slow drink of scotch.

"I was wondering who I should call to come for your corpse. And I was thinking about what I was going to tell your sons. Didn't you ever stop to consider what that would do to them?"

Hawken laughed. "That's a good question. Maybe you should just bury me out there on the savannah. But deep enough that the jackals don't dig me up. And you don't have to call anybody."

"It's not a laughing matter, Hawken. We need to have an understanding. You need to know that *I'm* the captain here in Africa, not you."

"What do you mean, Brenn?"

"I'm speaking of that action with the cartridges. It's not your right to make those decisions."

"Then you should have said something before the hunt, and maybe I wouldn't have done that. I knew you weren't letting me go alone," said Hawken.

"If you knew that, then you should have obeyed my wishes and not tested our friendship," replied Brenn. "It's difficult to be your friend when I see you making the mistakes that you make. Were you really hunting buffalo out there today, Hawken? Or hunting something that's already killing you?"

"What are you saying, Brenn?"

"I'm talking about your failure to put the past behind you and get on with your life. I'm talking about your habit of blaming your father, or lack there of, for your dubious behavior."

"Choose your words carefully, Brenn."

"I'll choose my words as I see fit. Didn't you ever learn anything from your family? Do you think that you have to mock their flaws and blame everything on your bloodline? Can you not learn from your bloodline…and take responsibility for your own life?"

"What are you saying?"

"I'm saying that you should look in the mirror and tell me what you see. What you will see is someone who is drunk, alone, and suicidal." Brenn took a drink. "Tell me about your father."

"My father?"

"Yes, your father."

"I never really knew him. God, I wish I had, but I didn't. I think he was probably a much better man than the ones I do know. And he was a great architect. He built things, he didn't kill them."

"When you look in the mirror, do you see a nice man? Do you know what happens to people like you? They drink until they die, or they die from the pain that they inflict upon themselves. You're not an architect's son, you're a bloody fool."

"You're drunk, Brenn."

"And what the hell's wrong with you, Hawken? Honestly, what the hell has twisted your knickers in this life for you to act like you do? You're just like the other fool who used to hunt here."

"Listen, Brenn. There are lots of outfitters in Africa looking for business. I don't have to take this shit from you."

"Bloody right you don't. Use another outfitter. I don't want you coming back here anyway. As a matter of record, I forbid it. You've lost the bloody plot."

"To tell you the truth, Brenn—and I'm sure you don't care—but life's not always been easy for me. I walk around every day feeling like I've been gutshot. I know you have no sympathy for that, but that's how it feels. Shot in the gut and bleeding out slowly. Every time I have my hands around something good in this life, something goes wrong. And I can't stop the bleeding."

"Why in the bloody hell not?"

"Gutshot is gutshot."

"Really? I don't see any blood on you. I don't see any bile leaking from your gut. You're gutshot in your head."

"Well, okay, Brenn. Here's to my imagination."

With those words, Hawken drank from his glass and tossed the remains into the fire. He left Brenn by the fire and walked to the perimeter where Motumba was standing in the darkness.

"What the hell's wrong with Brenn?" Hawken asked.

"He received a telegram last week."

"What telegram?"

"It's Hemingway's granddaughter. The one that came and stayed with us once as a young girl. She's dead. It was suicide."

"Oh, shit."

Hawken did not see Brenn Von Snierden the next morning as
he packed his bags for the bush plane back to Johannesburg.
Motumba helped load his bags into the Range Rover and sat in the
driver's seat. Hawken's head was spinning as he looked around to
see if Brenn would be joining. No Brenn, just him and Motumba.
Riding in the Rover with the silent Motumba was the same as riding alone. The landing strip at Brenn's camp was under repair,
forcing the plane to land at an adjacent camp approximately thirty
minutes away. Hawken's stomach was queasy, his head hurt, and he
was sweating as the African sun beat down on the plains.

Hawken tried to close his eyes and rest, but the dusty road was
pocked with holes, and the ride was rough. He looked over at his
driver, but refrained from speaking. Motumba held the steering
wheel tightly with both eyes fixed on the road. Hawken wished
that Motumba would say something, anything, to keep his mind
from wandering into forbidden thoughts. He took a drink from
a water bottle and offered it to Motumba. He paid no attention.
Maybe I should shoot him in the foot, Hawken thought to himself, *just
to make him say something.*

When they arrived at the camp, the bush plane sat waiting on
the airstrip with the engine running. The spinning propeller sent
clouds of orange dust into the hot African air, and the door was
propped open. Hawken gathered his bags and turned to say good-
bye to Motumba, but Motumba spoke first.

"There were two trips to Africa," he said.

"What?" Hawken could barely hear over the roaring engine.
He held his hat to keep the turbulence from blowing it from his
head.

"There were two trips to Africa," Motumba said. "Your mother was here in Africa two times."

"My mother was here two times?" Hawken was shouting over the noise.

"Yes."

"When was the second trip, Motumba?"

"The next year. The fall of the year before you were born."

"Who else was here? Hemingway?"

"No. Hemingway was not here."

"Who, then? Who was here?"

"Just Brenn and your mother."

"Brenn and Maggie? Just Brenn and Maggie?"

"Yes."

The pilot opened the window of the plane and yelled for Hawken to hurry.

"Was there something between the two of them? Tell me, Motumba!"

Motumba said nothing. He hung his head and stared into the steering wheel.

Hawken Turner boarded the plane and left Africa for good. As the Cessna sprung from the ground and gained altitude, he watched in silence as the green Range Rover drove along the bumpy dirt road. Trails of terra-cotta dust rose to the sky and fell back to earth, and Motumba clung tight to the wheel.

CHAPTER TWENTY THREE
Bolivia

Something changed him on the last trip to Africa. *Don't give a damn* became the answer to Hawken Turner's questions. He had lost Brenn, and the only friend he had left was the whiskey.

In February 1995, Hawken suffered a blow to his business. Due to deregulation of the airline industry resulting in unsustainable losses by the carriers, most major airlines cut commissions to travel agencies. Then cut again. And finally reduced to nothing. Thousands of agencies closed their doors. His business began to decline. Income from corporate clients had been the heart of his livelihood and then it was gone.

When empty whiskey bottles replaced the frozen dinners and takeout containers as the primary contents of Hawken's neglected kitchen at home, Hawken realized he had to stop drinking. But then he discovered he liked the taste of whiskey in his morning coffee.

A calico cat began to hang around the shed outside of Hawken's house. He watched the feral cat night after night slipping into some hiding place inside the shed. Hawken was out of family, out of friends, and out of money. He rarely left the house at night and declined all invitations to social functions. He had a cat. Or rather, he had the opportunity to have a cat. He considered the consequences. *If I feed that cat, I will like that cat, and if I start liking that cat…Never mind*, he decided. *Damn cat.*

The days seemed to last forever when Hawken worked in his office. He loathed the hours spent analyzing financial data, tax forms, sales reports, and industry forecasts. The bundle of cable wires, electrical plugs, cellular phones, log-ins, passwords, and security codes—they were sucking the manhood out of him. The drumbeats were beating louder. He needed a place to go. Somewhere new. Somewhere like the dusty wilderness where Butch and Sundance had died in a hail of bullets. Where Che Guevara had been gunned down like a dog. Where no one knew Hawken Turner. Somewhere like Bolivia.

Bolivia was closer and less costly than Hawken's other hunting and fishing venues in South America. At the peak of popularity for the famous dove-hunting operations in Colombia, drug cartels had moved in, making Colombia too dangerous for American hunters. Argentina took the place of Colombia and quickly earned a reputation as the new destination of choice for wing shooting, but one of the Colombian operators had found a hunter's oasis among the vast farms and prolific bird populations in neighboring Bolivia.

It would be a difficult sell. Bolivia was one of the poorest countries in South America. The government was unstable and complicated. Oil companies and drug dealers controlled its money. But the flight was shorter, and prices were lower. If Hawken could just establish a connection, it would be an attractive addition to his destination file. And if no one wanted to go, well…*what the hell?*

Hawken sat at his computer and typed Bolivia into the search engine. After two hours of searching the Internet, he found a Bolivian adventure company and sent an e-mail of introduction. Two days later, a reply came from Adriana, the owner's girlfriend, who was fluent in English and remarkably knowledgeable about the hunting operations. Hawken looked no further. Adriana had everything he needed, and she was cheerfully willing to share it. Her prompt responses and attention to detail indicated to Hawken that she was a bored woman with plenty of time to help him.

Hawken and Adriana exchanged e-mails every day as he studied the seasons, regulations, hotel options, food, and Bolivian culture. Adriana occasionally leaked details of her personal life, and though Hawken shared little of his own with her, he was a patient listener. She expressed herself and shared her secrets without hesitation. It occurred to Hawken that she never assumed that someday they would actually meet in person.

Adriana sent a photo of herself, and it was not the sort sent by business colleagues. It was the first of many. A sexy full-length shot of Adriana dressed in a bikini. A voluptuous body and the face of an angel. She was tall, with olive skin, long dark hair, and an arched European nose, features inherited from her Brazilian mother and a wealthy Italian father.

Before long, Hawken and Adriana were chatting online and sharing photographs through e-mail. Conversations drifted from business to personal, and the language changed from polite to flirtatious. Hawken had been taught to refrain from using foul language around women, but that didn't stop Adriana from cursing like a sailor.

Hawken asked for her telephone number, but lost it and did not call. Two days later, when he was into the better half of a bottle of scotch, he found the number and picked up the phone.

"*Hola*," Adriana answered. The phone line was remarkably clear for such long distance.

"Hello there. I just had to see what your voice sounded like," Hawken said. "Do you know who this is?"

"Yeah. Some asshole calling from the United States. What did you think? I would sound like a man? Or maybe a bitch?"

"No, but your voice sounds sweeter than I imagined. Even with the profanity. Where did you learn to speak so elegantly?"

"That's the way all you American men talk—the pilots, the DEA, the petroleum guys."

"Not all the American men—just the assholes," Hawken said.

"Are you one of the assholes?" Adriana asked.

"You can judge for yourself when I come to visit," he said. "How's your day been today?"

"I'm a little sad. My boyfriend broke up with me last night."

"Oh, no. I'm sorry to hear that. Will you stay there working for him?" Hawken asked.

"Not that boyfriend; my other boyfriend."

"You have two boyfriends?"

"At least two. Maybe more. I have the one who owns this business, and the other is a pilot for United Airlines. Well…the other *was* a pilot with United."

"That's intriguing," Hawken said. "Did they know about each other?"

"Not the particulars, but I think so. The one here is a Russian man, and he doesn't love me. The other was my American boyfriend, and he loves me, but he has a wife and babies."

"Which one do you like best?" Hawken asked.

"I don't know."

"Well…what does your Russian boyfriend think about the pilot?" Hawken asked.

"I don't know, but everybody here knows. Maybe he knows, but he has lots of bitches for girlfriends. He doesn't care."

"Uh huh—how the hell did you find a Russian boyfriend in Bolivia?"

"He's got a company here, and a business that he keeps secret from me. I don't give a shit. I only know this hunting business, but he's got Russian friends that work for him doing other things. He's the boss," Adriana said.

"And the pilot? Does he lay over there?"

"Yes, all the time. He and the other pilots party at Juanito's when they're here. All of them have Bolivian girlfriends. Chuck, Jim, Rusty—they're nice men. Some have Bolivian wives now who are living with them in the United States."

"Juanito's?"

"Juanito's. It's a bar. They have food, too. Lots of people go there—all the gringos and lots of beautiful Bolivian bitches."

"Maybe somebody can take me there if I come down to look around."

"Seriously, are you coming down here? You need to come here for your business," Adriana said.

"I know. Maybe soon."

"It's a dangerous place here. Are you scared?"

"I'm not scared of anything. Actually, I was looking at my schedule and thinking that maybe I can be there next week, if you can set it up for me. Think you can do that?"

"Next week? Are you serious? You have to get a yellow fever shot."

"Yes, I'm serious. And I already have the shot. Do you think you can get me in to see the lodge?"

"Of course."

"And I'd like to do some shooting if it's possible."

"I'm sure you can do that," said Adriana. "But I'm nervous now."

"Why are you nervous?" Hawken asked.

"I didn't think that you would really come."

"It's my business, Adriana. I need to come. Can you set it up or not?"

"Okay."

Adriana made the plans, and Bolivia grew more interesting every day. Hawken put away the mundane chores of his business, booked his flight to Santa Cruz, and sent the itinerary to Adriana. He had a strange feeling in his gut that he should not go, and he almost changed his mind when an e-mail arrived the day before his departure. The e-mail was from Melissa.

Hello Hawken,

I have not heard from you in so long! I hope that you and the boys are doing well. Mr. Murphy wants to look at an Alaska trip for salmon fishing in June. Do you have anything you can arrange for him there? He is still checking his calendar for the exact dates that will be available, but he wants to start gathering some information. First class, of course.

Call me,

Melissa

The e-mail from Melissa caught Hawken by surprise. The "call me" part gave him reason for hesitation. Maybe there was something there yet.

Nevertheless, Hawken kept his plan for Bolivia, and all doubts dissipated when he saw Adriana standing in the baggage claim area. She stood tall in stiletto heels, her long legs vacuum-packed inside skinny jeans. She wore a low-cut top with a red leather jacket that could barely contain her surgically enhanced breasts. Red fingernails and lipstick put the final touches on her seductive and questionable presentation. Hawken took a long look as he reminded himself he was there for the hunting. Adriana chatted nonstop and held his arm while they waited for his bags to arrive.

He dropped his luggage at the hotel, took a quick shower, and then they were off to dinner, as his flight had arrived in the early evening. As Adriana drove toward the restaurant, she studied his face as he was studying hers.

"What?" she asked. She looked at him shyly from the corner of her eye. "Do you like the way I look?"

"You're better looking in person," he said. "But that outfit doesn't look very professional. Or...at least not the kind of professional I was expecting."

"You're an asshole." Adriana turned and faced directly ahead.

"I know," Hawken Turner said.

"Are you gay?" she asked.

"No."

"So, you think I look like a prostitute?"

"I didn't say that."

Adriana turned around to face Hawken. "You're very handsome," she said.

"Thank you."

Adriana faced forward again. "I've made a plan for you," she said.

"Tell me."

"They're hunting at the cattle ranch tomorrow, and you're invited. It'll be a good day to go, because they're not always hunting down there. They're flying the plane in, and they have seats for us."

"Us?" Hawken asked. "You're going, too?"

"Yes, I'm going too."

"Early tomorrow?" he asked.

"Yes, early. But tonight I'll show you Santa Cruz."

Hawken and Adriana went to Juanito's for dinner that evening. The smoky bar was just as she had described it. There was the DEA section where the American agents drank and laughed with the petroleum engineers from Petrogas and the United Airlines crew. A small group of Russians sat at the far corner of the bar. Their conversation fluctuated between hushed whispers and boastful outbursts. Well-dressed Bolivians gathered at the center of the bar, flashing American dollars. Scattered throughout Juanito's was an ample supply of sexy Bolivian beauties. Adriana knew everyone in there.

Adriana stood close to Hawken, touching his arm and placing her hand on his shoulders in a flirtatious manner. She introduced him to all her friends.

"Aren't you worried that your boyfriend will say something about us being together?" Hawken asked.

"What are you talking about?" she asked. "We're doing nothing wrong."

"Not yet," Hawken replied.

"Are you scared?" Adriana asked.

"I'm not scared. I was thinking of you."

"He doesn't care about me. But he gets crazy sometimes and acts stupid. Maybe he'll kill you."

"This is a good country for dying."

"You don't care?"

"No, not anymore. My family is gone now. I lost my kids. My friends keep away from me. I don't care about anything anymore."

"That's good," she said. "Because we'll find out early tomorrow if my boyfriend is jealous. He's going to the ranch with us, and you can meet him then."

"Perfect."

Something did not feel right about the trip to the ranch. The early morning passed, and Hawken waited in his hotel until late afternoon when Adriana finally called. The plane that was supposed to fly then was "unavailable." She was leaving soon with her boyfriend, and Hawken would be traveling to the ranch in a Toyota Land Cruiser along with a mechanic and one of the ranch owners.

Neither the greasy mechanic nor the ranch owner was friendly, and Hawken hoped that the journey would pass quickly. He had been warned about treacherous road conditions, but the road was paved and straight for the first hour and a half of the drive, and he began to relax despite the absence of conversation.

"Oh, shit!"

The paved road abruptly ended. The Land Cruiser flew into the air and came down hard as it landed onto a rutted dirt road carved out of dense tangled brush. Steep ditch banks rose on each side of the road and extended well above the top of the Toyota. The hardened ruts occasionally snatched the steering wheel, causing the mechanic to cuss and fight to keep control. There were cows and goats in the road seeking refuge from the thorny brush. Hawken had seen rough roads before, but nothing like this. It took another three hours to get to the ranch.

When they finally arrived, Hawken was greeted by Adriana's Russian boyfriend, introduced as Yakov, and by Cole Stevens, an American outfitter who was in charge of the hunting. As they unpacked their bags, Hawken noticed a Cessna Centurion parked under a tree canopy tucked on the far side of an open pasture. Due to the poor road conditions, it was practical for such a farm to have a plane, but he had been told the plane was being repaired in Santa Cruz. Yet, there was the plane.

Hawken awoke early the next morning for coffee, fried eggs, and fruit before heading out to scout the fields and hunt for doves and wild pigeon. When they left the ranch, it was Hawken, Stevens, and a bird boy named Juan in the Toyota. Hawken sat in silence while they drove the farm roads past scattered fields and the occasional house tucked into jungle-like terrain. They passed Mennonite farmers driving tractors without tires because rubber tires were considered sinful by Mennonites. Strangely misplaced, the bearded Christians had somehow discovered the rugged outpost, hidden from most of the world. The existence of Mennonites was eerie, but the doves and wild pigeons swarmed in droves.

Hawken Turner knew exactly where he was. He was lost. Nothing there looked familiar to him, and he had never felt more alone, yet he did not care. He didn't worry about failure, his drinking, or the unattended responsibilities at home. There *was* no home, and this place suited him just fine. Maybe once, long ago, he had been a nice man, but he could not remember. No matter. He didn't want to be a nice man that day, and he didn't want to hunt; he wanted to kill.

They stopped at a field five miles from the ranch. Dense green jungle bordered the ragged cornfield. The sky was dark. A storm was coming, and thunder rumbled in the distance.

Hawken got out of the Land Cruiser with a shotgun, ten cases of shells, and Juan. He paid no attention to the storm, but focused on the doves, which were thick and swirling as they fed on the remnants of harvested corn. Hawken's brow was creased and his lips tight. He walked with the gait of a man on a mission to kill. A man who no longer cared about life.

He was methodical with his shooting, carefully choosing his shots as countless birds circled overhead. He began slowly by choosing one out of five from those birds in range of his gun. Then he increased his frequency, choosing one of three. His tempo increased, and he began to draw on every bird within range of his weapon. Dead birds began dropping from the sky and hitting the ground with every burst from the heated barrels.

"*Cartuchos!*" Hawken shouted at Juan as he thrust his hands into the shell pouch around his waist and found he was out of ammunition. He exchanged looks with Juan as they both realized that he intended to kill them all.

"*Más! Más!*" he said. The bird boy struggled to keep the pouch filled with shells as Hawken repeatedly placed the stock of the gun to his cheek, found a target, killed it, found another target, killed it, brought the gun to his waist, broke the gun, dropped two more shells into the smoking barrels, and fired again.

"*Cerveza,*" Hawken said. His lips were dry. The beer tasted good, and Hawken tossed the bottle on the ground and resumed hunting. He pounded the birds with three hours of relentless shooting, leaving the ground littered with feathers and a thousand dead carcasses scattered across the field. He had killed everything that flew within reach of his gun.

The storm was almost on top of them, and the wind began to blow loose feathers across the dirt field like tumbleweeds looking for a place to land. Nearby, a bolt of lightning thundered to the ground. Hawken Turner raised his gun high over his head, daring it to strike again. *Look at me, God, I am killing all your creatures. Come and get me now.*

Juan was speechless. He studied Hawken's face while the hunter stood there surveying the collateral damage that was laid out before them. Juan's expression was half amazement and half fear. He uttered an English word from cowboy Westerns he had seen on television.

"Keeler."

Hawken made up his mind on the drive back to the ranch; he was not going to bring clients there to hunt. The hunting was incredible, the ranch was suitable, but his gut told him there was more going on there than just hunting and raising cattle. It was the perfect setup to transport cocaine out of the country into neighboring Argentina, Peru, or maybe Paraguay as the new routes developed after the crackdown in Colombia. Perhaps the hunting operation was just another front to conceal the activity there. Or perhaps he just wanted to keep the place to himself.

Adriana walked onto the porch holding a cigarette in one hand and a glass of wine in the other. "How was your hunting today?"

Hawken was downing a strong scotch and browsing on a plate of cured meat and cheese. Cole, Yakov, and two others from the ranch had left him alone, heading inside amid hushed discussions.

"The hunting was good. Very, very good. How was your day?"

"I was bored here all day," she said. "I don't know why they wanted me to come."

"But it's paradise here, isn't it?" he asked.

"Oh, yes. Cows and trees. It's like Miami Beach, without the water."

Hawken laughed. "Nah, it's better than Miami Beach. What's going on inside?"

Adriana took a puff from her cigarette. "Juan is arguing with Cole. Juan says you are the best shot ever to come down here, but Cole says it's McNeill."

"If I had known it was a contest, I would have killed more. Maybe I should come back when the weather is better. Who's McNeill?"

"Relax. He came two years ago and set the record for shooting in the northern part of the Chaco. I met him in Santa Cruz and we're friends now. He's a handsome man."

"I bet he was shooting an automatic. Anybody worth a damn could set the record here with an automatic."

"Relax, honey, I was only making conversation."

"It's like cheating—using an automatic. That's for pussies."

"Are you jealous?"

"No."

"If you say so."

They chatted on the porch for a few minutes, and when they went inside, Hawken let Cole Stevens know that he was not interested in the ranch as a hunting destination for his business. Cole was disappointed, but offered to show Hawken more hunting lodges closer to the city.

"Maybe another time," Hawken said. "I have some things hanging back in Georgia and I need to get back."

"Nobody's going back for a couple of days."

"How about the plane?" Hawken asked.

"Still broken."

"I heard it take off this morning and it was gone most of the day."

"That was just a check-out ride. It's still broken."

"Anybody driving back?" Hawken asked.

Not for a couple of days. If you want to go sooner than that, you have to take the bus from Guaranda," Cole said.

Hawken cringed. "How's the ride?"

"Not too bad, but it takes all night."

After dinner, Hawken packed his bag and prepared to leave the ranch. On his way out, he stepped into the kitchen and poured a cup of coffee. When he came back into the den, Cole, Yakov, the ranch owner, and the mechanic stood around the dinner table.

Cole looked at the mug in Hawken's hand. "Do you want something a little stronger?" He reached into his pocket and brought out a fist-sized bag of white powder.

Time stood still while everyone waited for Hawken's answer. *Was this a test?* No one was looking, but everyone was watching. *They want to know if I'm DEA. Well…to hell with them, let's keep them wondering.*

"Sure."

Nobody blinked when Hawken accepted the package. Then they just looked at each other when he jammed the bag into his coat pocket and left the room.

Hawken had grown up in the age of drugs, sex, and rock and roll. He was familiar with cocaine, enough to know it was not for him. Whiskey was Hawken's drug of choice. Coke was a liar, luring users into a false sense of euphoria and enhanced self-worth, only to torment them later with the truth when the high was gone. But whiskey never lied. Whiskey spoke the truth and shared the pain.

The whiskey stood by his side. Others could have all the coke that they wanted, but whiskey was Hawken Turner's friend.

The town on the bus route was unfathomable. The village looked like a repopulated ghost town, with a dirt main street lined with masonry stores selling anemic produce, cheap clothing, and farm implements. There were a couple of dilapidated bars on the street with barstools occupied by red-eyed patrons drinking bottled beer, killing time. The scene was like a movie set from an old Western film, except the people in the streets were a mix of short, brown, indigenous Bolivians and tall, bearded Mennonites milling back and forth with no obvious destination. Every door in town was open, and the atmosphere was much like the carnivals Hawken remembered from his South Georgia youth.

Hawken wandered into the closest bar, bought a beer, and stepped into the street to drink it. He looked across the street and unexpectedly saw an Internet café in an open-doored building that looked like a converted saloon. Hawken took his beer inside, bought an access card, and settled into a plastic chair as he waited for the goliath computer to connect. The minutes passed painfully as the computer moaned and searched to grasp a connection.

"I'm going with you."

Hawken turned to see Adriana standing close behind him. She was dressed in a blue jogging suit, her jacket open and exposing a generous view of her cleavage. The sight of her contributed to the carnival atmosphere of the tiny town.

"Have a seat," he said. He slid an adjacent chair over to sit close to him. "I've been waiting ten minutes for this damned thing to connect."

"There's no connection here. They only take your money and let you wait for something that never happens."

"That's the story of my life. But I'll wait anyway."

They sat together, staring at the dusty monitor with the scratched screen. Neither of them seemed to care, or even expect the Internet to connect, but they sat and stared anyway. As they waited, a freckled Mennonite boy of about nine years old with inquisitive eyes walked in and stood behind the pair. Hawken was not sure if the boy was mesmerized by the computer or curious about the strangers. He wore gray pants and black suspenders. There was sadness in the boy's eyes, which peered beneath the stained straw hat on his head. Maybe he knew he had been born into a life of isolation. Maybe the boy knew that he would never swing a bat for a Little League baseball team. Or maybe it was his dream to do those things.

Hawken banged on the keyboard and then looked back at the boy. *Maybe it would be a good thing if he lives his whole life as an innocent boy. Never knows the taste of cold beer, or draws smoke from a cigarette. Maybe it would be better if the boy never knows a woman who smells of perfume, whiskey, and painted nails. He could be happy and live in a house with no electricity. He could spend his days plowing dusty fields on a tractor forbidden of rubber tires. He could die there too.*

When he gave up on the Internet connection and exited the café, Hawken looked back one last time to see the young boy still staring at them. *Damn*, Hawken thought, *so insignificant is his life, and he doesn't even know it.*

Hawken Turner recalled something that the Colonel once said to him when he went on his first date: "A man is born with two heads. Be sure to use the one that's above your waist."

Adriana sat close to Hawken when they boarded the over-crowded bus for the eight-hour ride to Santa Cruz. When everyone crammed into a seat, the bus crawled out of the station and onto the rutted trail to civilization. Adriana locked her arm inside of his and rested her head on his shoulder before drifting off to sleep.

Dawn was breaking when the bus pulled into the terminal. The trip had been long and rough, with several stops along the way for passengers to disperse into the roadside brush and relieve themselves.

Adriana rolled her neck and rubbed the sleep from her eyes. "Do you want to share a taxi to your hotel?" she asked.

"No, I'm going to your house."

She seemed to expect the answer. Without saying a word, Adriana located a taxi at the terminal, and they sat in silence as the taxi moved along empty streets to her house.

When they arrived at her house, she retrieved the key from her purse and opened the door to her sprawling home. It was richly decorated, with a shaded pool set among fruit trees and flowers in the back.

"My home," she said with a wave of her arm.

"Very nice. Are you going to make breakfast for me?"

"I'm not tired. Are you?" she asked.

"No. I'm not tired."

"Come with me."

Hawken had seen a few hard days, but his body was running on adrenaline, and his hormones were flowing as he followed her into the bedroom. Adriana did not wait for words as she turned and kissed him on the lips. The kisses were deep and hard. She bit into his lip and Hawken tasted blood. Suddenly, she broke away, drew back her hand and slapped him across his face.

Hawken licked the blood from the corner of his mouth. "What the hell are you doing?"

She drew back to strike him again and Hawken caught her hand just before she delivered the blow. She eased the attack and looked at him with a vicious smile.

"Why don't you fight?"

"I don't hit women."

She drew back again, but Hawken took her firmly by the shoulders and laid her on the bed.

They spent the following three days in a swirling tornado of lust. They hardly left the bedroom for food or drink. Yakov had left a well-stocked bar in her house, which further fueled their lustful affair. The combustible concoction of sex and alcohol began to wear on Hawken's mind, but he didn't leave Adriana. He didn't leave her even though he was restless. As they lay in bed together on the third night, every sound reminded him that her Russian boyfriend might come through the door at any moment.

"Does Yakov have a gun here?" he asked.

Without saying a word, she opened the dresser drawer and pulled out a Glock 9 mm pistol. Hawken ejected the clip, confirmed that it was loaded, and placed the gun under the bed.

"Are you going to kill my boyfriend?" Adriana asked.

"Only if he tries to kill me first," Hawken said. "But I need to be leaving here soon. There're some things that I need to take care of. And I think we are pushing our luck."

"You have another woman here in Bolivia?"

"No. There's no other woman in Bolivia. I'm thinking of your boyfriend—and trying to figure out which culture is calling the shots here. I don't want to end up with a Colombian necktie for making love with the Brazilian-Italian girlfriend of a Russian *businessman* in Bolivia."

"What's a Colombian necktie?" Adriana asked.

"That's what the Colombian *narcotraficantes* do to their enemies. They cut your tongue loose, then make a slit in your throat and pull the tongue out like a necktie." He took his hand and drew like a knife on Adriana's throat. "A friend of mine in Colombia said that it all started when one of the cartel bosses caught his girlfriend with another man. Necktied him."

"Baby, you don't have to worry about anything like that. I'll kill you first." Adriana rolled on top of him. "With this Bolivian necktie."

Hawken wasn't convinced.

On his last day at her house, Hawken awoke and looked over at Adriana sleeping peacefully in bed. There was not a line in her face, and her lips appeared baby soft, frozen in an angelic smile. Her hair was not tousled, belying the torrid sex of the night before. Hawken wanted to place his hand to the side of her face and kiss her gently. He wanted to taste her breath and run his hands softly through her hair. He wanted to feel the warmth of her body and bring her close to him. He could not take his eyes from her sweet angel face.

Hawken fought the urge to wake her. He eased out of the bed and took a shower. When Adriana woke, his bags were packed and breakfast was on the table. Adriana joined him to share one last cup of coffee before he departed. She reached across the table and touched a large bruise where her teeth had clamped onto his bicep.

"Oh, look what I did to your arm. I'm sorry, honey."

"I don't understand why you want me to hurt you," Hawken said.

"I don't want you to hurt me, but I don't care if you do. I want you to love me."

"Damn. The crazy part about that is the fact that I believe you. So I'm the lucky one?"

"Yes, you're the one," she said. "You can do anything you want with me. Do you want to marry me?"

"No," he answered.

"Do you love me?" she asked.

"No. It's just sex," he answered.

"I don't think so. I think you love me."

"Men don't always know the difference. I hate to tell you that."

"You don't believe in love?" she asked.

"I used to believe in love, but it makes me angry now."

"How can it make you angry?" she asked.

"It's the curse of a man like me. We can't believe in forever love because we know we'll lose it. It's inevitable. We don't acknowledge it, but we know what our eventual fate is. There's no such thing as forever."

"So you have never loved a woman?"

"I was very, very in love once. And like a fool, for a long time, I thought I could fall in love like that again. I still dream about it sometimes."

"Tell me about the dreams. The details."

"Okay." Hawken took a drink from his coffee. "The dream is like a river, you know. And the river is taking me someplace that I have to go, but it's flowing with swift waters and rapids that never end. I can't leave the river, so I wait for every bend, thinking that just maybe *this* will be the one, and there it will be—the big, calm, beautiful ocean. Just like before."

"Go on, my lovely poet."

"That's it. The dream just follows the river. But it changes from time to time. Sometimes there are different people in the dream and sometimes the landscape changes, but it never goes anywhere."

"So, what does your river look like now?" she asked.

"Like Africa. Dark and covered with jungle canopy. Lots of animals," he said, taking a drink from his coffee. "You should go to Africa. It's wild there. Raw and dangerous. You'd like it."

"Will you take me?"

"Maybe—one day. I have a good friend there."

"A woman friend?"

"No, a man friend. Brenn Von Snierden. He's like a father to me sometimes. And a great safari hunter. We've been good friends for a long, long time. We had an argument the last time I was in Africa and I've got to go back and make peace with him. I need to hunt with him again. My favorite hunting partner. Well—one of my favorites."

CHAPTER TWENTY FOUR
Going Home

Hawken Turner imagined there was a reason for Adriana's dark side. No, he was sure of that. Somewhere beneath her sexy exterior and desire to be hurt was a woman with a sensitive soul hiding scars from the past. That was the reason he was drawn to her—she was just as broken as he was. It was time for Hawken Turner to go.

After checking his bags at the airport, Hawken stepped into the bathroom before going to his departure gate. He looked at his reflection in the cracked mirror above the sink and saw a desperate man with red eyes and a crease in his forehead. He splashed his face with water and opened his shirt to reveal the bite marks and scratches as he tried to make sense of his affair with Adriana.

"Damn, mister, you look like you been laid up with an alligator."

It was one of the Texas oilmen standing at the urinal next to him wearing a cowboy hat and dark sunglasses.

"I *feel* like I've been laid up with an alligator," Hawken replied.

"You got to be careful down here in Bolivia," the cowboy said. "There's all kinds of shit you can step in down here."

"So I see," Hawken said. "You on the Miami flight?"

"Yes, sir. Then on to Houston."

"Good. I'll see you on the plane."

Just as Hawken gathered his laptop and camera from the X-ray belt after clearing security, a gut-wrenching thought hit him. He had stayed up all night with Adriana. He had carelessly thrown his belongings into his luggage. He swallowed hard. His belongings, he just remembered, included a ten-year-sentence worth of cocaine.

The bag had been tagged and had long since disappeared into the baggage chute behind the counter. Hawken stood in the boarding area sweating profusely. He worked his brain trying to think of any conceivable excuse to retrieve the bag without suspicion, but he knew it was too late. He was too tired to think his way out of this disaster. He found a seat at the far end of the room and waited for airport security to call him.

To his relief, security never called. He boarded the plane and took off for the United States. When the plane touched down in Miami, Hawken was sure that he had used up all his luck. His bag would be searched there, and he would pay for his defiance at the ranch, and his recklessness in Santa Cruz.

He began to prepare his defense as he waited in the baggage claim area watching suitcase after suitcase circle around the conveyors and wishing that one of those could have been his. Maybe they were already looking at his bag. It was too late. There was no way in hell he could intercept it before it reached customs and the drug-sniffing canines.

Then he saw it. Hawken allowed his bag to travel around the carousel three times, standing back and watching to see if anyone was waiting for the owner. He thought about leaving it, just walking away, but that would be an admission that he knew about the contents. It would have been hard to deny ownership with luggage tags on the outside, business cards and a copy of his passport tucked inside. Maybe he would be out in five years for good behavior.

He had to claim his bag. Nobody came to stop him. When he got to the exit, the customs officer took his declaration form and pointed him to the no-check line, bypassing additional screening. He walked through the door of customs and into the reception corridor crowded with anxious friends and family waiting for loved ones arriving in Miami. There was no one there to greet him. No family, no friends, no DEA squad.

Hawken found a quiet area in the corner of the downstairs baggage claim to check e-mail messages from his phone. He scanned through thirty-seven e-mails, deleting the spam, jokes from his friends, and annoying solicitations. Then he found a bar in the concourse and drank two fast scotches before returning to his e-mail.

From June: *Burlington group canceled Alaska trip. They are asking about refunds.*

From Robin: *I have not received your check for Hayden's braces. Please send to me this week.*

From Great Plains Outfitters: *Unable to accommodate your Jackson party in November. Lodge is booked until next season.*

From Robin: *Hey. Did you forget about Thomas's birthday last Thursday?*

From June: *We need to meet and talk about money. We need to pay several suppliers, and our line of credit is down to zero.*

From Hayden: *Dad, I bought this really cool bat, and I have been on fire at the plate. We have two games this weekend if you want to come up.*

From Elizabeth Von Snierden: *Dear Mr. Turner, I understand that you were a close acquaintance of my brother, Brenn. I regret to inform you that Brenn was killed in a hunting accident on November 30 while on safari in Tanzania. He was accidentally shot from behind by one of his clients while tracking a wounded buffalo. Services were held...*

The words dissolved into the page, and Hawken could barely focus enough to read the last of the message: *Before he died, Brenn instructed Motumba that you should have his rifle. The double rifle that was a gift from Ernest Hemingway.*

Hawken thought about the cocaine as he started toward the departure gate for his domestic flight back to Tallahassee. He knew that a sane man would stop at the nearest bathroom and flush it down the toilet. He walked to the elevator; he stopped, turned around, and headed for the rental cars instead. He would keep the coke, and he would drive to his home. *What the hell.* There was nothing waiting for him at home. Maybe he would stay a night or two in Miami before driving back.

Miami was crowded that time of year. The frigid weather up north sent waves of tourists down to spend the holidays in the warm Miami sunshine. Hawken stopped at three rental car agencies before he found a car available at National. He had a choice of a champagne minivan or a red Mustang. He chose the red Mustang.

Hawken knew what was waiting for him when he got back home, and he was in no hurry to get there. He called the Eden Roc Hotel on Miami Beach and made a reservation for the night. Then he called Gabriela. She was living in Miami, and he was certain she would be happy to hear from him.

"*Hola, mi amor*," Hawken said when Gabriela answered the phone.

"Hawken!"

Hawken forced a smile. "How are you?"

"Good! Where are you?" she asked.

"I'm here, in Miami."

"Where in Miami?"

"I'm staying at the Eden Roc. How about dinner tonight?"

"Yes, of course!"

Thinking of Gabriela comforted him. Their relationship had been complicated before, but at the heart, it had always been simple. There were no expectations and no rules. They did not belong together, but they had a long history of pleasant days from the past. Gabriela often teased him about having girlfriends all over the world, and he never hid the truth, but he had always thought of her as special. He kept her at a distance, but they made mutual exceptions from time to time. Hawken was in need of one of those exceptions.

Gabriela picked him up at his hotel and drove to Lincoln Avenue, where they walked the sidewalks, window-shopped, and watched the eclectic collection of pedestrians soaking in the Miami nightlife. She was lovelier than he remembered, dressed in a long linen dress and looking more like a barefoot angel than a Miami Cubana. Like always, she allowed her natural beauty to speak for itself, with a minimum of makeup or accessories to detract from her God-given charm. They settled into an outdoor café and ordered two coffees, sharing conversation of family and old times in Cuba. Adriana called his cell phone, but Hawken did not answer.

"I have a boyfriend now," Gabriela said.

"Oh, really?"

"Yes. The teacher at my English school."

"Is it serious?" Hawken asked.

"Not yet, but I like him."

"Does he like you?" Hawken asked.

"I think so. He's an American man, and you know the Americans are more cold than Cubans. Like you." Gabriela nodded toward Hawken and smiled.

"Well, he's a lucky American man."

"Thank you."

"So why did you come with me for coffee tonight?" Hawken asked.

"I don't know. You're special to me. And all of my family loves you. They're very happy that you're here."

Hawken chuckled at the thought. "Too bad that I'll be leaving tomorrow. I'd like to see your mother."

"I know," said Gabriela. "Are you okay? You look sad tonight."

"No, I'm fine. It was a long trip to Bolivia. Do you want to stay with me at the hotel tonight?" Hawken asked.

Gabriela did not answer and Hawken did not ask again. When they finished their coffee, she dropped him at the hotel and left with a kiss to his cheek. Hawken could not sleep. His circadian clock was as lost as the man who owned it. *Too much of everything except the good stuff.* Hawken remembered the coke, still in the trunk of the car parked in the hotel garage. Being busted for drugs that he never wanted in the first place was the last thing he needed. He packed his bags and left the hotel at two in the morning. He stopped at an all-night liquor store and bought a pint of driving whiskey.

The streets of Miami were quiet as he pulled the Mustang into the toll lane to pay the three-dollar-and-fifty-cent toll and merge onto the interstate. When Hawken left the toll booth, the highway became pitch black except for the halo illuminated by his head-lights. He drove for several miles until he found a secluded road that ran beside a bridge and decided it was a good place to throw out the coke.

The dirt road turned away from the bridge, then followed the bank of a black river and eventually came to a desolate end with a small clearing and a short pier extending into the river. He pulled the car to the side, opened the trunk, and found the bag of coke hidden in his luggage. He took the pint bottle of whiskey from under the front seat. He had been foolish to buy it and risk another traffic citation.

The South Florida night was hot and humid. Frogs bellowed, crickets chirped, and the river flowed toward darkness. Hawken stood on the end of the pier with whiskey in one hand and cocaine in the other. He would keep one of them, but he did not know which one. He hesitated for a moment, then took the bottle of whiskey, threw it as far as he could and then listened as it splashed into the black river. "That's for you, Brenn Von Snierden. You son of a bitch."

Before driving off, Hawken took his American Express card from his wallet, shoved the corner of the card into white powder and snorted a mound of coke into his nostril. He started the car and turned the radio dials until he found a late-night rock station.

He turned the volume loud when a soulful song came on and fueled the flames:

> *Who has heard your forlorn cries*
> *Jesus rolls his eyes*
> *Who says you have to compromise*
> *I will ease your pain*

He cranked the volume louder.

> *Take the cup I offer*
> *My tea will help your throat*
> *Wrap my coat around you, and step inside my boat*

Tires barked as the car lurched onto the interstate and Hawken weighed heavily on the accelerator. The lights from his speeding car punched a hole into the darkness, revealing only more darkness ahead, as if chasing a light that did not exist. His thoughts dissolved into a whirling fog of confusion. Right was wrong, wrong was right. Strong became weak, weak became strong. He was facing the truth, but Hawken Turner did not see it. The coke was lying to him, and he was feeling good. Lost and alone…but feeling good.

> *Forget about salvation*
> *See your savior flee*
> *Firestorm lights the horizon*
> *Now you belong to me.*

The day after he returned to Lewisville, Hawken drove his truck to Tallahassee and traded it for a black Porsche using the last of his savings. Christmas was coming, and the storm was closing in for Hawken Turner. Poor conditions and his own malaise continued to drain away his business. The bank account was empty, credit cards at the limits. He had no spirit left for Christmas, and dreaded the forthcoming holiday's obligations with friends and family. He felt guilty knowing he would not contribute joy to his sons' Christmas celebrations. Hawken held warm memories of the holidays from his childhood, and though it had not been perfect, it was much more than he could provide to his children. His heart was not into gifts and he feared his boys would notice.

Two days later, Hawken pulled the dirt-covered Porsche into the parking lot of Hanrattty's Irish Pub. Every country he had ever visited had an Irish pub, and this was Tallahassee's. The car went there like a train on tracks. He drank there often. He knew the whiskey would drag him deeper into the black hole, but he needed to purge his thoughts. He was not the nice man he once thought he would be. That much he knew. He was bitter and losing his grip on the skills he had once used to survive and continue his search for the one thing he needed. The thing he failed to find.

He walked into Hanratty's and noticed the laughter from two lawyers sitting at the bar—a stark contrast to his belligerent mood. Obviously, it had been a good year for them, and they looked confident and pleased with themselves as they ordered another round of drinks. Hawken had learned not to judge a man's success by the way he was dressed, but these lawyers were dressed well. Their hair was cut and professionally styled. They wore perfectly fitted suits with perfectly loosened ties. Likely, they had just left jobs at offices with leather chairs, walnut paneling, and window-dressing receptionists. One of the lawyers answered his cell phone, and, judging from his wedding ring, the woman he was sweet-talking was obviously his wife, expecting him home…or maybe not.

Damn lawyers, Hawken thought. *They probably come from some half-assed family that failed to teach them the skills that I possess. They probably pray to God when they want something they don't have. Hell, maybe God even gives it to them. They could be hunters—the kind who hunt to make themselves feel like men. Probably buy their food from expensive boutique markets with fancy names and drink overpriced lattes at Starbucks. Son-of-a-bitching lawyers.*

Hawken did the only thing he felt like doing at the moment—he ordered another whiskey.

While he sat at the corner of the bar, he surveyed the collage of characters joined together by spirits. There were old men with wrinkled faces leaning on the bar. There was a table near the window filled with giggling college girls drinking beer. There were businessmen in suits and expensive shoes, and construction workers with dirty faces and calloused hands. The one thing that linked them all was the glass sitting in front of each one. Before Hawken realized what he was doing, he whispered to himself, out loud, as if someone were speaking the words for him. *Drink from this well and you will thirst again.*

He finished his drinking at the bar when he ran out of money. When he was done, he stumbled to his car, pulled the plastic bag out of the corner of the glove box, poured the powder onto his leather briefcase, and snorted the coke into his nostrils. He leaned his head back allowing the membranes to absorb every particle. Hawken Turner was at rock bottom, and he knew it.

When he lost control of the car that night and slammed into the unforgiving oak, Hawken was determined to fight to the end. The end which was growing closer by the second. Flames grew larger, and smoke filled the cabin. He was out of options. He had traveled all over the world, faced all kinds of controversy, seen dangerous situations, and solved unsolvable conflicts—yet there he was—out of options.

There was only one—no, there was *no* hope for survival. He swore to himself he would not yell out when the flames began to sear his flesh. He didn't want his sons to learn of his pain. His heart filled with shame and regret at so many things he had left undone. So much blame that should have been extinguished long ago. So many simple words he longed to say. So many friends he failed to thank.

He was no longer in control. *This is the time when people ask God for help.* When Sam died, he had begged God for one more day with her. To speak with her just once more. He had asked God to wake him from the dream. There was no answer from God. He had been ashamed of his begging, and he would not beg again. No, he had had opportunity to live for God, and he had lived for himself instead. He could ask God to forgive him for the destruction he had left in the wake of his life, but he deserved to suffer, and suffer he would. Like the buffalo he faced eye to eye in Africa—if God chose mercy, that would be God's choice.

The physical pain was nothing to Hawken, but the loss of control terrified him. He fought against the tide and struggled to free himself, but God held him in the palm of his hand. He fought for strength with all he had, but found none. Seconds turned into minutes. Then minutes turned into what seemed to be hours. When he could take it no more, and when he finally gave up, the anguish that engulfed his soul began to dissolve and a strange feeling of tranquility flowed into his heart. He took his hands off the wheel and his foot off the brake. He closed his eyes, let go his breath, and surrendered to God's will. Then, the gift…

A woman stepped in from the darkness and appeared at his window. "Give me your arm." She spoke quietly and sweetly in a familiar voice from his past. Her sweet breath washed away his suffering. He was afraid to turn toward her for fear of it was only a dream. But it did not feel like a dream. The voice was clear and just as present as the hissing and popping sounds coming from the burning car. Without hesitation, and without turning to look, he extended his arm through the open window.

When he regained consciousness, Hawken was lying on the hard pavement of the dark road that had been his demise. He kept his eyes closed and tried to grasp the reality of what was happening. *Was he dreaming, or was he dead? Was this the miracle that he had asked God to grant him so many years ago?* He could sense her kneeling over his body, looking into his eyes. He could envision the carefree smile and the soft lips that spoke to him. He could see the faint lines of concern and feel the brush of her hair as she leaned close to his face and placed her hand softly to his cheek. He squeezed the seconds like hours, and a faint smile broke through his pain. He struggled to open his eyes, but they would not open. *This is not a dream,* he thought to himself.

"I can't open my eyes," he said aloud.

"Yes, I know."

A wave of warmth soothed his trembling body.

"You're here for me?" he asked. He held his breath, fearing her answer. He knew the answer the moment he asked the question. The sudden clarity of his thoughts opened his eyes and brought him back from the brink of unconsciousness. You cannot lose something that was never yours to lose.

The smile left *Mona Lisa*, and a look of sadness took its place. She leaned closely to his ear and quietly whispered the last words he would ever hear from her: "No, I'm not here for you."

He was lying on the centerline of the narrow country road. The soothing white image from his past was on one side, and the burning fire of hell on the other. Flashing lights clouded his thoughts and denied his mind access to logic. This was it. *Heaven or hell?* He wondered.

When the answer came, Hawken Turner felt himself lifted up to the heavens—not in the arms of a sweet angel dressed in flowing linen, but strapped to a cold aluminum gurney slid into the belly of an orange and white medevac helicopter.

CHAPTER TWENTY FIVE
The Ocean

The gifts kept coming for Hawken Turner after the accident. An unexpected call came from Robin shortly after he returned home from the hospital. When she'd heard about the wreck, she had offered to come to Lewisville and help him during his recuperation at home. Hawken was shocked; he had caused her much misery and pain, but she must have decided that she could put the past behind her and care for the man who would always be the father of her children.

Robin had been as unlucky in love as Hawken. Her marriage had dissolved after she caught Stan in an affair, and Robin did not forgive easily. She had retired from the library and was teaching aerobics at a neighborhood gym, but she took time off from the gym and came to stay with Hawken for the Christmas holiday. And, most important to Hawken, she brought Hayden with her.

Having Robin and Hayden living in his house as a family again brought happiness and hope to Hawken. When he was healed enough to hobble around on crutches, he awoke one day and found that Robin had left for groceries. He made his way into the study, went straight to the carved wooden cabinet, and opened the door where he kept his whiskey. An agitated voice startled him as he reached for the whiskey.

"You're not supposed to drink when you're taking pain medication." Robin stood with a bag of groceries at the kitchen door.

"I know that. I'm throwing it out." Hawken hobbled into the kitchen and waited for Robin to face him. They stood there for a moment looking at each other until Hawken broke the silence again.

"You know, it was never a disease for me," he said.

"What do you mean?" she asked.

"I never drank because I had too. I just drank because I thought I was supposed to."

"There're bottles all over your house," she said.

"I know. I didn't say that I didn't like it. But that's in the past. I don't need it. And I don't want it anymore. I'm throwing it out now. All of it...for good."

"I hope you're right," she said. She began putting groceries in the cabinet.

"I need to give you some money for the groceries," Hawken said.

"No need. I used your credit card," Robin answered.

"Okay. Good."

There was an awkward silence as Hawken hobbled closer until they stood face to face.

"You know, I'm a different man now, too," he said. "I've been through hell and back."

"So you had a near-death experience, and now you're different?"

"I know it sounds dramatic, but it's true. That's exactly what happened," he said. "If you stay around here for a little while, you'll know it too."

Robin placed the receipt on the counter as Hawken continued.

"For a long time, I've wanted to tell you that I'm sorry for the things that I let happen to our marriage. I made a lot of mistakes, but I didn't know it at the time."

Robin said nothing.

"I wish you'd consider staying for a while longer. It would be good to have you and Hayden here so we could spend more time together. Things happened so fast with us before that we never got to know each other as we should have. And I'd like that. I'd like to know you better."

"You'd like to know *me* better, or Hayden?" she asked.

"Both of you," he said.

"It's too late for that, Hawken," she said.

"I know. I have lots of regrets. I'm sorry that I let things fall apart for us. I could have done better, but I just didn't know how at the time. I know that it was selfish of me, but everything got twisted, and in my mind, I thought some time apart would be best for everybody."

Robin continued putting groceries away.

"Just think about it."

There was another long moment of silence.

"I'm going to Africa as soon as I get well enough to travel. Maybe you and Hayden could go with me. Maybe Thomas and Garrett too."

"I don't want to go on a safari," she said.

"No hunting. Just looking at the animals and taking pictures. Sleeping in tents at night and going on game drives during the day. I have to go anyway. There's a gun over there that I need to bring back."

"You're going all the way to Africa to get a gun?"

"Yes. It belonged to a friend of mine, but it's mine now. It's got sentimental value. And…it's a great gun."

"I don't think so," she said. "And I've been meaning to talk to you about something. You owe money for the boys' college and they have some medical expenses too that you owe me. I brought the bills with me."

The cast on Hawken's left arm and the heavy boot on his right leg made it difficult to use crutches, but Hawken was getting better every day. He knew it would be months before he could walk well, but time was running out. There was something he had to do.

On the first afternoon when he felt able to leave the house, he turned to Hayden to help with his quest. "Come on, I have a favor I need from you," Hawken said. He dangled the truck keys as he spoke.

"Where are we going?" Hayden asked. He opened the door for his father and waited for him to limp toward the truck.

"Let's go to the florist first."

Hayden started the truck as Hawken directed him to the main street florist located in the center of town.

"Go in and buy me one red rose. No vase, just the flower," Hawken said. Then as a second thought, Hawken shouted to him as he was reaching the building, "Hey, Hayden, get two flowers."

As expected, Hayden asked no questions and dutifully did as he was told. He returned with the rose and started the truck back toward the house.

"Let's go to the cemetery out on Highway 78," Hawken said.

"What for?" Hayden asked.

"Just something I should have done a long time ago. I don't like secrets, but I don't want you to tell your mother about this. Sometimes it's better to let the past stay in the past."

Hayden said nothing.

Hawken studied Hayden's face as they entered the highway. His face was serious and mature. *Confident and controlled*, Hawken thought to himself. It was a look that Hawken recognized as his own, and this worried him. A look that hid any sign of weakness, pain, or fear.

Though Hawken had driven by the small cemetery a thousand times, he had never stopped. He had carried the casket to the final resting place—a duty bestowed upon him by her family. They never could have imagined the pain that it caused him to know that the weight he was bearing was a burden that would be with him all his life.

"How was your prom last year?" Hawken asked.

"Pretty good," Hayden answered.

"Good. How was your date?"

"She was nice."

"Have you been out with her since then?"

"No, sir."

"Have you been out with anybody else since then?" Hawken asked.

"No, sir."

"You're a good-looking guy. How come you don't have a girlfriend?"

"I don't want to be pussy-whipped like Thomas and Garrett."

Hawken laughed. "Listen to me. Your pussy-whipped brothers are probably going to be a lot happier than you with that attitude. There is nothing better than a solid relationship with a good woman. A good woman will make you a better man. Trust me on that."

Hayden continued driving the truck, wearing no emotion while he processed the information. Hawken recognized the look. Hayden was sorting the words and storing the moment to be kept in the dark corners until he felt the need to resurrect them sometime in the future.

"Let me tell you—I've been all over this earth and seen more things than most people will ever see, but I've never been happier than I'll be when I walk back into that house and see your mom there."

"How long do you think we're staying?" Hayden asked.

"You can stay as long as you like. I like having the two of you around here."

"Mom says we're going back in two weeks," Hayden said.

"When did she tell you that?" Hawken asked.

"Yesterday."

"Are you sure?" Hawken asked.

"Yes, sir."

"Is that what you want to do?"

"It's not up to me. But I'm pretty sure we're going back."

"Even if your mom goes back in a couple of weeks, you can stay as long as you want," Hawken said. "As a matter of fact, I'd be very happy if you wanted to live here. You can finish your school here. We've got some pretty good schools around."

"I'll think about it," Hayden said. "But I want to play football at my school next year."

"Maybe you can stay for just a little longer. We can take it day by day, you know," Hawken said. "There were lots of things that I wanted to tell you and your brothers when I was sitting in that car after the accident and feeling sure that I was going to die. But now, when I try to remember, I can't seem to find the words that I wanted to say."

"That's okay," Hayden said.

"I do know that I want to tell you boys that I'm sorry that I haven't been a better father. I always wanted to be the perfect father. That was always a big part of my dream. It's the dream part that has been the problem. Things aren't always what they seem."

"What do you mean?" Hayden asked.

"I'm talking about spending my whole life chasing a dream that wasn't coming true. Sometimes you have to let go of one dream before you can have another. I didn't know how to do in the past, but I know how to do it now. Slow down and pull in here." Hawken pointed to the driveway leading inside the cemetery, and Hayden eased the truck along the drive until Hawken raised his hand for him to stop.

They sat silently for some time until Hawken finally spoke.

"You know, having you and your mom with me now makes me think of something your Grandma Maggie used to say." Hawken turned to look at his son to be sure that he was listening before he continued.

"What's that?" Hayden asked.

"No man is an island."

Hayden stared straight ahead. "No man is an island?"

"Yes, no man is an island. Think about those words, and trust me, there's a lot of truth there. Keep that in the back of your mind, and roll it around in your head every now and then. Once you grasp that concept, you'll know one of the lessons that it took me way too long to realize."

Hawken gathered his crutches and carefully stepped from the truck. "Hand me one of those roses," he said. "We're taking the other one home to your mom."

Hawken and his son searched for twenty minutes before Hayden found the modest headstone on the far side of the cemetery. It took another five minutes before Hawken was able to make his way to the gravesite, inching his broken body forward with the aid of his crutches. When he got there, his eyes became heavy with tears. He had never shed a tear over her. Not one. Years of forbidden tears began building in his eyes as he fought hard to hold back the flood. If not for his son standing nearby, Hawken would have surely fallen to his knees and begun sobbing out loud. He propped his crutches against the granite headstone and bent down on one knee. He carefully laid the rose on the slab of gray marble. After a deep breath and moment of hesitation, Hawken Turner closed his eyes and said the words that he had waited so many years to say...

"Good-bye, Sam."

CHAPTER TWENTY SIX
Without Sam

Two weeks after Hawken visited the cemetery, Robin and Hayden packed their bags into the Chrysler minivan and prepared to leave. As they stood in the driveway, Hawken joined them at the rear of the vehicle. It was too late to stop them.

Hawken gave Hayden a strong hug and held him tight before letting go. He stood and watched while the van with Robin and his son disappeared from sight. A light breeze rustled the leaves high in the oaks as Hawken Turner realized he had no place to go and nothing left to search for. As he walked toward his house, he gazed at the dogwood tree he had planted the day Hayden was born. The tree was as tall as his house, and the branches spread wide. He thought of Cuba and the warm beaches there, and then he remembered José Marti.

A man should do three things in his life, José Marti once said. *He should have a son, he should plant a tree, and he should write a book.*

Acknowledgements

After many months of pouring heart and soul into a manuscript, I turned to handful of friends and family seeking their advice for the next step towards strengthening this story. I would like to thank those of you who read the early version of this book, the much-too-early version of this book, and the *who are you kidding?* version of this book. Those readers include Linda Moore, Greg Edwards, Donna Edwards, Mary Chason, Susan Philbrick, Jamie Emge, Dena Strickland, Glen Webner, Nan Ghivan, and Tracy Tata.

In addition, a special thank-you goes to Zoe Alonso, the best guide in all of Cuba, a dear friend, and a literary advisor—all rolled into one. And lastly, I would like to thank Nina Moskovskaia, my friend and wonderful guide in St. Petersburg, Russia.

For those of you who choose to read the published version of this novel—thank you. I hope you enjoy it.